"Poor Jill. I can't imagine losing both parents."

"Even worse, she acted so badly that no one would keep her."

"She was hurt and fighting her pain. That little girl is a fighter," Carly said.

"I can never hope to replace the home she's lost."

Carly tried to not let it bother her that Sawyer spoke as if he was alone in this. She gently corrected him. "No, we can't. But we can give her something else. A new beginning. A chance to learn that love is still an option."

They had stopped walking and faced each other. He searched her gaze so intently that her eyes stung. She didn't look away. Didn't want to end this moment and prayed he would see that she included him in her hope of a happy future.

A smile began in his eyes and spread to his mouth. "Love is an option. That sounds very hopeful."

She sensed an unasked question. Did he wonder if love was available to him? She'd married a stranger. Their agreement was to remain businesslike. But did he sometimes want more?

Linda Ford lives on a ranch in Alberta, Canada, near enough to the Rocky Mountains that she can enjoy them on a daily basis. She and her husband raised fourteen children—four homemade, ten adopted. She currently shares her home and life with her husband, a grown son, a live-in paraplegic client and a continual (and welcome) stream of kids, kids-in-law, grandkids and assorted friends and relatives.

Books by Linda Ford

Love Inspired Historical

Big Sky Country

Montana Cowboy Daddy
Montana Cowboy Family
Montana Cowboy's Baby
Montana Bride by Christmas
Montana Groom of Convenience

Montana Cowboys

The Cowboy's Ready-Made Family
The Cowboy's Baby Bond
The Cowboy's City Girl

Christmas in Eden Valley

A Daddy for Christmas
A Baby for Christmas
A Home for Christmas

Lone Star Cowboy League: Multiple Blessings

The Rancher's Surprise Triplets

Journey West

Wagon Train Reunion

Visit the Author Profile page at Harlequin.com for more titles.

LINDA FORD

Montana Groom of Convenience

HARLEQUIN® LOVE INSPIRED® HISTORICAL

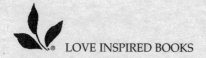 LOVE INSPIRED BOOKS

ISBN-13: 978-1-335-36950-5

Montana Groom of Convenience

Copyright © 2018 by Linda Ford

www.Harlequin.com

Printed in U.S.A.

Thy word is a lamp unto my feet,
and a light unto my path.
—*Psalms* 119:105

Dedicated to mothers who teach their children to find answers in the Bible, who help them commit verses to memory so that the Word guides their footsteps. My mother was such a woman and this book is especially dedicated to her memory.

Chapter One

Bella Creek, Montana, 1891

They were dead! His plan had been to deliver his eight-year-old half sister, Jill, to her mother's cousin and her husband in Bella Creek. The local sheriff's explanation that the couple had passed away several months ago had brought a stop to that idea.

Twenty-three-year-old Sawyer Gallagher stared at Jill as she devoured her breakfast. He didn't know the first thing about little girls, nor what they needed. He didn't even have a home. For years, he had wandered from place to place. Now what was he supposed to do with his little sister? He couldn't take her with him on a cattle drive or even if he got a job as a ranch hand. That sort of life wasn't suitable for a young girl.

As he pondered his problem and how to solve it, the words of the conversation at a nearby table reached him.

"He's going to sell the ranch."

Sawyer angled his head to study the woman who spoke with such feeling. He couldn't say if she expressed anger or pain. His position gave him a view of the woman's profile. She leaned toward her friend, strands of straw blond hair drifting about her face. The rest was in a loose braid hanging down her back. She wore a dark blue print dress.

His gaze went downward and he grinned at the sight of a sturdy pair of cowboy boots peeking out from under her skirts. Both the boots and hem of her dress were caked with mud.

He returned his attention to the pair at the table. Her companion was also blonde though much darker. And much neater.

"No! You can't reason with him?"

"You do realize we're talking about my father—the most stubborn Scotsman I've ever encountered."

Her friend chuckled. "I dare say he's the only one you've ever encountered."

The girl shuddered. "Don't care to meet another." She leaned closer to her companion. "Do you know what he told me? That I need a man to run the ranch now that he's been injured. Doc says his leg won't mend properly. Says he will never be able to use it like he used to. He can't ride anymore. Can't walk behind the plow. Can't drive Big Harry." With each item on the list, the gal's voice grew more sorrowful and her shoulders sank.

"I'm sorry to hear that. But, Carly, he's never allowed you to work with the Clydesdale."

She sat up straight. "I could." Her shoulders sank again. "But he forbids me to do so. Says it takes a man."

Amusement sparkled from the second woman. "So you're out to find a man?"

Carly, as her friend called her, jerked forward. Her jaw jutted out. "That's exactly what I'm going to do. I said I would hire someone but Father says only marriage will ensure stability so I need to find someone to marry." Her gaze circled the room, momentarily rested on Sawyer, lowered to Jill across from him and returned to her companion.

Sawyer's breath whooshed out. He had the feeling he'd just escaped disaster.

"You'd marry to save the ranch?"

Sawyer shared the speaker's astonishment.

"Indeed, I would. Too bad your brothers are already married. You don't happen to have some male, unmarried cousins I haven't heard of?"

"I can't believe you're asking."

"It's not like I'm expecting love and romance. I only want a man to sign a piece of paper and pretend to be my husband."

"Carly Morrison! Dismiss this notion at once. It's folly. Better to pray God changes your father's mind."

"Might as well ask for the mountains to disappear." Miss Morrison sank back.

"There's always Billy Cameron." The woman laughed.

Carly shuddered. "Please, I'm not that desperate. You can smell the man coming a mile away. I've been with Father to visit him. The man never washes his dishes. Just lets his dog lick them clean. Yuck."

"Glad to hear you aren't that desperate." Her companion rose. "I must go. I'm going to ask Hugh to pray for you."

"So long as you both pray I'll find a husband." She scowled. "Father has given me two weeks to do so."

"That doesn't even give you time to find a mail-order husband." The friend pulled on her gloves. "I'm sorry but it doesn't sound very hopeful, does it?"

"There must be someone." Miss Morrison brightened. "I just have to find him."

Her friend left, shaking her head.

Sawyer shifted so he could see the woman still sitting at the table. Youngish, maybe twenty though that was but a guess. He wasn't able to judge a woman's age. She was pretty enough from what he could see. He'd been mildly surprised to see her brown eyes…unusual in someone with such fair hair. She was a little on the small size. He supposed, like most places in the west, there were a dozen men to every woman. So why wasn't she already married? Instead, she was desperately looking for a husband.

He was desperately seeking a home for Jill.

His mind clicked like a tightly wound watch.

Jill burped loudly and he made up his mind.

"Jill, stay here while I speak to that lady." Taking her compliance for granted, though compliance and cooperation had been sadly lacking from the beginning of this journey, he pushed his chair back and rose to his feet.

Carly planted her elbows on the table and buried her face in her palms. Father could be so unreasonable. Two weeks to find a husband! That was impossible. Besides, she didn't want a husband. But she did want the ranch. She'd been mostly running it for several years now, though Father had steadfastly refused to let her handle Big Harry, insisting the plow horse was too much animal for *a bitty thing like her*.

The chair across the table scraped on the floor and someone sat down. Carly jerked up, expecting Annie had returned, perhaps having recalled an unmarried cousin. Instead she stared at a stranger.

Wasn't this the man who had been seated at the next table? She darted a glance out of the corner of her eyes. Yes, the little girl sat alone, watching Carly and the man.

"Excuse me," Carly said, returning her attention to the stranger. "This is my table."

He didn't pay any heed to her hint that he should leave. Didn't even address her comment. "I couldn't help but overhear part of your conversation."

How dare he listen to her painful discussion with Annie? "Didn't your mother teach you it was rude to eavesdrop?"

He lifted one shoulder dismissively. "She might have if she hadn't died when I was seven."

"I spoke out of turn. I'm sorry." Wasn't Father always telling her she was far too free with her comments? Given that he wasn't opposed to speaking his mind, he could hardly expect otherwise.

The man across from her dipped his head in acknowledgment. "It would seem you have a problem."

She gave no indication that she understood what he meant, her insides burning to think someone had overheard her conversation with Annie.

"I also have a problem." His gaze went to the little girl.

Carly's eyes went the same direction.

The untidy little girl scowled at them, then turned away, swiped her plate with her dirty fingers and sucked the bacon fat from them. She gave them a look of pure challenge that brought a fleeting smile to Carly's mouth. It was a look she herself had honed over the years. For all the good it did her in the end. Father told her he didn't care how much fire she shot from her eyes, there were certain things he would not let a daughter of his do. Remembering that brought her thoughts back to her quandary.

Carly could see the child might be a problem but didn't see how it involved her. She didn't have time to deal with a child. She had to find a husband.

"That's my little sister, Jill. She's eight and her parents are dead."

"Poor little girl." Carly studied the child more closely. She had light brown hair that hadn't seen a brush in days. Brown eyes that challenged everyone and everything they encountered. A trail-dusty brown dress. Scuffed shoes that were swinging back and forth. Her heart went to the child. She must feel very alone. At least she had a brother.

How often Carly wished she had a sibling, preferably a brother or two or more.

The man continued, "I thought to turn her over to her second cousin but I just learned the cousin and her husband died last summer."

"Poor child." She revised her earlier assumption. It sounded very much like the little girl had no one who cared about her despite the brother sitting across from Carly. Jill, he'd said, shifted her gaze to Carly's and Carly glimpsed the child's pain and fear before the little one turned away and began dragging the fork over the tabletop, scratching the worn surface.

Dorie, sister to the owner of Miss Daisy's Eatery, hustled over and gathered up the used dishes and cutlery, taking the fork and leaving only a glass of water in front of Jill.

Carly realized the man opposite her waited her attention.

"I find myself needing a home for Jill."

Carly wished him well with his search but she didn't have time to discuss the matter. Nor anyone she cared to suggest who might offer the child a home. She had to find a man willing to marry her.

Though she had her doubts that she'd meet with any man's approval. She had the ranch to offer as enticement even though she hated to use it that way. Hadn't she long ago promised herself that in order for a man to marry her, he'd have to care for *her*…not the ranch?

Bart Connelly had made her see how important that was. He courted her ardently. She'd admired his interest in everything to do with the ranch operation. Her admiration had cooled considerably after he let her see his real reason for the courtship. He told her he intended to have his own ranch some day and he didn't mean to wait until he'd saved up enough from his wages. That would take far too long. Nope. There was more than one way to get started.

Didn't take Carly long to realize she was his shortcut. She might have been agreeable to a partnership but then he started to tell her how to do things. Started telling her to run along and get prettied up for him. She finally told him he should run along and get himself prettied up.

After that, she refused his company. Let him find someone else to marry in order to get his ranch.

Seems most men expected she'd change for them, get prettied up and let them order her about. She soon stopped bothering with them. But now, here she was needing to marry someone. Bart was long gone, which was a mercy. She shuddered at the thought of giving in to his demands.

She pushed her chair back. She didn't have time to listen to the man's woes. She had to save the ranch.

"I'm sorry about your plight but I don't know what I can do to help."

"You can marry me."

She sat down with a thud and opened her mouth but not a word came out. She stared. Blinked. Blinked again. Closed her eyes and told herself she was in a bad dream but when she opened her eyes, the man still sat there, watching, waiting.

She found her voice, though it sounded a bit rusty. "Marry you? You're a stranger. I don't even know your name. I don't know anything about you."

"Name's Sawyer Gallagher. I'm twenty-three. Been on my own since I was fourteen. Been working on ranches or riding herd on a trail ride. That's about it."

That was it? Who was he? What sort of life did he plan to live?

She studied him with narrowed eyes. Dirty blond hair. Blue-green eyes. Three days' growth of dusty beard. A trail-soiled faded blue shirt. A look that shouted *don't mess with me*. A man used to being in charge.

She almost shivered. No. She could not see herself married to this man.

Except to save the ranch?

He leaned forward, his eyes challenging and fierce enough to make her want to sit back and put more distance between them. "You need a husband so you can keep your ranch. I need a home for Jill." He looked down as he continued, not allowing her to read his expression. "I know what it's like to grow up homeless and drifting. It's how me and my pa were until he married Judith and they had little Jill." He paused.

When he resumed speaking, his voice had deepened

and his words came slowly as if he found them difficult
to say them. "I learned not to care about people or places
'cause I knew they weren't going to last. It killed something inside me so that I don't feel things anymore."
He lifted his head and she sat back at the way his eyes
blazed. "I don't want Jill to end up like me." The fire
in his gaze died and she could have been looking into
a bottomless pit for all she saw.

She swallowed hard. Not often a man made her feel
small and vulnerable but something about this man did.
He wasn't big. Annie's brothers were far bigger. But his
soulless eyes unnerved her.

He went on, not hurrying, yet she felt his intensity.
"I want nothing but a permanent home for my sister.
No emotional ties. No expectations except for me to do
the ranch work and you to teach Jill how to feel safe."

Their glances went to the child. She picked her nose
and wiped it on her already soiled dress. "I don't suppose learning a few manners would hurt either."

"No strings attached?" Why was she even considering this? One reason and one only…to keep the ranch.
She looked again at the little girl. Maybe two reasons.
The second, to give a child a home where she would
be safe and secure.

"No strings." His voice was flat but firm.

"You'd have your own bedroom?" Her cheeks burned
at the question but she had to be sure they were clear
on this matter. She did not want to be controlled by a
man indoors or out.

"Either that or I'll sleep in the barn."

"No need for that." There was a small room next to
Father's that was used mostly for storage. It would be
adequate.

Except this wasn't going to happen. She wasn't seriously considering his suggestion. No. She wasn't that desperate.

"I heard you say your father gave you two weeks."

She stared at the wall behind him. Could she find someone else to marry in two weeks? As Annie said, it didn't allow time to advertise for a husband, and even if it did, there would not be enough time to get to know and evaluate any man who responded. No one from around here would marry her knowing how she conducted herself. Every man she'd ever met wanted her to go to the house and pretty herself up. The few single men in the area who might be desperate enough to marry her had already been dismissed as old, ugly, mean or simpering. Old Billy Cameron was but a sample of what she had to choose from.

She simply didn't have the luxury of picking and choosing.

She squirmed in her chair. But to marry a complete stranger!

Jill got down from her chair and kicked at the table legs.

"Jill," Sawyer said. "Don't do that."

The child kicked harder, causing the table to hop away. Then she gave Sawyer a look full of disdain, challenge and—

Despair.

Carly saw it. She felt it and her heart went out to the orphaned child who didn't know where she belonged. She couldn't imagine the pain of not having a home, no place to call one's own.

If Carly didn't marry and present her father with a

man to help run the ranch, she was about to lose the place she called home, the place she considered her own.

"Okay. Let's do it." She would marry the man, ensure her own home and give Jill one at the same time.

Sawyer didn't move a muscle. Didn't blink. Didn't so much as allow his eyelids to flicker, even though the woman's ready agreement left him feeling like he teetered at the brink of a bottomless ravine. Shouldn't she have asked a lot of questions about him and his character?

"I'm an honest, honorable man." The words fell out of his mouth. "I'll treat you right."

Carly gave him narrow-eyed study with those dark brown eyes. He had to concentrate not to shift his gaze away. "Mr. Gallagher, you might hit me once, but you'll never hit me twice. I'll see to that. I'll not tolerate a man who rules with his fists."

He didn't know if he should laugh at the idea of this little gal getting all feisty or congratulate her on her stand. "Warning duly noted." He wondered if she heard the humor in his voice, then remembered she wouldn't. He'd kept his responses cooled for so long that he seldom felt them and even less often did others recognize them. "But completely unnecessary. I'd never hit a woman or child."

Her lips pursed. "I won't abide rough treatment of my animals, either."

He nodded. "You and I see eye to eye on that matter."

She studied him so hard he felt something inside shudder.

To avoid her gaze, he turned to Jill. "Her parents died right after Christmas." It was the last time he'd been home and he'd stayed only two days, anxious to be on the move. Mostly from not wanting to feel like an outsider to the happy family of his pa, Judith and Jill, although Judith did everything she could to include him. He'd seen the pain in her eyes and Pa's when he rode out.

The neighbor said they had taken sick shortly after he left and the fever had claimed their lives. "I was away and when I came home, I found Jill living with an elderly woman who provided nothing but a roof over her head and some meals. From what I could see, Jill took care of herself, which meant she ran wild. She'd been shuffled from home to home. No one wanted to keep her."

He studied his little sister. Already he saw the evidence of her reaction to losing her parents and having a home where no discipline or affection was given. "She accepts no affection. Rebuffs attempts of people to befriend her." He gave a sound that was half snort, half amusement. "Course I'm hardly one to judge what a normal reaction is." He subdued a sigh. "Like I said, I don't want her to end up like me."

"I expect she's just wanting someone who will accept her as she is and be there for her every day."

Those words ricocheted back and forth inside Sawyer's heart. Every day? He'd long ago learned there was no such thing as counting on someone every day. He'd discovered the best way to keep from being hurt was to not allow himself to feel anything, not to trust anyone to always be there.

He'd gotten really good at it. So good that women considered him cold and distant. He'd tried to change when he met Gladys Berry. She talked of home and family…things he thought he wanted. He soon learned he couldn't become what she wanted and she'd stopped letting him call on her. Accused him of having no feelings—something he could not deny. Said he was a loner and would always be so.

He'd been better off than Jill. He'd had his pa. Sort of. Pa was there in body but absent in every other way until he had met and married Judith.

By marrying Carly, Sawyer could hope to give Jill what Pa had found. He wasn't sure what to call it but figured security best described it.

"How soon you want to get married?" he asked.

"Today suit you?"

Long years of hiding emotions enabled him to sit perfectly still, revealing none of his surprise. "Today is fine by me." There seemed nothing to be gained by waiting except to allow her time to change her mind. "You know someone who will marry us on such short notice?"

She rumbled her lips. "Now that might pose a problem."

"How much of a problem?"

"I don't know if I can find anyone to agree to our plan."

He should have known this wouldn't work out. With studied indifference, he got to his feet. "In that case, I'll be moving along. Nice talking to you." He grabbed his worn and battered cowboy hat from where it hung on the back of the chair and reached for Jill's hand. "Come on." Jill raced ahead and was out the door before he'd made three steps.

Knowing she could get into all kinds of trouble in less time than it took to say her name, he rushed after her.

"Mr. Gallagher, wait just one minute."

He ignored Carly Morrison's imperative call and hurried out the door just in time to see Jill dash into the middle of the street, right into the path of an oncoming wagon. He rushed after her, praying he'd get there in time to prevent a tragedy.

Chapter Two

Carly stood with her hands on her hips, staring after Sawyer as the door slapped shut behind him. What had caused him to up and disappear like that? All she'd said was…

She groaned as she recalled her words. Did he think the problem she mentioned was unsurmountable? Her only concern was that the preacher, Hugh, who was also Annie's husband, might decide to object. She sniffed. Not that he had any right to. Hadn't he and Annie planned to marry solely to provide a home for his little son? Of course, they had soon fallen in love.

Not that Carly had any intention of doing that. She wanted nothing but to keep her ranch. Certainly didn't want a man thinking he had the right to tell her how to act or dress.

Either Sawyer thought she meant there was no one to marry them or else Sawyer had changed his mind. But would it hurt for him to come right out and say so instead of leaving her standing in the middle of Miss Daisy's Eatery, trying to gather her thoughts together?

Annie had paid for their tea so she chased after

the man with every intention of making him explain himself.

Before she reached the door, she heard people shouting and a woman screaming. She hurried outside to see what the fuss was all about.

Her breath stalled in her chest at the sight before her. Sawyer held the head of two struggling horses that tossed their heads and reared. A man in the wagon the horses were harnessed to stood on his feet and reared back on the reins, trying to get control of the frightened animals. And then she saw Jill and her heart slammed into her chest.

The child lay in the street. Carly knew in a flash what had happened. Jill had run into the street without checking to see it was safe. It happened far too often. She remembered when Annie's niece, Mattie, had almost been run over last summer. Mattie's father had ridden up and swept her to safety. Jill had not been as fortunate.

She was annoyed at how her skirts hindered her—she'd only worn a dress to town because of some foolish hope it would make a man consider her as marriage material. Now they were a hazard to her. Carly grabbed the hem and lifted the fabric to free her to run as she dashed into the street.

Ignoring the flashing hooves of the rearing horses, she scooped up the girl and carried her to safety in front of Marshall's Mercantile. Paying no attention to the questions from the spectators, she laid Jill gently on the step and bent over to wipe the tangled brown hair from the child's face. Her eyelids fluttered, then brown eyes went wide with shock.

"Are you hurt?" Carly checked each limb. A lump bulged on Jill's forehead.

"I'm okay."

It was the first time Carly had heard her speak, so she couldn't judge if the huskiness was from her fright or if that was the child's normal voice. She looked around, hoping Dr. Baker or his daughter were among those hovering nearby.

"Kate." Relief flooded her at the sight of the doctor's daughter pushing through the crowd. Kate had light brown hair that she often wore in a careless bun. So typical of the woman. Caring for others mattered far more than looks. Her brown eyes filled with kindness.

"Is she hurt?" Unmindful of the dusty wooden sidewalk that would soil her dark skirt, Kate knelt beside Carly and deftly ran her hands over Jill's legs and arms, then pulled down each bottom eyelid to look into Jill's eyes. "Take her over to the doctor's office. I'll examine her more closely there."

Carly shoved aside the offers of help to carry Jill and lifted her against her chest. Jill crossed her arms and stiffened. Poor child to be in the arms of a stranger. Something warm and protective blossomed in Carly's heart. This motherless child deserved to be sheltered and cherished. "I'll take care of you," she murmured to Jill.

It was a promise she meant to keep. Somehow she would persuade Sawyer there was no need to retract his offer of marriage…an agreement between them was in the best interests of all three of them. No. Only two of them. She didn't know what Sawyer needed, nor did it matter so long as Jill got her home and Carly got her ranch.

She reached the doctor's house and glanced back to see Sawyer looking about. His gaze found her and when he saw she held Jill, he handed the calming horses to another man and trotted in Carly's direction. She didn't wait for him but carried Jill inside to the examining room.

Kate brought a basin of warm water. "I need to see what's under the dirt."

"I'll do it." Carly took the wet cloth and gently washed Jill's face. All the while, Jill watched her solemnly. Carly smiled. "Tell me if I hurt you."

"It don't."

Kate stood beside Carly.

"Kate, this is Jill. She's eight years old." She smiled at the child. She was quite lovely with all the dirt removed. "Jill, this is Mrs. Marshall." Kate had married Conner Marshall, one of the three sons of the Marshall family who had built the town. "She's a nurse. She'll see if you're hurt."

Carly stepped back to allow Kate more space.

The door banged open and Sawyer strode through, jerking off his worn hat but not slowing until he was at his sister's side. "That was a foolish thing to do. You could have been killed."

Jill's eyes went from hungry to angry. "I'm not even hurt."

"I was about to see if that is so or not," Kate said.

Carly introduced Kate to Sawyer.

Kate waited for Sawyer to realize he needed to step back. "Can you tell me what happened?" She examined Jill as she talked.

Sawyer answered though Carly wondered if Kate had directed the question at Jill. "She ran full speed into the street without looking to see if it was safe. The horses saw her and reared in fright. If she hadn't tripped and fallen, she would have been kicked." He spoke in a flat tone.

Carly wondered if he was as unfeeling about seeing his sister in such dire straits as he sounded.

Kate stepped aside. "Apart from the goose egg on her forehead, she seems unhurt. I suggest you keep her awake for the next eight or twelve hours to make certain she's okay."

Now was the time for Carly to speak her mind. "Kate, can you watch her for a minute?"

Kate nodded, her brows raised in curiosity.

Carly turned to Sawyer. "May I speak to you in private?" Not waiting for him to agree or otherwise, she headed for the door that led to the doctor's living quarters. With Sawyer on her heels, she crossed the front room and entered the kitchen, sparing a quick glance around.

Last spring, Kate, her friend Isabelle and Sadie, the teacher, had all arrived in town, along with Dr. Baker. The doctor and teacher were to replace those who had left after the devastating fire that had leveled a block of buildings in Bella Creek. Now the three female newcomers were married—all to Marshall men. And Annie Marshall, Carly's best friend, had recently married Preacher Hugh Arness. Carly had never thought to be joining them in wedlock but her father had left her little choice.

She reached the outer door, was about to grab the handle and head outside, then changed her mind. It would be much harder for him to escape her demands with her back pressed to the closest exit. "Did you offer to marry me only to mock my need?"

He sank back on his heels. "Did you not say there would be a problem in getting married?"

"Nope. Sure didn't. Said it might be a problem getting the preacher to agree to marry us."

His eyebrows lifted marginally. Barely enough for her to guess that he wondered what she meant.

"That woman you saw me with earlier is my best friend, Annie. She's one of the Marshalls. Of course that means little to you at this point but you'll soon learn that the Marshall family is pretty much in charge of Bella Creek."

His eyebrows remained arched in question.

"Grandfather Marshall started the town so people would have a safe place to live. Until then, Wolf Hollow was the only town in the vicinity and it's a rough mining town."

He nodded, though she wondered if anything she said was making sense to him.

She continued, "Annie married the preacher. Preacher Hugh Arness. Likely they'll have an opinion about my decision to marry a stranger." She considered the alternatives and could come up with nothing but asking Hugh to marry them. There was no other preacher nearby and the judge wouldn't be around until who knew when.

Of course, it might not be a problem if Sawyer had changed his mind. "That is if you were serious about marrying me." Life had come to a pretty pass when she had to beg a complete stranger to agree to a marriage… or rather, a pretend marriage.

"I'm serious about getting a home for Jill."

They studied each other.

Carly wasn't sure what she expected from him but after a moment of silent study, one of the other, she realized he'd said all he meant to say on the matter. "Then we are agreed?"

"I'd say so."

"Then let's get Jill and go find the preacher." She pretended she didn't feel an uncomfortable tremor in the pit of her stomach. This marriage would change nothing except to have a man in the little bedroom and a child chasing after butterflies.

They returned to the examining room where Kate waited with Jill who now sat cross-legged on the gurney. They both watched Carly and Sawyer step back into the room; both wore curiosity-filled expressions. Carly knew that Kate must wonder what Carly needed to say in private to a stranger, and Jill likely wondered how their conversation would affect her.

"She's fit to go," Kate said. "Bring her to Father if you have any concerns."

"How much?" Sawyer asked.

Kate named a sum and Sawyer pulled the coins from his pocket and gave them to her.

Carly watched Jill. What they planned to do was partly on behalf of this child. Didn't she need to be informed?

"Let's go," Sawyer said.

Jill jumped down and headed for the outer door.

Sawyer caught her arm. "No more running into the street."

They exited into the empty waiting room.

"Wait," Carly said.

Sawyer stopped and gave her a hard look. "You're changing your mind again?"

"I never changed my mind before and I don't plan to now. But I think we should tell Jill our plans."

His gaze went to his sister. "Why?"

Annoyance colored her voice. "Because it concerns her."

Sawyer and Jill both looked at her, one as silently demanding as the other. Carly sucked in air. Fine. She'd be the one to tell the news.

She sat on the bench so she'd be face-level with Jill. "I'm very sorry about your mama and papa. You must miss them very much."

Jill blinked twice and then grew impassive.

Carly glanced at Sawyer. His expression matched Jill's. The child had already learned to hide her feelings, had learned it well from someone who admitted to being very good at it.

"Sawyer—" She stumbled a bit at using his name so freely, but seeing as they were to be married... "Well, he wants you to have a home where you'll always belong."

Jill's eyes darted toward her brother. "He's gonna leave me here, isn't he?"

"No, sweetie. That isn't what he has in mind at all. You see I have a very nice home that needs a—" She couldn't bring herself to say *a man*. "A family. You need a home. I need a family. So your brother and I are going to get married and we all get what we need."

Jill stared, her brown eyes intense but Carly couldn't tell if she approved of the idea or found it loathsome. "Is that okay with you?"

"What kind of home you got?"

"I live on a ranch with my father. We have horses and cows—"

"Puppies and kitties?"

"Not at the moment." Carly promised herself she'd get one of each as soon as possible. "We had a dog but he died during the winter. He was old." Carly missed him and hadn't considering replacing him yet. It was time to think about one now. Every child needed pets.

"I'd have to work?"

"You'd have chores. We all would. It's how families operate."

Jill nodded. "That's what Mama said, too." She nodded. "Okay."

Sawyer cleared his throat. "Seems we're all agreed."

"Then let's go find the preacher." Carly led the way out of the doctor's house. She turned left, marched past the schoolhouse where Jill would soon be attending, past the town square with trees budding and flowers pushing up through the sod. They turned by the church and went to the manse where Hugh had his office. The three of them stood at the doorway. It felt strange to be coming to this entrance. Carly always went to the door that opened to the kitchen. She knocked.

Hugh opened the door, a smile driving deep dimples into his cheeks. "Carly, go round to the kitchen. Annie's there."

"I've come to see you." Remembering the other two, she corrected herself. "We've come to see you."

Hugh's mobile face sobered and a hard look replaced his smile. He surely must wonder why Carly had brought a man and a child to his office.

"Then by all means come right in." He waved them toward the pair of chairs facing the desk, realized he needed another chair and snagged one from against the wall.

They sat. Carly to the right, Sawyer to the left and Jill in the middle. Hugh took his place across the desk from them.

Carly had always liked Hugh. He was darkly handsome with a quick smile and those lovely deep dimples in his cheeks. And single-minded. He'd come to town to find his missing son, Evan, and hadn't given up until he'd rescued the boy. Not unlike Sawyer's situation. Surely he'd see the similarities and it would make him eager to help.

Hugh directed his gaze toward Sawyer. "I don't believe I've had the pleasure."

"Hugh, this is Sawyer Gallagher and his sister, Jill."

The men shook hands, Hugh unmistakably curious. Then he offered his hand to Jill and she solemnly took it.

Hugh returned to a seated position. "Now what is it I can do for you?"

Carly and Sawyer glanced at each other, turned back to Hugh and spoke at the same time.

"Marry us."

Hugh sat back, shock and surprise making his mouth fall open. He sucked in air. "Marry you? To each other?"

Carly nodded.

"How do you know each other?"

"We don't. First time I saw him was this morning after I had tea with Annie."

"I see." He tented his fingers and tapped the ends of them together. His gaze was serious and not exactly affable. "Then may I suggest that this is rather sudden? Perhaps you should wait and get to know each other better."

"Why?" Carly and Sawyer asked at the same time.

Sawyer continued, "We know what we're doing."

Hugh shook his head. "You know nothing about each other."

Carly made a derisive sound. "This from a man who advertised for a mail-order bride."

Hugh had the grace to look embarrassed. "I would have wanted a few details before I actually tied the knot."

"I know all I need to know," Sawyer said, his voice calm. "Like she said to Jill, we need a home and she needs a family."

"She does?" Hugh didn't have to sound like this was unexpected news to him. Even if she'd never before mentioned this need. The truth was she'd never considered such a thing before, but thanks to Father's ultimatum, it had become imperative.

"Does Annie know of your plans?"

"Not yet." Carly hadn't had time to inform anyone.

"Do you mind if I ask her to join us?"

Annie knew why Carly had to do this. She would support Carly's decision. "It's all right by me if it's all right by Sawyer."

"I've no objection." He sat still and patient. As if it didn't matter that he was about to marry a stranger.

Carly eased back until she pressed to the wooden chair. She slowed her breathing and did her best to appear as unconcerned as Sawyer.

Hugh hurried from the room. They heard his murmured conversation with Annie though they could not make out the words. Heard her surprised response, then the pair returned, Hugh carrying a chair for Annie. He put it beside his own.

"You want to get married?" Annie asked, her voice and expression full of shocked surprise.

"I told you I would."

"Yes, but I didn't think…" She shook her head. "I didn't think it was possible."

Carly chuckled, seeing the humor in this situation. "I told you to pray I'd find a husband."

"Yes, but—"

"Is there a problem?" Sawyer asked.

"We know nothing about you," Hugh said.

"There's not much to know."

Carly needed to prove that she had found out the essentials. "He's twenty-three. Been working on ranches or cattle drives since he was fourteen. Guess that qualifies him to work on the Morrison Ranch. His parents are dead. Jill is his half sister and her mother is dead, too. He came to Bella Creek hoping to find a cousin and her husband but they've passed on." She sat back, feeling quite triumphant.

"Cousin?" Hugh said. "And who might that be?"

His tone carried just enough doubt for Carly to know he wondered if Sawyer made up the information. She had never thought to ask and she really should have.

"Ida and Henry Brown. They had a young son, Hank."

"The Browns. They passed last spring. Their chimney blocked and they died of fumes."

Hugh continued to press for more information. "What was your plan when you found them?"

"I thought they would give Jill the sort of home she deserves."

"And you'd do what?"

"Look for a job. Maybe head to Texas and get on another cattle drive."

Carly sat up tall and straight. She would not let anyone guess at how this information troubled her. She could live with a man who cared nothing about feelings. Suited her just fine. But a wandering one? How would that meet Father's requirements? She had no wish to be saddled with an absent husband and a father who believed an able-bodied man was necessary in order for her to keep the ranch.

She knew Annie watched her and guessed at her worry. Again, she smoothed her expression, wanting to hide her feelings from her friends. Soon she'd be as good as Sawyer at revealing nothing.

Perhaps Hugh understood the situation as well for he asked another question. "Once you marry and Carly takes on Jill's care, what's to stop you from heading for Texas and leaving her to carry the load on her own?"

"I won't. I give my word. I keep my word." A beat of heavy silence met his answer.

Carly knew Annie and Hugh were thinking the same as she. How were they to know if they could trust him?

"A man is only as good as his word." Sawyer's voice rang clear.

Carly was convinced. Or perhaps, she admitted, she wanted to believe him so they could proceed with their plan.

Hugh continued. "I can't marry the two of you without knowing what your religious beliefs are."

Carly looked at Sawyer. Another question she should have asked.

Not a muscle twitched anywhere on him. Nothing about his expression changed. He was very good at hiding his feelings. If, indeed, he had any. She couldn't be sure he did at this point.

"I believe in God," he said when he realized Hugh would not go on without an answer.

Hugh gave a mirthless laugh. "Perhaps you could tell me what you believe about God. Who is He to you?"

The preacher's question snaked through Sawyer. He had long ago stopped thinking about God. He couldn't say when it had happened. "My mama taught me that God loves me." A rush of long-forgotten memories swept over him. Mama reading the Bible and praying. She'd loved God and yet God had let her and Johnny perish in the fire. How could he trust a God like that?

"How would you describe your relationship to God?" the preacher asked.

Sawyer understood the man on the other side of the desk was reluctant to marry Carly Morrison to a stranger and would leap on any reason to refuse. This would be the reason if Sawyer let it be.

He couldn't lie, not even to gain the preacher's approval. As he said, a man was only as good as his word and once that was gone, so was honor and self-respect. It was about all he had left that mattered to him. And now the responsibility of his little sister.

"I believe in Jesus Christ, God's only Son, our Lord, who was crucified, died and was buried. He descended to the dead. On the third day, he rose again." The words rolled off his tongue as he said them from memory. But when had they been committed to his memory? Who had taught him those words? The answer was simple. His mama had taught them to him long ago and they had lain dormant in his brain until he needed to recall them. *Thank you, Mama.*

"Are you a believer?" the preacher asked.

The preacher hadn't been specific about what Sawyer believed in. He believed in lots of things. Doing a job to the best of his ability. Never quitting until the task was done. Being kind to children, women and animals. Keeping one's word. And of course, a God who ruled the world. "Yes."

Preacher Arness dropped his hand to the desktop. "I'm still not convinced this is the right thing to do." He pondered in silence a moment, then brightened. "Sawyer, perhaps there are things you want to know about Carly before you commit yourself to spending the rest of your life with her."

He knew marriage was forever but to hear it in those terms—*the rest of your life*—gave him pause. Between them, Jill swung her legs. Her hands moved restlessly. He knew the signs. His little sister had about reached the end of sitting still and that could lead to all sorts of unwanted events.

Just then, the door leading to the living quarters creaked open and a small boy peeked through the opening. "Mama, I finished the picture." The lad looked about the room. "Hi, Auntie Carly."

"Hi, Evan." Carly turned her gaze to Sawyer. "This is Annie and Hugh's son. Why not let Jill play with him while we finish up here?" She had no idea what she suggested. She couldn't begin to know what disasters Jill was capable of.

But Jill had already gotten to her feet and pushed past Sawyer. He caught her arm and stopped her. "I don't think it's a good idea."

Jill favored him with a scowl fit to curdle his stomach.

"Evan would like that, wouldn't you?" Mrs. Arness said. "We can leave the door open so we can see them."

Jill squirmed from Sawyer's grasp and followed the woman into the other room.

The two children sat in plain view with an assortment of toy animals between them. A small dog flopped down beside them and Jill began to pet it. The preacher's wife returned to sit by her husband.

Sawyer tried to relax but it was impossible. Every muscle in his body tensed, ready to react to whatever might occur.

"Now back to the business at hand," the preacher said. "You were wondering about Carly."

He wasn't but Sawyer let the assumption go unchallenged.

"I don't know what she's told you so I'll provide a few details. Carly is nineteen years old."

Sawyer nodded. He would have guessed her older than that but her age made no difference to him. At least she wasn't forty.

The preacher went on, "She's a believer. She lives on a small ranch four miles southeast of town along with her father. Mr. Morrison was injured in a wagon accident a few weeks ago. Doc says his leg will never mend properly. Carly's been doing most of the work around the place since even before her father's accident but he has never let her handle their big Clydesdale."

"He's too much for a wee lassie like you."

Sawyer knew by the strong brogue with which Carly said the words that she quoted her father.

Preacher Hugh leaned back. "There's lots more to know about her. And I know there's lots more to know about you. Why not spend some time learning about each other and come back in a few months to get married?"

"I don't have a few months. I don't need to know more." Carly's opinion was clear.

"I see no reason to delay." The sooner Sawyer got Jill settled into a permanent home, the better he'd like it.

Carly planted her fists on her knees. "Nor do I."

"You'll need your father's permission."

Sawyer knew the preacher was stalling.

Carly bolted to her feet. "He can't ride but I'll go ask him."

The preacher and his wife exchanged looks and grinned. Hugh got to his feet. "I think I better be the one to talk to him." He grabbed his hat and headed for the door. "Annie will serve you tea."

"Wait," Carly said. "At least let me write him a note." She grabbed paper and pencil and hurriedly wrote down some words. She folded the paper and handed it to Hugh.

Sawyer didn't fancy the idea of spending the afternoon in the company of two women. "Can't you just marry us and be done with it?" He congratulated himself at keeping any annoyance from his voice. No need for any of them to guess that he was finding this all rather unsettling.

"An hour for some serious second thought won't hurt." And with that, the door closed behind the preacher.

Carly huffed. "I don't need any serious second thought." She grinned at Sawyer. "Father will agree once he's read my note."

Sawyer couldn't imagine what she'd written that

made her so certain. The women left the room. He had little choice but to follow them, though he did so reluctantly. He paused by the two children. Jill ignored him and ran to the kitchen after Evan who followed his mama.

Every carefully honed instinct told Sawyer he should turn left, exit through the door and not look back until he was fifty miles down the road.

"Would you children like some cookies and milk?" Mrs. Arness asked.

"Yes, please," her little boy said.

"Me, too." Jill's tone was almost demanding.

When he last saw his little sister, she was well mannered and full of laughter. He wanted to see that child return to replace the demanding, unruly one she'd become. He recognized all the signs of someone turning her back to the world, to kindness and love. He would do everything he could to reverse that process.

But as he turned right and joined the others in the kitchen, he couldn't decide whether or not he wished Mr. Morrison would refuse to grant permission for a marriage between Sawyer and Carly.

Chapter Three

Carly and Annie normally had no difficulty carrying on a conversation but with Sawyer at the same table, suddenly Carly could think of nothing to say. She felt Annie's glance on her and looked up.

Annie tipped her head toward Sawyer. *Talk to him,* she mouthed.

Carly understood she had to do so if only to prove to her friend…and herself…that it would not be uncomfortable sharing her table with a stranger. Of course, Father would be there. But he could be dour at times.

She'd be sharing her table. Her house. Her ranch. Her life.

Her throat tightened so she couldn't speak. Thankfully, Annie set a cup of tea before each of them just then and Carly sucked back a mouthful of the hot liquid.

Annie took pity on her and spoke to Sawyer. "Where are you and Jill from?"

"We've come from Libby, Kansas."

"My, that is a long ride for a little girl."

"I suppose so." Sawyer's tone communicated nothing. Carly couldn't tell if he was surprised at the idea or if he had already considered it or if, indeed, it mattered not at all to him. If she had to guess, she'd go with the last thought simply because he revealed no emotion.

Annie turned to Jill. "Did you enjoy the trip?"

Jill bumped her glass of milk and the contents splashed across the table.

Carly jumped up. "I'll get it." She grabbed the dishrag and mopped up the liquid.

"It's okay. Accidents happen," Annie said.

Carly studied Jill. Surely she was mistaken in thinking the accident had been deliberate.

Jill kept her face downturned. Her shoulders hunched forward.

Carly's heart went out to the orphaned little girl. Perhaps the bump on her head had put her aim off.

By the time Carly had cleaned up the spilled milk, the children had finished their cookies.

"Mama, can we go outside?" Evan asked.

"Yes, of course. Stay in the backyard. And take Happy with you."

The pup ran for the door and barked. The children let him out and followed. Their voices, raised in play, reached those around the table.

"I apologize for the spilled milk," Sawyer said.

"No need. She's just a child."

Something flicked through his eyes before that bottomless empty pit opened up again and swallowed every hint of feeling but it was enough to make Carly wonder if he had a secret concerning Jill.

Now she was getting fanciful. Jill was an eight-year-old. But she did not look at Annie for fear her friend would see a hint of Carly's worries. This time for serious second thought allowed for far too much second-guessing. The reasons for marrying Sawyer were just as valid now as they had been an hour earlier.

She took a cookie from the plate in the middle of the table and passed the plate to Sawyer. He also took a cookie and bit into it.

"These are good." He turned to Carly. "You can cook, can't you?"

Carly caught Annie's eyes, silently signaling her not to reveal anything, then she turned to Sawyer and gave him her best innocent look. "Why? Can't you?"

He held her gaze, allowing her to see nothing. She did her best to do the same.

"What I do best is open a can of beans with my pocketknife. Peaches, too. I can stir up a batch of biscuits if I have to but I'll be the first to admit they aren't very good."

"Might be as good as anything I make." *For all you know.*

He continued to look at her and she kept her expression bland.

Annie chuckled. "I can assure you, you won't starve to death."

"I could say the same about my own cooking."

Carly laughed at the wry note in his voice. Good to know he could express some feeling, though food might be the only reason he did so. "What more can you ask?"

He swirled the contents of his tea cup round and round, stared at them and gave a little sigh. "I guess it's too much to hope for crispy fried chicken, sweet berry pie and melt-in-your-mouth biscuits."

Carly decided she'd let him wonder about her cooking ability until he got a chance to see for himself. "I don't recall cooking being part of our agreement. You going to start adding in things now?"

"No." One shoulder rose ever so slightly. She wouldn't have noticed had she not been paying close attention. And likely closer attention than one normally would as she tried to figure out what sort of man she was about to marry. Hopefully he wouldn't turn out to be the demanding type that wanted meals served by a gal who had prettied herself up.

Annie shook her head and Carly knew she would abide no more teasing.

Carly shrugged, grinning and feeling rather pleased with herself. It had been fun to try to get some sort of reaction from Sawyer.

A cry from outside jolted all three of them to their feet and they rushed for the door.

Annie was the first into the yard and yelled, "Evan!"

Evan stood in the middle of the yard, pointing toward the tree in the back corner.

Three pairs of eyes followed the direction he indicated.

Jill perched in a branch a goodly distance from the ground, holding Happy, who shivered and whined.

Annie rushed to Evan to console him. "Don't worry. We'll get him down." She turned to Sawyer, her meaning plain. She expected him to settle this problem.

Already Sawyer had crossed to the bottom of the tree. "Jill, come down immediately."

She shook her head.

"Right this instance."

"Can't." She sounded quite certain.

"You must."

"Can't," she yelled.

"Can't or won't?"

Carly went to Sawyer's side. "Can you go up there and get her to hand you the dog?"

"I don't think the branch will take the weight of both of us."

He was right. Only one thing to do. She pulled the back of her skirt up and fixed it at her waist forming a pair of loose trousers. Not for the first time and certainly not for the last, she wondered at the impracticality of women's wear. Thus girded up, she quickly climbed the tree until she came alongside Jill and reached for the dog. "Let me hand him down before he falls." She managed to pluck the animal from her arms and shinnied down far enough to hand Happy to Sawyer.

"Are you coming?" she called up to Jill.

"No."

"Do you want us to leave you here?"

"You can't leave her," Annie protested. "It isn't safe."

"I've climbed lots of tree. Never got hurt. Besides, she got up there. She can get down." She jumped to the ground, freed her skirts and shook out the wrinkles as best she could. Then she faced Sawyer. If seeing her like this was going to shock him to the core, best they all find out now.

"Thanks for getting the dog." He put Happy in Evan's arms.

Carly headed for the house. When she realized no one followed, she turned. "Anyone coming?"

The two adults remained rooted to the spot, watching Jill.

"I can't leave her," Sawyer said. "What if she falls?"

Carly slowly retraced her steps. "I don't think someone who climbed a tree with a pup in her arms will have any trouble getting down with her arms empty."

Sawyer gave a low sound of disagreement that could be best described as a grunt. "I have no desire to stand by and do nothing and then see harm come to her."

"Me, either. But I simply don't think Jill needs help." Was the child playing games with them? Perhaps testing them to see if she could make them jump to her tune? Like Carly had done when she was younger. Before she learned it was easier to do what needed to be done without waiting for or expecting approval.

"Then why isn't she coming down?" Sawyer moved closer to the tree and looked up through the branches and spoke to his sister. "You can get down easily. Just lower your foot to the branch below you."

Jill kept her gaze locked on the distance.

Carly studied the child. There was something about her expression that made Carly change her opinion. Jill's knuckles were white where she clung to the branch. Her lips were pressed into a narrow line. Perhaps the bump on her head had affected her balance. Whatever the cause, Carly knew the child feared to climb down and she nudged Sawyer aside. "I'll help her down."

"I should be the one."

"As you already pointed out, the branches aren't strong enough to take your weight." Already she had her skirts tucked out of the way and began to climb. Again she came alongside Jill. "Can you let go of the branch?"

"Not going to."

Even though Jill tried to sound tough, Carly caught the thread of fear in her voice. "Okay then, let's try something else." She edged closer to Jill, pushed herself to her tiptoes. "Climb on my back and I'll give you a ride down." If she made it sound like fun, maybe Jill would forget her fear.

"Don't want to."

So she wasn't going to let go of that branch. Praying the branch would hold the weight of both of them, she hoisted herself up beside Jill. "Will you let me carry you down? It will be fun. Just like when I carried you off the street." She pried open the fingers of one hand as she talked, hoping her conversation distracted Jill. She freed the hand and pulled one arm about her neck. Then talking softly to Jill, as she would with a frightened colt, she pulled the other arm about her neck. "Hang on." She needn't have told Jill to do so. The child's arms about her neck almost choked her.

Carly began to inch toward the trunk.

The branch upon which she sat, creaked, cracked and bent.

Sawyer held his breath when he saw the branch under Jill and Carly bow. He would not stand here and be a spectator. He couldn't live with that sort of memory to add to another he could not erase. He reached the trunk of the tree in seconds and pulled himself upward from branch to branch, ignoring the way they creaked under his weight. He drew even with Carly's foot and clamped his hand around her ankle. He would stop her from falling no matter what.

"I have you," he called.

"I'm on my way down."

They hadn't fallen. His lung released a gust of spent air.

"You'll have to get out of the way." Her voice sounded

a little thin but then he had no way of judging whether that was normal or otherwise.

"I'm easing down." He moved one branch at a time, staying close enough he could catch the pair if they fell. He didn't jump from the last branch until Carly and Jill were safely on the ground and then he stood face to face with Carly, Jill still clinging to her. He touched the back of Jill's head. Felt her twitch. Dropped his hand. Did his sister find his touches objectionable? He wouldn't let himself care about anyone else but this little girl. It pained him to think she resisted his affection. Though he knew he wasn't good at showing it.

"Everyone is safe and sound." His voice seemed calm and steady. That was good.

Carly eased Jill to the ground. "Go with Mrs. Arness."

Jill hesitated, then sauntered toward the woman.

Mrs. Arness took each child by the hand and led them inside.

Carly shook out her skirts, then stood straight as a post, her arms crossed. "I'm trying to decide if I should thank you or be angry at you."

"Angry? Why?"

"For treating me like I couldn't manage on my own."

A shudder snaked through his insides but he remained impassive and unemotional on the outside. "Didn't you feel the branch give under you?"

"I did and knew I had to grab the tree trunk. Which I did." She tipped her head from side to side. "I didn't need help."

"I didn't know that. All I could think was I wasn't about to stand by and do nothing. I know how awful that feels."

Her interest sharpened. "Perhaps you'd care to explain."

"Not really."

"Then let's be clear that I need no mollycoddling." She leaned closer. "I can manage fine on my own. I don't need a man. That's Father's idea."

Something about her anger lit his own and he stuck out his chin. "I watched our house burn down with my brother and mother inside. I didn't do anything to help. I was afraid to move. To this day, I live with regret over that and I've vowed I will never stand by and do nothing when I think someone is in danger."

She continued her solemn study of him. Something soft flickered through her eyes. "I'm sorry you experienced that and I accept your explanation as apology."

He choked back a sputter. "It wasn't meant as apology. Or even explanation." He reached for his hat, then realized he'd left it in the house and had to settle for scrubbing his hair back. "And you can forget I said anything about the fire. I don't want to talk about it ever again."

She smiled ever so slightly but it was enough for her brown eyes to darken to molten chocolate and make him wonder if he was about to step into a vat of the warm, sweet liquid.

He scrubbed his hair again and wished he had his hat so he could slap it on his head. He needed something physical to release the tightness in his chest as he stared at Carly.

"Then why did you mention it?" she persisted.

He stepped back and shifted to look toward the house. Anywhere but at her warm expression. "So you'd realize that my actions had nothing to do with you. I only reacted because of my vow." He turned back to scowl at her. "And because you made me angry."

Her smile grew. "There goes your certainty that you feel nothing."

He rumbled his lips. "Won't happen again."

The preacher rode into the yard and dismounted. He approached them. "Carly, your father gave his go-ahead. Don't know what you put in that note but he chuckled when he read it and said, 'Let the lassie marry that man. It might prove interesting.'"

The preacher glanced from Carly to Sawyer. "Have I interrupted an argument?"

Neither of them answered.

"Perhaps you've changed your minds about this marriage?"

Sawyer's heart bounced against the walls of his chest. He should have been more careful of how he spoke. Not that it was something he usually had to concern himself with. But now, having seen a glimpse of his soul, Carly would have cause to refuse this marriage.

But to his surprise, she took his arm and marched him toward the house. "Nothing's changed. We both have reason for this and I think we understand each other well enough."

Sawyer firmly dismissed any doubt he had. As far as he could see, he didn't have much choice. Besides, how hard could it be to have a pretend marriage, a job on a ranch and a home for Jill all with the same agreement?

Chapter Four

Carly had it all figured out in her head. Marry the man. Go home and life would go on as it had since she'd started working the ranch when she was fifteen. Against her father's wishes, although she had done plenty to help before that. His protesting noise meant nothing as he clearly needed the help. He didn't like riding the range, didn't like pushing cows out of coulees or roping an ornery steer to tend a hoof. She did like it and she did it well, so they had settled unto a comfortable routine. He farmed the few acres he had plowed to raise feed and wheat for their flour. She did the cow stuff.

The roles were perfectly clear.

Sawyer would help her maintain those roles. He could take Father's place in the way the ranch was run.

But if he thought she'd agreed to marry him because she needed him—

Well, she hoped she'd set him straight on that matter.

She resisted an urge to bend down and rub her ankle where he'd grabbed her. Indignation rose within her. Even if he'd promised himself to not stand by when he saw someone in danger, it didn't give him the right to be so indiscreet.

But marriage would.

She shook her head to dismiss the idea. They'd agreed on the terms of their marriage and it did not include any privileges.

At least Father had given his permission. She ducked her head to hide her smile as she thought of the note she'd written to him.

You said we needed a man at the ranch. I found one. He's strong. Has a little sister. They need a home. So we're going to get married. I think you'll like Sawyer. He appears to be a lot like you—stubborn, a man of his word and when he speaks, he means what he says. Though I doubt he is as stubborn as a Scotsman. I've made up my mind and intend to do this but I would appreciate your blessing.

She hadn't added that Hugh might refuse to marry them without Father's approval.

Her thoughts returned to the present when Hugh asked Annie to be witness to the exchanging of vows. "I'll call Augie East to be the other witness." Hugh left to go ask the blacksmith who also served as undertaker to join them.

When the door closed behind him, Annie broke into tears, trying to wipe them from her face before the children noticed.

"You two go play with Evan's toys on the hearth," Carly said and waited for the children to settle down in front of the cold fireplace to play before she pulled Annie aside. "What's wrong?"

Annie sobbed her reply. "I always dreamed of you

walking down the aisle in a lovely white gown as I stood up front to share your wedding day with you."

Carly glanced over to Sawyer, saw that he watched them but he might have been deaf for all she could read of his expression.

She turned back to Annie. "We could get married in the church if it means that much to you." Though she preferred not to take vows before the pulpit. Not that she didn't mean to keep the vows but not in the sense of marriage as God had instituted.

"It's not the same." Annie wiped her tears on the corner of a kitchen towel. "But I know you won't change your mind." She looked past Carly to Sawyer. "She's stubborn like that."

"Hush, Annie, do you want him to change his mind?" Some men saw stubbornness as contentious.

"Better now than to have regrets later."

"I'm not about to change my mind," Sawyer said. "I've given my word and I stand by it."

Annie sniffed. "You're as stubborn as she."

"Not stubborn, ma'am. Just going to do what has to be done."

Hugh returned with Mr. East. He looked from Carly to Sawyer and back again. "I can't say as I like this but it seems you've both made up your minds. Do you want to get married in the church or—"

"Can we just do it in the front room?" Carly knew it didn't make any difference in God's sight where they spoke their vows but she did not want to do it in the church.

"That will be fine." They went into the next room. Hugh stood with his back to the fireplace.

Feeling as awkward as a newborn foal trying to find

her legs for the first time, Carly faced Hugh, with Sawyer on one side of her, Annie on the other and Mr. East at Sawyer's far side. She'd never envisioned herself as getting married and if she had, it would not have been like this. But as Sawyer said, they were only doing what had to be done.

Hugh opened his black book of ceremonies. "I will ask yet again, are you sure of this?"

Carly nodded as did Sawyer. The children sat on the hearth, watching. Somehow, seeing Jill in her soiled dress with her hair tangled about her head made Carly straighten her spine. This was the right thing to do.

"Very well," Hugh said. "Even though the circumstances of this marriage are unusual, the vows are the same. You are about to enter into a union which is most sacred and most serious. It is most sacred, because it is established by God himself. You are swearing before God to uphold the tenants of this holy institution." He paused long enough to give them a chance to withdraw their request.

Neither did.

"Very well. If you would face each other." He waited while they slowly turned. "Take each other's hands."

Neither Carly nor Sawyer moved.

Hugh sighed a little. "How do you expect to be joined in marriage if you can't even hold hands?" He half closed the book. "I don't know if I can go through with this."

Carly and Sawyer reached for each other. She was not surprised to learn his hands were work worn and his grasp firm. She tightened her fingers and gave him an equally firm hold.

"Good. Now let's proceed. Sawyer, repeat after me."

Hugh spoke the wedding vows and Sawyer repeated them, his voice strong and sure.

And then it was Carly's turn. She met Sawyer's gaze without flinching and echoed Hugh's words. Every word a promise to be forever united to this man.

"You have exchanged vows before God and these witnesses. Those whom God hath joined together, let no one put asunder. You may now kiss the bride."

Carly couldn't say if Sawyer dropped her hands or if she dropped his but they faced each other with their hands at their sides. She was not going to kiss him. For one thing, he was a stranger. And more important, they had agreed this was purely a contractual union for mutual benefit. Not for romance or any such thing.

Sawyer moved back. "That's not necessary."

She also took a step back. "I agree."

Hugh sighed. "Why am I not surprised? Everyone needs to sign the register." Hugh led them into his office where the necessary paperwork was completed.

Annie wrung her hands. "I feel bad. You should have a special wedding meal. But I'd be pleased if you'd join us for dinner, plain as it is."

"Fine. Thank you," Sawyer and Carly said in unison.

Carly followed Annie back to the kitchen and stood in the middle of the room. She'd been here any number of times and yet nothing looked familiar. Her brain seemed stuck back at the fireplace, saying the words she would now live by.

"I have enough roast pork to make sandwiches if you'd like to help make them."

"Of course." But she couldn't think what to do.

Annie gave a little laugh and pushed her toward the cupboard, handed her a knife and put a loaf of bread on the cutting board. "Slice the loaf and butter it while I slice the meat."

Carly did as she was instructed. All the while, Annie talked and yet her words echoed inside Carly's head, making as much sense as the clanging of harness bells.

Annie nudged her aside and laid the meat on the prepared bread. "Would you set out six plates?"

She did so, though she miscounted the plates and had to return one to the cupboard.

Somehow the others appeared and they all sat at the table, Jill at Sawyer's side, Sawyer straight across from Carly. Carly stared at the man. Her husband. In name only. But it still felt unreal. "Hard to believe I left home this morning, worried Father was about to sell the ranch and now I'm going home with a husband to save the ranch." Her voice sounded hollow to her and she hoped the others wouldn't notice anything amiss.

"The Lord works in mysterious ways." Hugh's ironic tone was impossible to miss.

Carly laughed a little. "He should have made me a boy so Father would have a son. Then this marriage wouldn't be necessary." Her words fell into a pool of silence. She jerked herself to attention. She'd never mentioned such a thing before. Not even to Annie. Such thoughts had been buried long enough for her to think they were dead. Why had they suddenly resurrected? "These are good sandwiches, Annie. Thank you."

"Like I said, if I'd known you were to be married today, I would have at least baked a cake."

Carly shrugged. "It doesn't matter." She pushed back from the table. "I'll help you clean up, then we best get home."

Annie waved her away. "That's not necessary. You

go on ahead. You'll have lots to do when you get home."
She hugged Carly. "This should really be your honeymoon."

Carly almost choked. Surely Annie didn't think—

She didn't dare look at Sawyer, afraid he had overheard the comment.

"You're right. There will be much to do at home."
Not the least of which was introduce her husband to her
father. That might prove interesting. To put it mildly.

Jill clung to Sawyer's back as they rode south of town
toward the Morrison Ranch.

"You're married to her?" Jill asked.

"Yup. You saw us."

"So she's my aunt now?"

He hadn't thought of it. "No. She's your sister-in-
law."

"Maybe I don't like her." She kept her voice flat as
if she didn't care but he knew better. Knew his little
half sister had endured too many sorrows and disappointments and had begun to tell herself she didn't care
about anything. He didn't want her to believe it as completely as he did. It didn't happen immediately and he
couldn't say when he'd gotten so good at it that it was
now his very nature.

"We'll have a home."

"That don't matter to me." He couldn't see her but
knew she lifted her shoulders and let them sag.

"I think it will be nice. Your mama and papa would
care."

"Well, I don't."

He tried to think how to make Jill care. Make her
realize they were going to stay here. But how could he

give her reassurances when he had married a woman he'd met only a few hours ago? He clung to his only hope—she needed him as much as he needed her. That was enough to keep them committed to their vows.

They rode on in silence even though he longed to make Jill believe things would be different now but he couldn't find words. He was too long out of practice at thinking about such vague things.

He glanced about himself. He'd been to Montana before and had liked what he saw. Now he looked at the rolling hills to his left covered with lush spring grass and the trees to his right…some leafed out. Beyond the trees would be the mountains and he promised himself he would go camping in the mountains the first chance he got. Alone.

Now that Jill had a home, he could make such plans.

Carly rode a little ahead of them. She made no attempt at conversation, which suited him fine. Though he might have liked to ask a few questions about the ranch.

She reined in. "Our land starts here. The buildings are there." She pointed to the left.

A cluster of buildings by some trees—pine and cedar perhaps. Plus deciduous trees. Probably aspen. He'd seen a variety of trees in his travels through Montana.

He made out a small weathered house with a rock chimney, a low barn, also weathered, surrounded by corrals and several other outbuildings.

They turned off the road and started down the trail leading to the homesite. As they drew closer, he could see that everything was neat and well maintained. He drew in a satisfying breath for the first time since they had left town.

As newlyweds.

No doubt Preacher Hugh expected the marriage would be real enough even if rushed. If he'd known the exact details of the agreement between Sawyer and Carly, he might have refused to marry them.

But what did it matter to others if the arrangement suited them?

And it did. If he had any doubts, he wasn't about to admit it. Not even to himself. Especially not to himself. He had given his word and would fulfill his vows to the best of his ability and within the boundaries they had agreed upon.

They reached the yard and turned toward the barn. She swung off her horse, less hampered by her skirts than most women he'd seen. And he'd seen a few who rode astride. Didn't have much of an opinion about it except to think riding sidesaddle looked mighty uncomfortable.

He drew to a halt next to her horse but before he could reach back to let Jill down, she slid off, holding to his leg until her feet hit the ground. She put a distance between herself and Sawyer. Perhaps Carly, too, and stood with her arms crossed and a look of pure challenge on her face.

Carly began to lead her horse to the barn, then turned to Sawyer. "There's room for your horse and feed and—" She broke off as she saw Jill. She gave the girl a moment's study, then brought her gaze back to Sawyer, silently asking for an explanation.

He shrugged and led his horse after her. Not until they entered the barn and were far enough away that Jill couldn't hear did he answer. "Too many changes. She's getting so she resents them."

"Then it's up to us to make sure she knows this is permanent."

"It will take time for her to believe it."

She pointed him toward a stall and indicated where to get the feed and find a currycomb. She led her horse into the adjoining stall. As she brushed the horse, she murmured to it.

He tipped his head trying to catch her words but he only made out a few.

"Good boy...changes...surprise..."

He grinned. That about summarized it. Changes and good surprises. At least he hoped they would be good. Only time would tell but he meant to do what he could to ensure things went well. He glanced back to where Jill still stood. Her hands were now at her sides and she looked about, taking in their new surroundings.

Carly put away the grooming tools and straightened. The cowboy hat she'd worn while riding home hung down her back. She smoothed her tousled hair back. He decided he liked the straw color of it. She glanced at her skirts, gave them a shake and then looked at Sawyer.

"You ready to meet my father?"

The thing he'd been ignoring could no longer be ignored. "Ready as I'll ever be." He removed his own hat and smoothed his hair. "If I'd known I was getting married, I would have gotten a haircut and a new shirt."

She eyed him long enough that he ached to turn from her. He didn't. It was far more important to let her see that he was unaffected by her sharp study.

"Too late for that." Her words were flat as if it didn't matter one way or the other to her.

He glanced at his boots. Wouldn't hurt to clean them up a mite but already Carly headed for the door and, seeing how Jill resumed her former stance, he hurried after her, knowing Jill wouldn't move if he didn't.

Jill looked from one adult to the other. Her eyes darted away.

Sawyer guessed at her intention and before she could run, he caught her hand. She tried to jerk away but he had a good hold and they followed Carly toward the house.

He studied it carefully as if it might reveal what sort of life was lived within its walls. A low, log structure. The roof sloped down to cover an open veranda. Matching windows stood on either side of the door. An attached woodshed with its own door. They reached the veranda and climbed the steps.

"It's small," Carly said. "But I think it will be adequate."

For all of us, he added for her. "It looks warm and dry. That's what matters the most." Jill dragged her feet so that he was forced to haul her along. He would tell her everything would be okay but she had no reason to believe him given he didn't have any basis for such an opinion.

Carly straightened her shoulders, making him realize this was equally awkward for her.

She turned the knob and pushed the door open, stepped inside and beckoned them to follow.

Jill skidding at his heels, Sawyer entered a kitchen. He barely had time to register his surroundings before his gaze came to a man sitting at the table, his right leg stretched out, immobile in a splint.

Sawyer's gaze darted from the leg to the man's face. Full white whiskers, snapping brown eyes, a full head of white hair. A big man. How did he sire a woman as small as Carly?

"Dinnae stand with the door open. Come in and show your face."

At the man's robust voice, Jill stopped tugging at Sawyer's hand and pressed to his back.

"Ack, now, no need for the lassie to be afeared of me. I dinnae bite."

Carly snorted. "But you growl a lot. Father, this is Sawyer Gallagher and his sister, Jill."

"Aye. Yer husband I presume." He struggled to his feet and held out a ham-sized hand to shake with Sawyer.

"Pleased to make your acquaintance," Sawyer managed as his hand was swallowed up.

"Well, now that remains to be seen. Aye?"

Aye, indeed, Sawyer thought as Mr. Morrison leaned over to look at Jill.

"There, there, little lassie. You and I will soon enough be friends." With a groan, the man sank back to his chair and faced Carly. "And you, Carly Morrison—no, wait. It's now Carly Gallagher—I suppose yer well pleased with yerself that you found a husband so quickly. Could be you've jumped from the frying pan into the fire." He laughed heartily.

"Sorry about your accident," Sawyer said, taking in the strain about the man's eyes despite his laughter. "What happened?"

"Ack. What can I say? A foolish old man trying to be a hero."

Sawyer looked at Carly for explanation. "He tried to stop a runaway wagon and slipped on a patch of ice. The wagon ran over his leg."

"Aye and it would not have happened if some fool had not blasted his gun beside the horses." He eased himself to a more comfortable position, then leaned forward. "Now let's have a look at the wee lassie."

Sawyer peeled Jill off the back of his legs and pulled her forward. "Say hello to Mr. Morrison."

She didn't respond. Her jaw jutted out and he knew she wouldn't.

He couldn't force her to. Instead of trying, he glanced about the house. A big kitchen with the table in the middle of the room, the stove and cupboards to one side. A wide doorway opened to the living room. From where he stood, he saw a couple of comfortable looking armchairs, one with a table beside it and a scattering of newspapers and books. A footstool to one side of the chair. He wondered if that's where Mr. Morrison spent some of his day.

Across the kitchen was a closed door. To one end of the kitchen, another closed door. No doubt the bedrooms. He eased slightly to his left and saw another door off the kitchen. The house was small, as Carly said, but more than adequate. He'd shared crowded quarters with a dozen men and slept in the open under the stars. This would do fine for a home for himself and Jill.

No doubt he would soon learn where he and Jill were to sleep and which rooms were used by Carly and her father.

Mr. Morrison took the initiative with Jill. "Hello, little Jill. So yer going to be living with us now." Mr. Morrison eyed the child without saying another word. The silence grew heavy and uncomfortable.

Jill lifted her head and looked at the older man.

Mr. Morrison smiled. "That's better." He nodded.

"You have beautiful eyes. You should let people see them more often. 'Tis my guess you have a beautiful smile, too. I can't wait to see it."

Sawyer could have warned the man it might be a long time before he did.

Mr. Morrison sat back and Jill shuffled to Sawyer's side. She didn't touch him. She wouldn't. Sawyer understood. But perhaps living here and being settled would help her remember a time when it was okay to feel something besides caution.

"Well, if you're satisfied," Carly said. "I need to get some beds ready for these people."

Mr. Morrison chuckled. A pleasing sound that spread a little honey to Sawyer's insides. "You mean your husband and his little sister?"

"Uh-huh. I'm going to clean out the little storeroom."

"Aye. It will be a nice bedroom for the wee lassie."

"Or for the big brother."

Mr. Morrison sat upright so suddenly he groaned with pain. He quickly recovered. "Are you telling me your husband is going to sleep there? What kind of nonsense is this?" His voice rose.

Carly dipped water from the bucket on the cupboard and had a long drink. "You said I needed a husband to keep the ranch. I got one. The ranch is safe. But I have no need of a man for any other reason." She refilled the dipper and offered it to Sawyer.

He drank, more to distance himself from this situation than because of thirst. "Thanks." He returned the dipper to her and she again refilled it and offered it to Jill, who likewise drank rather desperately. She might try to distance herself from people but she couldn't help but feel the tension in the room.

"Are ye telling me this marriage is a mockery?"

Carly seemed unaffected by the man's loud voice. "Nope. Just a contract between two adults."

Mr. Morrison's eyes came to Sawyer. Hard, challenging.

Sawyer met the gaze without flinching.

"Yer agreeable to this?"

Sawyer nodded. He was getting tired of explaining it. "We need a family. She needed a man."

"That so? Seems to me a married man would be wanting to share his wife's bed."

"Father! Enough. We agreed the marriage was for mutual benefit and that wasn't one of them. We know what we're doing."

Her father sat back. "Aye. So you say." He grinned and stroked his beard, as content as a cat full of warm milk. "This will be interesting." He rolled the *r*.

Carly stared at her father, turned to look at Sawyer and he saw something that made his nerves twitch. A look of surprise, a flicker of fear and then she shrugged.

"I expect it will."

A little tremor twisted Sawyer's neck muscles. Had he bitten off more than he could chew?

Chapter Five

Carly refused to let Father's amusement trouble her.
She knew what she was doing. She wasn't being naive.
There would be adjustments to make, things she might
be surprised to learn. But she'd faced tough challenges
before and always overcome them. She felt duty-bound
to point out the fact to her father.

"Remember the time I brought home that wild horse?"
She turned to Sawyer. "The gelding wasn't really a wild
horse, just a horse that had been mishandled and turned
bad and then the owners turned him loose rather than
bother with him or feed him. But he was a beauty. He's
a golden palomino. His coat glistens like sunshine. Or
at least it did once he regained his health." She shifted
her gaze back to Father, reminding him of how that had
turned out. "I made up my mind to gentle him and turn
him into the best horse one could ask for. And now he is."

She'd named him Sunny and rode him everywhere.
Did Father see that marrying Sawyer was much the
same? Not that she thought she had to tame the man but
she had worked out the problem of dealing with Sunny.
She would do the same with Sawyer.

Father continued to stroke his beard, his gaze shifting from Carly to Sawyer to Jill and then back to Carly. "Aye? Is that what ye have in mind for Sawyer? Taming him to be a pet?"

Jill snorted behind her hand, a sound of amusement and derision combined.

"Of course that's not what I mean." She didn't dare look at Sawyer to gauge his reaction. "Father, you're impossible." She ground around so her back was to the men, which had her facing the door of the storeroom and a reminder of the need to get Sawyer and Jill settled. "I have to get beds ready." She hurried to the small room, more than half tempted to pull the door shut behind her and slip the hook in place to secure the door. Except the hook was on the other side of the door. So she settled for squaring her shoulders and looking about the room.

Sawyer's boots thudded on the floor as he followed her.

She pushed back her annoyance. Of course, she wouldn't have the same degree of privacy and the ability to be alone as she'd had prior to their arrangement. She could live with that. And if she couldn't, Sunny and a ride in the open were but a few steps away.

Sawyer stopped at the doorway.

Jill ducked past him and looked about the room. Her eyes lit as she saw the trunk in the corner. "What's in there?"

"My mother's things." And baby things Mother had saved, always hoping for a baby boy who survived. But Carly was the only baby to live past a few weeks and grow to adulthood. She was aware of four baby boys who did not live that long. Their little graves were on the hillside and her mother lay next to them.

"Where's your ma?"

"She died when I was fourteen."

"Oh." Jill pushed her way through the boxes and other items until she reached the trunk. She examined the latches and tried to release them.

"Jill," Sawyer spoke with a hefty degree of warning. "You don't have permission to touch that."

"Can't I look?" Jill asked.

Carly had crossed the room and pressed on the latches to stop the curious child. "I prefer you didn't."

"Fine." Jill stomped away, crushing an old hat of Father's beneath her feet.

Sawyer grabbed it and punched it back to shape as best he could. "I apologize."

Carly nodded. She wasn't about to excuse the child but neither could she blame Sawyer. "Help me move the trunk to my room." Not only would it clear out room for Sawyer, it would be safer where she could keep an eye on it.

She grabbed the handle on one side, he grabbed the other and they carried the trunk across the kitchen to her bedroom. She put it down outside the door. "Wait here a minute." Jill would have followed her but Carly closed the door and leaned against it. She'd carelessly tossed a few items of clothing on the chair and floor and bent to pick them up and shove them into the wardrobe. She pushed the bed against the wall to make room for a cot for Jill. A little sister! She grinned. How many times had she hoped for a little brother or sister only to have her hopes dashed when the newborns didn't live? Seems she was about to have her dreams fulfilled this way. It ought to be fun.

Someone kicked at the door. Sawyer spoke Jill's name in a warning tone.

Carly faced the door. It might not be as much fun as she'd imagined. Oh, what was she thinking? The child was only eight. Soon enough she'd be chasing butterflies and playing with imaginary friends.

She opened the door. Sawyer had a firm grip on Jill's shoulder and the little girl wore a mutinous expression. Carly wasn't sure what to do…or even if she could do anything. Seems the child was Sawyer's responsibility. Though Carly meant to do everything she could to help Jill feel secure. Everything, she added with a bit of foresight, that Jill would allow her to do.

"Are you ready?" Sawyer asked.

Carly nodded and grabbed her end of the trunk. They carried it into the room and parked it at the end of her bed. She dusted her hands off. "Now let's get the other room ready."

They tromped back across the room, Father watching them with a great deal of interest.

Sawyer stopped inside the storeroom. "Where do you plan to put all this stuff?"

Carly raised her voice. "I figure a bonfire out back will take care of most of it."

"Dinnae burn me treasures," Father roared, making Carly chuckle.

"I knew he'd do that," she whispered, then spoke louder so she would be heard in the other room. "Father, it's just junk."

He thumped his crutch on the floor.

She rushed to the door. "Sit down. I'll not burn it." She released a heavy sigh. "Can we put some of it in your room?"

"Aye, that's a fine idea." He sank back, his mouth set in a hard line at the pain of moving.

With Sawyer's help and Jill's watchful supervision, several crates were stacked in the corner of Father's bedroom.

Carly didn't give Father's crowded quarters much thought. He insisted on keeping all this stuff so she reasoned he must enjoy having it crowding every corner.

They returned to the storeroom. It still held far too much.

She and Sawyer stood side by side in the little cleared area. "There's a cot under that pile of—" she lowered her voice to a whisper "—rags. I'll have to move them, though I itch to get rid of them."

Sawyer glanced over his shoulder. "Your father likes to keep stuff?" It was as much statement as question.

"Aye," Carly said, imitating her father. "Lassie, you never know when ye might have a need for this very item."

Jill covered her mouth in an attempt to stifle her giggle.

Liking the child's sense of humor, Carly grinned at Sawyer.

His blue-green eyes shifted to more blue than green as he met her gaze. He seemed a bit startled at her grin and blinked. His mouth twitched and for a moment, she thought he would smile. But he looked away without doing so. Like he said, he didn't allow himself to have feelings.

What a sad way to live. She could understand why he wouldn't want Jill to end up the same.

"I suppose we need to find that cot," he said.

She returned to studying the room. "It'll be more

comfortable than sleeping on the floor." They stood in silent contemplation for two seconds. She couldn't think of him as her husband but at least if he slept here, she could accept him as a hired man. "Besides, I've been wanting to clear out this space. Father planned this to be a hallway to more rooms. But he never needed them, to his great disappointment."

"No brothers or sisters?"

"None that lived." She was so used to thinking that way that she didn't consider how her words would affect Jill.

Jill had been poking through the piles of old newspapers. Her hands grew still. Carly thought she heard the child suck in air. "You got dead brothers and sisters?" Jill asked.

"Four brothers. Maybe I'll show you their graves someday."

"Sawyer gots a dead brother, too." She tipped her head. "Does that mean I have a dead brother?"

Carly waited for Sawyer to answer. But his face had turned to granite and he stared at the wall.

"I suppose it does," she answered in his stead.

"Huh. His name was Johnny." Jill spoke with a degree of authority as if she thought Sawyer might have forgotten.

Carly wasn't sure how to respond, so said words that might mean anything. "I see."

Sawyer had still not moved.

"Let's take some of these things out to the woodshed." She gathered up a bundle of old clothes and stepped past Sawyer, making her way to the small building at the side of the house. She didn't bother looking to see what he did. The man had agreed to marry her.

That was all she expected of him. But she was mildly pleased when he followed, his arms holding the rest of the clothing.

He traipsed on her heels into the shed. She looked about. "If I put shelves along the top of the wall, I can store all this stuff on them." She lowered her armload to the nearby bench.

Sawyer did the same.

She headed for the door, intent on getting to the barn. Her skirts tangled around her ankles. The first thing she would do was trade these cumbersome skirts for her customary trousers. She'd only worn a dress to town because of some vague hope she would find a man willing to wed her.

A smile tugged at her mouth. It hadn't been so much hope that she'd find a man as desperation. Truth be told, she would have married almost anyone to save the ranch. Even if she'd had to drag him from the gutter. She shuddered as a couple of men came to mind. Thankfully, she had found a man in Miss Daisy's Eatery rather than the gutter.

Sawyer followed on her heels. "I'll help you."

"I can do it. But got something to attend to first." She hurried to her room and closed the door firmly after her. The pesky buttons on the bodice of her dress took forever to undo but she'd learned the folly of hurrying. It took even more time to sew buttons back on. She slipped the dress and petticoats off and donned her baggy shirt and fitted trousers, stuck her feet into her pair of well-worn cowboy boots and returned to the main room.

Jill sat on a chair opposite Father, giving him solemn study. She turned as Carly left her room. Carly knew she tried to hide any expression—having learned it from an expert—but her eyes rounded. Her mouth gaped and then she blinked and turned deadpan.

Carly didn't care what Sawyer thought of her attire and yet she looked his direction. Would he see the warning in her eyes to keep his opinion to himself?

"Lassie." Father sighed heavily. "Is it too much to hope ye'd be content to be the woman of the house?"

Carly snorted, her attention still directed toward Sawyer. Would he be as disapproving as Father? He might as well learn right now that she didn't intend to be the sort of woman Father meant.

Sawyer's gaze ran down the length of the woman he'd married. Brown trousers with worn creases informed him she made a habit of dressing like this. He tried to decide what he thought about it and realized he didn't have an opinion. Why should he? Who she was and what she did had little importance to him. He'd agreed to do the ranch work in return for a home for Jill. He expected nothing more, nothing less, from either of them.

Jill looked at him. Something about her expression sent tension up his spine. What was his little sister scheming now?

"I'm going to make shelves." Carly marched past him, the challenge in her voice unmistakable.

He saw no point in telling her she had no need to feel threatened and followed her to the barn.

She grabbed a board, a handful of nails and a hammer. The long board teetered in her grasp and he caught it.

"I'll take this."

She hesitated, then nodded. "Fine."

He had long ago learned to hide his feelings, to deny them until now he hardly even had any feelings he could identify but Carly did not have the same skill. Her annoyance was as evident as the golden sun in the blue sky. He couldn't imagine why she was upset.

"Did I do something to offend you?"

Halfway out the door, she stopped, slowly came about to face him. Her brown eyes narrowed as she studied him. He got the feeling she wanted something from him, but he had no idea what it might be so he stood motionless and waited.

"I hope I've made myself clear that I don't need a man."

"Seems your father has a differing opinion."

"My father is a stubborn Scotsman."

"I believe you've said that before. No need to remind me."

Her shoulders sank and her expression cleared. "Guess I should apologize for getting upset. It's just that—" She didn't finish. "I need to get this shelf made."

He followed her across the yard. Just what? he wanted to ask. But if she wanted to tell him, she would. Until then, he was content to simply follow her back to the shed.

Jill stepped from the woodshed as they approached. She wore too-big trousers, rolled up at the ankles and a baggy shirt. A length of rope held her pants in place. She crossed her arms and scowled at Sawyer.

"Where'd you get the clothes?"

"Found 'em."

"Were they lost?"

"She said they were rags." Jill tipped her head toward Carly but did not look at her.

Nor did Sawyer as he tried to think if she would be offended that Jill had helped herself to some items.

Carly chuckled and he jerked his head round to look at her.

"You're welcome to the clothes. They're too small for me. Of course, you might need your brother's permission to dress like that." The challenge in Carly's eyes sent a twitch down Sawyer's spine. He had hopes of Jill learning to be a lady, like her mother had been.

Jill crossed her arms and scowled at them. "I don't need nobody's permission." She gave Sawyer a hard look. "She wears pants."

"They're a lot more comfortable and safer even when I'm working around the ranch."

"I like 'em." Jill's tone dared Sawyer to try to stop her.

He considered his options. How Carly dressed was none of his business. She clearly didn't heed her father's opinion, so why would she heed his? Not that he cared if she wore trousers. A grin bubbled below the surface. Truth was, she looked fine in them. But Jill was a different matter. Her parents would not approve. Shouldn't he teach her the same things they would have if they lived?

"What'd you do with your dress?"

"Threw it out."

"Jill, we can't afford to replace clothes."

Carly edged past the girl into the woodshed. "The dress is right here." She held up a bundle with fabric that he recognized. "It needs a good scrubbing." After a second of letting him stare at it, she tossed it into the pile on the bench. "I'll get that shelf made." She reached for the board but he shook his head and carried it in, passing Jill who continued to give him loads of defiance.

We'll settle this later, he promised himself. *In private.*

He lifted the board to where he thought she would want it. "Is here okay?"

"It's fine." She grabbed shorter pieces and made shelf brackets, nailing them into place.

He could have driven in the spikes in half the time but wasn't about to offer to trade places with her. Even he—blind as he was to emotions—understood she didn't care for offers of help. Perhaps she had had to fight her father so long to gain her independence that resisting help had become part and parcel of her.

Neither of them talked as they worked. He was used to working in silence, preferred it to useless chatter. But something bothered him and he had to get it off his chest. "Jill's mother was a lady."

She let the hammer hang from her hand and jerked back to give him a hard look. "So was my mother. What are you trying to say?"

One thing about Carly, he didn't have to try to guess at her feelings. "Don't get all offended."

"Offended? Me?" She swung the hammer in a circle. "Why would you think that?"

Not liking the narrow confines of the shed and the swinging hammer, he eased toward the door. "Do you need more things brought out for the shelf?"

She tossed the hammer to the corner. The one nearest where he stood, though perhaps that had been unintentional. He couldn't say.

"I don't know." She didn't move and something warned him he should not either. Not until she finished with her anger. "Are you by any means, referring to her wearing trousers?"

He was getting good at understanding her thinly veiled warnings and answered cautiously. "There's people who would consider it inappropriate."

She closed the distance between them until they were toe to toe. "Sawyer Gallagher, let's get a few things straight."

He gave her his best steely-eyed look.

"I long ago decided my comfort and safety were far more important than what people thought."

He continued his expressionless stare.

"I suppose you're entitled to your opinion but best you keep it to yourself." She half turned away. "How you deal with Jill is your problem."

He allowed one eyebrow to flick. "Dealing with Jill has been a problem."

Carly nodded. "I gathered that. So why bother her about something that truly doesn't matter?" She swiped a hand at her trousers. "Does anyone really think wearing these makes me less of a woman, less moral?"

He let his gaze go up and down her length as if looking for clues and then shook his head. "I don't suppose it does."

Carly's cheeks stained pink. "Well, then. That's settled." She pushed past him and went to the house. "Best I get a bed made up for you."

He followed at a safe distance, not knowing if she was given to words or actions when she was upset, and she was clearly upset.

Jill trailed along after them, her eyes wide and if he wasn't mistaken, full of interest. Having her care about something should please him but it didn't. Not if her only interest was in seeing others in conflict.

They single-filed into the room where he was to sleep. A cot with a bare mattress stood on one side of the room. Piles of old newspapers nested against one wall.

"What's a person to do with old papers?" she asked. "Father?" She raised her voice. "Can we burn the papers?"

"Ack. No. I haven't finished reading them."

"Nor will you ever." She stared at the piles.

"Shove them under the bed." He waited for her response.

"Good idea." Seems her good humor had returned and she grabbed an armload and stuffed it under the cot.

He did the same.

She hurried to get another load. So did he. He stuffed from one end, she from the other until their piles jammed against each other with a thud that made her laugh. "There won't even be room for dust bunnies in there."

Jill watched every move as Sawyer swept the room and Carly made the bed and spread a crazy quilt on top. "My mother and I made this one winter. Mother had been expecting another baby and hoped if she took it easy, this baby would live so she'd spent much of her day sitting with her feet up."

Carly patted the quilt once, then stood back to look around. "You need a cupboard of some sort."

"Surprised there wasn't one or several in this room."

She studied him a moment, decided he was joshing and laughed. It sent a jolt of pleasure through his heart to know she'd appreciated his little attempt at humor.

"Father keeps all the cupboards in his room so he can guard his stuff."

Sawyer nodded. He'd noticed how jam-packed the man's room was. "He likes to keep things."

She grinned at him, her eyes sparkling with humor. "I guess that's pretty evident."

Deep inside Sawyer, something responded. He couldn't say what it was. Couldn't name it. Could only think it was frightening and alluring at the same time.

She turned to again study the room. "There are some apple crates in the loft you can use for a cupboard. And you can pretty the room up any way you like."

"Pretty it up?" He could hardly choke the words out.

"Yeah. You know with pictures and things."

"Oh. That." He hadn't stayed in one place long enough in the past few years to even have a wall to put things on. Last real room he'd had was with Pa and Judith and it had never felt quite right.

Now he was here with a promise to stay. Until death parted them. Seemed like that might be a very long time. He expected that would be a good thing for Jill, though he hadn't expected she'd be wearing trousers. He'd planned to deal with the matter later but Carly's words caused him to reconsider. Seems there were enough things in life to deal with. This one didn't seem all that important. "I might hang a calendar."

In a few minutes, the floor was clean, the bed made. His room was ready and he looked around. A small room. Maybe eight by eight but plenty big enough for him.

Jill perched on the edge of the cot. "Where'm I gonna sleep?"

"In my room," Carly answered. "There a small bed

out in the barn. Used to be mine but when I outgrew it, we didn't give it away." She sighed. "We don't give away, throw away or burn old stuff."

Jill pursed her lips. "What if I don't want to sleep with you?"

Carly stopped at the door. "Then where will you sleep? With your brother?"

"No. I don't want to sleep with him, either. Don't want to be with anyone. I want to be by myself."

Carly sent Sawyer a look that he thought meant she wanted him to deal with this but he had nothing to offer. He'd learned a rebellious Jill was difficult to reason with. Perhaps Carly would have better success.

She turned her attention back to Jill. "There's no other place. As you can see, it's a small house." After an expectant beat, she continued. "You have to sleep someplace."

"Who says?"

Carly laughed. Stopped at the rebellion in Jill's face. "Everyone sleeps."

"Who says?" Jill wouldn't look at either of them, tried to look disinterested.

Sawyer recognized the way she pulled her expression blank and tried to look as if nothing mattered to her. He did the same. This was why she needed a permanent home.

Carly grinned widely. "You'll change your mind soon enough."

"No, I won't."

"I'll get the bed ready just in case." She left.

"Stop being ridiculous," Sawyer murmured to Jill as he followed Carly. He didn't wait to see what his little sister would say. Or do.

Carly headed for the barn, went to the far corner where the pieces of a bed leaned against the wall. She reached for them.

"I'll get it." And before she could voice disagreement, he picked up the headboard, footboard and spring, leaving the side rails for her. He glanced about for a mattress. Didn't see one.

"I'll stuff a tick," Carly said.

They returned to the house and went to Carly's room. He let her enter first, feeling somewhat awkward at being in her bedroom.

She stopped so suddenly he almost collided with her. She dropped the rails to the floor and rushed forward with a little cry.

He didn't need to look to guess that Jill had done something wrong. But it did cross his mind to wonder if Carly might be having regrets about their agreement.

Chapter Six

Carly's breath caught halfway up her throat as she looked at Jill. The child had opened the trunk and pulled out two little nightgowns Carly's mother had lovingly stitched for one of the babies.

At Carly's cry, Jill spun around and dropped the little china shepherdess that had belonged to Carly's mother. The head snapped off and rolled in one direction, the little lamb broke from the shepherdess's arms.

Jill's expression went from surprised to impassive.

Carly didn't give it a thought as she fell on her knees and reached for the broken pieces. She was vaguely aware of Sawyer stepping into the room, taking Jill by the arm and leading her away. With a distant part of her mind, she heard Sawyer speak, heard her father say something. She held the broken ornament in her palms and let her tears wash the pieces.

Through the haze of her silent weeping, she saw Sawyer's legs and boots. She didn't look up. He squatted beside her. "I'm sorry."

She rocked her head back and forth. No amount of regret would fix the broken ornament.

"Your father said it had belonged to your mother."

She sniffed back the tears. "She called it her Twenty-third Psalm reminder. You know, 'The Lord is my shepherd.' She said all she had to do was look at the tenderness in this girl's face—" She turned the broken head over to see the serene smile. Her throat choked closed. When she spoke again, the words edged past the tightness. "She said looking at this made her remember how much God loved her despite the pain of losing so many babies and her failing health." Her heart slowly shattered as she recalled her sweet mother. "I promised her I would never forget that fact." She filled her lungs and spoke firmly, confidently. "She used to quote Romans chapter eight, verses thirty-eight and thirty-nine. Nothing, she said, can separate us from the love of God."

"Hmm." The sound revealed nothing.

She shifted slightly to look at him. He watched her with those expressionless eyes. Could he really feel nothing? Her own emotions and Father's simmered so close to the surface that they continually spilled over. Sometimes they erupted explosively. "You believe in God's eternal love, don't you?"

He held her gaze, revealing nothing of his opinion.

She waited, wanting to know what he felt. Perhaps hoping to find comfort in hearing him confess, as Mother did, that God's love was unchangeable, never wavering.

"I don't know much about love. Not man's nor God's. I can't say if I believe in it as you do." He lifted one shoulder. "Can't say I don't believe, either."

They had both settled to the floor, carefully studying each other. This man was her husband. She knew so little about him but it seems she had a lifetime to learn everything…at least, as much as he was willing to let her know. She shivered a little. Perhaps it would be nothing.

He picked up a fragment of china and handed it to her. "Can it be mended?"

She held the pieces in her palms, studied them a moment. "I doubt it." She met his gaze. Did she detect a lingering question in his eyes? She studied him. "Are you talking about the shepherdess or something more?"

He nodded. "Are you going to change your mind?"

"About what? The shepherdess? It will never be the same."

"I don't mean your ornament." His blue-green eyes darkened to nighttime sky. "Are you going to change your mind about us?"

"Our marriage?"

"I'm sure we can go to the preacher and tell him we've changed our minds. He'll understand."

"Have we changed our minds?"

"I haven't," he said. "My reasons and my decision still stand. But you might think you've made a mistake." He indicated the broken ornament.

She plucked a baby blanket from the trunk and wrapped the pieces carefully. "I know it's beyond repair but I can't bear to throw it away." Her chuckle was as much self-mockery as amusement. "Guess I'm my father's daughter…nothing is every ready to be discarded." She put the bundle in the trunk, then plucked the two little nightgowns off the floor. "Mother put so much love into making these, hoping and praying to have another child to raise." She rang her fingers along the row of neat stitches at the hem.

"And yet she never lost her belief in God's goodness." His softly spoken words settled her heart. Odd that they should do that. She couldn't explain why they did.

"If anything, her faith grew stronger. She often said adversity forced one's roots to grow deeper."

"Sometimes adversity has the power to tear one from their roots."

She couldn't say how she knew but she did—he wanted to know if Jill could be fixed. Perhaps if he could be fixed. But he would never ask. Never admit it.

She pushed to her feet. He did the same and they stood three feet apart, each watching the other. "I'm not sure about Jill but I remember something Mother said. 'Today is not the end. Tomorrow is full of surprises and possibilities.'"

He held her gaze, searched it, seeking to understand, perhaps looking for hope.

She hadn't answered his original question. It wasn't fair to keep him waiting and wondering, perhaps expecting the worse. Though, she realized with a hint of humor, did he think her saying she didn't want to continue with their marriage agreement was the worst? Or did he think the worst would be for her to say she wanted to continue?

"I haven't changed my mind about our agreement." She meant to do everything in her power to make it work.

He studied her. Then released a barely audible sigh. And nodded.

She shifted her gaze from his. He might not reveal his feelings, yet his eyes sucked at her very soul. "I'm going to set up the bed for Jill. It's up to her if she uses it or not."

"She hasn't been very cooperative."

Carly chuckled. "Father would call it a streak of contrariness."

They both turned toward the door where they could hear Father's rumbling voice as he talked to Jill. "He'll be telling her about his childhood. He and Jill have a lot in common. He was orphaned at a young age. Had no family, so at nine he was on his own, trying to support himself." As she talked, they put the bed together. "He found a good family to work for when he was fifteen and began to work for Mother's uncle. Before that, he encountered some cruel people."

"Maybe Jill will realize that things could be worse than they are."

She placed the final side rail and straightened. "When Mother died, I don't think I could have believed that things could be worse. Now, in hindsight, I understand they could have been. But it takes time to work through pain."

They considered each other. Silently sharing something they had in common. For the briefest of moments, she thought she saw a flash of acknowledgment. As if he saw her pain. Admitted his own.

And then it was gone. Perhaps it had only been her imagination.

"Now for a mattress." She didn't invite him to accompany her but half expected he would. Since they arrived at the ranch, he had followed her on every task. Not that there was any need for his help but with him holding the mattress and her stuffing in sweet hay from the stack in the loft, she admitted how much easier it was than struggling on her own.

Jill still sat at the table with Father when they returned. Carly spoke to Sawyer.

"I don't need any help to make the bed. Sit and talk with Father."

"Aye, you do that, laddie. Jilly has been telling me about your travels. Seems you've had a few adventures."

Carly made sure to leave the bedroom door open so she would be in on any stories Sawyer told. She listened shamelessly as he told of being followed by some wolves and encountering a winter storm.

As she smoothed the last cover on the bed, Sawyer said, "We found shelter with an old man in a cabin by a river." His voice deepened. "A loner with a mean streak."

Carly shuddered. She'd sooner deal with marauding animals and Mother Nature at her worst than a man with evil intent.

"Aye, I've met a few of those nasty sort. What did this one do?"

"He snatched Jill from her bed and said he would kill her if I didn't give him all my money."

Carly went to the door, needing to see Jill's reaction to the story.

She sat at the table, motionless, staring at her hands. Hiding her feelings as well as Sawyer.

But Jill was a little girl, she would have been so frightened. So powerless. Carly went to Jill's side. "How awful. I'm glad you're okay." Jill showed no emotion. Carly looked at Sawyer. He too was impassive, revealing nothing. She wasn't convinced that meant he felt nothing. "What did you do?"

"I agreed to give it to him but it was in my saddlebag. So was my gun. I couldn't be certain he wouldn't hurt

Jill, so I hid my gun at first. When I made as if to give him my money, Jill kicked him and bit him."

Father and Carly looked at each other and grinned. No doubt he was thinking Carly would have done much the same.

"I pulled out my gun then and he backed away. We left. Better a snowstorm than a crazy man."

"You've had an awful time. And not just that man." She longed to offer some sort of comfort but both Sawyer and Jill sat stiff and expressionless. Both believing they felt nothing and no one could hurt them. "You're a very brave little girl." She squeezed Jill's shoulder, then moved away, sensing the child didn't know how to deal with such gestures.

"I wasn't brave. I was angry."

"And scared, too, I think. I know I would have been." Jill didn't answer.

"Good thing you had Sawyer to take care of you."

Two Gallagher heads came up and Sawyer and Jill looked at each other. Both seemed surprised at Carly's observation. If only Mother was alive. She would know how to help this pair. Carly could only do what she thought Mother would have said and done. Right now, she knew Mother would have hugged them both but Carly didn't feel free to do it. She patted them both on the back and then moved on before either could react.

Father, perhaps sensing the awkwardness of the others, spoke. "Shouldn't you show them around the place?"

An excellent idea. "Come with me." She signaled them both to join her and they left the house. "You've already seen the barn, so we'll skip that for now. Behind the house is the garden." She led the way to the right. "That way is where we grow the crops. Wheat and oats. To the left is the corrals for the horses. That's Big Harry. He's a black Clydesdale." As if they couldn't see that for themselves. "He's a gentle giant but Father forbids me to handle him."

"'Too much for a wee lassie like you,'" Sawyer quoted getting the accent exactly right.

It sounded so funny coming from his mouth that Carly laughed.

Her gaze caught his and refused to move on. His lips barely lifted. But she decided she would call it a smile. His eyes lightened as if humor had caught him by surprise.

She shifted his attention to Jill just in time to catch a fleeting grin.

Feeling rather pleased with their reaction, she pointed past the corrals. "Our ranch runs down to the river. We have a hundred head of cows. I try and keep them close to home rather than let them roam too far afield. It's still open range."

"Grass looks good," Sawyer said.

Jill headed for the barn and they followed her. They reached the building in time to see her disappear up the ladder into the loft.

Sawyer looked after her. "I never know if I should try and control her or let her find her own way."

She didn't know if he was asking for her opinion but she offered it anyway. "I remember hearing Mother tell young mothers that they should give their children enough freedom to learn things but not enough they could get hurt."

He nodded. "Sounds good to me."

They wandered up the alley, looking at the dozen

pens, stopping at the tack room to examine the harnesses. He checked the collar Big Harry would wear to pull the farm implements.

"It's in good shape. It appears your Father is a careful man."

She chuckled. "He is that. Especially careful not to throw anything away." She indicated the tangle of leather scraps in the corner.

Sawyer glanced at them and this time she knew he smiled though it disappeared before he looked her direction. Still, she felt more than a little pleased with herself.

It was time to return to the house and prepare supper. Time to let him learn what sort of cook she was.

Sawyer felt rather pleased with himself. He'd made her laugh. And no amount of telling himself he didn't care changed the fact that it made him feel good. She'd laughed at him imitating her father's accent, too. Maybe he was getting good at this.

The thought scared him and he turned to study the harnesses hung neatly from pegs, oiled and polished. He perceived he had landed in a family that showed care and concern in everyday things. And likely in big, occasional things, too. The way Carly quoted her mother filled him with reassurance. As if his own mother spoke through her.

He spoke almost as if in a dream. "I can't remember my mother very well but I do recall something she said often. 'Look for sunshine and you'll find rays even on a cloudy day. Look for darkness and you'll find it even on the sunniest of days.'" He couldn't think why he had told her that or even why he had remembered it. Except there was something about Carly's sunny nature that brought it to remembrance.

She smiled brightly, sending a shaft of light into his dormant heart and stirring it to life.

He wasn't sure he wanted that to happen and yet he wasn't ready to refuse it either.

She tipped her head. "Didn't you say you were seven when your mother and brother perished?"

"I was."

Her eyes narrowed. "But you said you regretted standing by and not doing anything. What could a seven-year-old do?"

His heart died a thousand deaths. He'd told her too much. Should have guessed she'd see the flaw in his confession. "Pa tried to get in to save them. It took three men to hold him back. I just stood there shaking with fear as the flames licked at the walls and consumed the roof. I was too afraid to even try. It wasn't right for me to be more concerned with my own safety than rescuing them."

Her smile left her mouth but not her eyes and the look she gave him felt like a caress. "Sawyer, do you think your mother would have wanted you to perish, too?"

The question stunned him. He'd never considered it.

"If she could see you, I'm sure she'd be so happy to see you all grown up. Jill's parents will also be happy she's alive and will grow up and have children of her own."

"Pa was never the same after. Not until he met Judith." He'd shut Sawyer out. As if he couldn't bear to see a surviving son while his other had died.

"We've all lost so much. Why don't we do our best to help each other find joy in what our lives are now?"

"I don't have much to offer. But if you'll help Jill…" She already had by offering encouraging words and touches. His shoulder warmed where her hand had rested briefly so he knew it felt good. Just what Jill needed.

Carly patted his arm, sending a bolus of warmth to his heart. He couldn't decide if there was something about her touch that did that or if he had something wrong with him.

"You might discover you have more to offer than you think."

The idea flared for the space of two seconds and then flickered out.

Her eyes sparkled as if she'd read his mind. "You might have a lot of surprises ahead of you."

Again the idea flared with hope. He didn't completely succeed in dowsing it. "Not too many, I hope, and none bad."

She tossed her head, making her wheat-blond braid flip back and forth. "You'll have to be the judge of that. Now, if we aren't all going to starve to death, I best go make supper, though I can't say how close to starving you'll feel after you eat my meal."

He followed her from the barn. Jill shinnied down the ladder and fell in behind them. "Are you warning me again that your cooking might not be real good?" he asked.

"You'll have to see for yourself." She laughed, a merry sound that held more than a note of teasing… or was it warning?

"It can't be worse than my cooking." He couldn't keep resignation from his voice.

"Or could it?" She laughed again.

He glanced back at Jill and saw the concern in her face, though she masked it as soon as she realized he looked her way. "We'll survive, won't we, Jill?"

She answered with a scowl.

They reached the house and Carly hurried into the pantry, returned with a basin and gave him instruction to bring potatoes from the root cellar. Jill followed him.

Jill sank to the ground by the entranceway. "I might not like this place."

He couldn't say if she meant the root cellar or the Morrison Ranch but he decided it was the latter. He filled the basin with last year's potatoes, still firm from good storage. "Doesn't appear either of them is mean. That's a good thing." He considered all he'd observed. "Carly likes to laugh a lot."

"Her pa is funny."

"But nice."

"I guess."

They returned to the house with the potatoes. He sniffed. Something smelled mighty good but he wasn't getting his hopes up. Though he was mightily tempted to open the oven and see what it held.

Carly took the potatoes and soon had them peeled and boiling. "It will be a few minutes. Why don't you two bring in your things and get settled?"

He eyed her for a moment. Was she trying to get rid of them? But for what reason? With a start, he realized he'd immediately jumped to thinking of long-term leave-taking. But hadn't they agreed she needed him and Jill needed her?

Jill only? a little voice questioned.

He refused to dignify it with an answer.

Carly smiled and nodded, tipped her head toward the door to encourage his cooperation.

There seemed little reason to disagree. "All right." He and Jill tromped to the barn and he took his saddlebags and the carpetbag that held her few belongings. He'd thought about buying her more clothes but had decided her cousin was better suited for the task.

Which brought to mind her present outfit. He had to try to convince her to dress like a young lady and he faced her. "Jill, I don't think your ma would want you to dress like a boy."

Jill stuck out her bottom lip and glowered at him. "Ma's dead so she don't care."

"Don't you want to do what would please her?"

"I don't care anymore. Besides, Carly dresses like a man. And you married her."

"True." But she'd worn a dress when he married her.

"Just 'cause she wears pants, you don't like her?"

Well, put that way, it did seem a little unreasonable. "I guess I don't care what she wears." Her mode of dress had not been part of their agreement. Of course, he had no idea at the time.

"Then you can't care what I wear."

He sighed deeply and with a great deal of frustration. Were all females so argumentative? So adept at twisting what a fellow said? But rather than be upset at the notion, he realized he felt like smiling. Having someone other than Jill challenge him might be amusing.

They returned to the house. Carly stood at the stove, her back to the room. If he wasn't mistaken, she grinned rather widely and hummed a little tune.

Seems she was enjoying herself just a bit too much.

Well, he'd signed up for this marriage and neither her dressing like a man nor cooking like an old cowboy was going to make him change his mind.

Besides, how bad could her cooking be?

Chapter Seven

Carly had never had so much fun preparing a meal. She could barely contain her amusement as Sawyer passed through the kitchen, his mouth set in determination. Seems he was prepared to make the best of it no matter how bad her cooking turned out to be.

She'd really had to hustle to get the pork chops browned and in the oven stewing in gravy while he went out for the potatoes. Then she mixed up biscuits and got them in the oven while he attended to getting his room organized. Everything was ready. She couldn't wait for him to see what she'd made for their meal.

Before she called them, she put the bowls of food on the table. Everything looked perfect. Mounds of creamy mashed potatoes, tender pork chops in rich brown gravy and fluffy golden-brown biscuits. She'd heated a jar of beans from last summer.

"Come and get it," she called. If Father wondered why she grinned so widely, he didn't ask but he watched everyone with keen interest.

She indicated Sawyer should sit on her right, Jill on her left. Father sat across the table as usual.

As Sawyer took his place, he looked at the food on the table and his eyes widened. "You did this?"

She forced herself to stop smiling and nodded.

"It looks good. Smells good."

"Proof is in the tasting. Don't say you weren't warned."

"I'll ask the blessing," Father said after watching them a moment without comment.

Carly was a tad surprised Father kept his opinion to himself. She held Sawyer's gaze until the last second before she bowed her head.

At Father's *amen*, she passed the potatoes to him and then Jill. Sawyer took a moderate amount, less even than Jill.

The rest of the food was passed from hand to hand and then Sawyer took up his fork.

Carly grinned at him. "Father and I are still alive, so you must know my cooking won't kill you."

He scooped up a forkful and lifted it to his mouth. His eyes widened and he sighed. "You have been teasing me. You're an excellent cook."

"Aye, she is that." Father gave her a scolding look. "Did ye lead the poor man to think otherwise?" He shook his head at her acknowledging shrug. "And yet he still entered into this arrangement of yours. Brave man he is."

Brave or desperate? Seems they were both a bit of each.

Both Jill and Sawyer ate with much enthusiasm. And then she brought out the chocolate cake she had baked the day before.

Jill edged forward, her eyes wide. "I love chocolate cake." Her expression went from eager to hard in a flash and she sat back. "My mama made the best chocolate cake."

Carly shot a quick glance at Sawyer. His hands had grown still. His face revealed nothing…or at least she guessed that's what he hoped. But she detected a flicker of something in his eyes. Couldn't say if it was sorrow or frustration. Perhaps both.

She turned back to Jill. "I know mine won't be as good as your mama's but you might enjoy a small piece."

Jill's gaze went from Carly to the cake. "I guess I could try it."

Carly cut off a big enough slice that she hoped would satisfy Jill's desire for a sweet without making her feel disloyal to her mother's memory. She put the plate holding the cake in front of the child. Jill had her hands stuffed under her thighs and stared at the treat.

Giving the child lots of time to fight her inner war, Carly served the others.

Sawyer took a bite and closed his eyes. A look of bliss filled his face.

Carly stared. For a man who claimed not to have any feelings left, he surely did know how to express appreciation for her baking.

His eyes opened, as blue-green as the water of a high mountain lake. Their gazes caught and held and she felt something she had never felt before. A connection or perhaps a longing for connection. He turned away and she roped in her foolish thoughts. Their agreement had no room for anything but a work arrangement.

She finished her own piece of cake without looking at any of the others, then pushed back from the table. "I'll do up the dishes."

Jill's cake had disappeared, though she didn't look

at Carly or give any indication if it tasted good or not. Carly knew enough to let the girl hang on to her loyalty to her ma.

Carly scurried from table to cupboard where she had a basin of hot soapy water. She did her best to remember exactly what their agreement entailed. He needed a home for Jill. She needed a man to appease her father's demands. Nothing more.

"We'll help," Sawyer said, carrying a handful of cutlery. He reached past her to drop the items in the wash water. His arm brushed against her. She felt his strength, breathed in the outdoor scent of him and immediately forgot the details of their agreement.

He turned to his little sister. "Jill, you can help, too."

Jill's chair scraped back and she made a sound of disagreement.

"It's not necessary," Carly murmured, having no desire to get on the bad side of the child.

"I think it is." Sawyer held a towel out to Jill. "You can dry."

Carly shifted so she could see them both. They wore identical expressions, jaws set, eyes unblinking. Not so much as a twitch from either of them.

"Well, fine." Jill stomped over to grab the towel. Carly hurriedly started to wash dishes while Sawyer continued to clear the table.

"'Tis good to see the spirit of cooperation," Father said.

Carly glanced at him to see if he teased but his dark eyes were full of gentleness and approval.

"'Twill be pleasant to have you finally married and you even got a little girl."

"She ain't my ma," Jill said.

Carly wondered if that might be a blessing but her annoyance at Jill's rejection lasted only a second. Of course the child wasn't about to embrace Carly as mother. Carly wasn't even sure she welcomed the idea. She'd only offered a home in exchange for a wedding certificate.

"Aye, child, one never forgets their mother. Just ask Carly."

Jill's attention jerked toward Carly but if Carly thought she saw any sign of understanding, it disappeared so fast she likely only imagined it.

As she turned back to her task, her gaze grazed Sawyer's. The man met her eyes, his brimming with sympathy, startling her so much she let her wet hands drip at her sides. She couldn't tear her gaze from his. Couldn't think beyond the feeling of having fallen into something warm and fuzzy.

Then he blinked and his face grew impassive.

She turned back to washing dishes. But her mind whirled. She expected him to keep his feelings to himself. After all, he'd said he no longer had them. Just that little glimpse of what lay behind his mask of indifference had the power to leave her dry-mouthed. If he should open his heart up, she didn't know what she'd do. How she'd be able to handle it.

Stop being so dramatic, she scolded herself.

Easier said than done, she discovered. She emptied the water and put away the last of the dishes. "Thanks for the help."

Sawyer nodded. "Thanks for being a good cook."

She promised herself she wouldn't meet his eyes but couldn't keep that promise and she looked at him, saw a flicker of humor. Why had she never noticed how handsome he was even unshaven?

Not that it mattered, she firmly informed herself. They each had their expectations of this arrangement and it was strictly business.

She faced the room. Father watched, a twinkle in his eyes as if knowing how uncomfortable she was. Jill plunked down on a chair and stared at the tabletop. Several times she'd studied the child, trying to assess if the lump on her head caused her any problem but she was only guessing that it wasn't. "Jill, how is your head? Does it hurt?"

Jill drew back and gave Carly an angry look. "Nothing wrong with me."

Father was immediately concerned. "I saw the lump on your forehead, child. What happened?"

"I fell."

Carly understood Jill didn't want Father to know the whole story but he needed to be aware and mindful of the need to watch Jill for a few more hours.

"She ran into the street and got knocked down by some horses."

"I almost got run over by a wagon." It seemed that Jill decided if the incident had to be discussed, she would make it as dramatic as possible.

Carly sketched out the details of the accident.

"Ack, child," Father said. "'Tis a painful thing to get run over. I'm that glad you were spared."

After a few minutes, that conversation ended.

Sawyer lounged against the cupboard, close enough she felt his presence in every pore.

What was she to do with the rest of the evening? Normally she and Father would read or talk. Or she'd go for a ride...an appealing thought. But she could hardly leave two almost-strangers in the house on their first evening.

As she mulled over possibilities, she heard an approaching wagon and hurried to the window. Not one wagon, but three.

"What is it?" Father asked and Sawyer came to her elbow to look out the window.

"Looks like we have company." Who would visit them and why?

Sawyer welcomed the idea of visitors. Maybe the presence of others would ease the tension vibrating in his veins. He had married Carly solely to get a home for Jill. Not because he wanted anything on his own behalf. He was quite content being a lonely wanderer. He was quite used to spending evenings alone with no one to talk to. But now he faced the necessity of making conversation.

He felt a grin tug at his lips. He'd never enjoyed his own cooking and was prepared to endure Carly's efforts. He certainly had no objection to learning Carly could cook a fine meal. Best he'd ever had, in fact. He barely managed to stifle a chuckle at the way she had led him to believe otherwise. Gladys never teased like that. She certainly never would perpetrate a trick. There was something strangely appealing about a woman who could pull off such a joke.

Jill had made it plain she didn't care for the plans he and Carly had but she'd soon learn to appreciate the benefits of a good home. She might already like Mr. Morrison with his Scottish brogue and long white beard. He'd watched her as the older man told stories and had seen something in her expression she would have erased if she guessed he saw…he wasn't sure what to call it. Perhaps yearning. That was good.

The lead wagon drew close enough for him to recognize its occupants. "Isn't that the preacher and his wife?" Before Carly could answer, Annie held up a cowbell and rang it.

Carly made a sound of frustration. "I should never had told her how it was for Mother and Father's wedding."

Mr. Morrison's chuckle seemed to come from deep inside him. "You mean the ringing of the bells?"

"Yes, Mother always said it was the happiest sound ever." She turned to explain to Sawyer. "When they were married, the church bells all rang out. First one church and then another until the whole city rang." She glanced out the window again. "Annie's brothers and their wives and children are here as well." As she spoke, the wagons drew to a halt before the house and the occupants jumped down. He counted at least a dozen people, all ringing cowbells. They circled the house and continued to ring.

"Ye best go out and greet them," Mr. Morrison said.

Carly faced Sawyer. "What do you want to do?"

It pleased him immensely that she asked his opinion. "Do I understand that they expect the newlyweds to go out to them?" Newlyweds? The term hardly fit them and yet their friends and neighbors had no way of knowing that.

She shrugged. "I'm sorry. We don't have to do it."

Did she want everyone to know the details of their arrangement? Why did it matter what she thought? And yet, strangely it did. He couldn't explain why, but he wanted to show off the woman he had married even though these were all her friends. "I don't mind." He took her hand before he could think better of it and led her outside to stand on the doorstep.

The crowd gathered round and rang the bells until his ears hurt.

Carly laughed. "Enough now."

At a signal from Annie, the ringing ceased, though it continued in his ears.

Annie rushed forward and hugged her. "I remembered the bells. How you said you hoped someone would ring bells when you were married."

Carly pulled her hand free of Sawyer's, leaving him adrift among strangers. She faced the crowd. "Everyone, this is Sawyer Gallagher."

"Your new husband," Annie added. "Or have you forgotten?"

"Haven't had time to remember, let alone forget," she said.

Although her answer tickled his funny bone that he thought he no longer had, it also brought him back to reality. He'd almost let himself believe she would like to be his wife. Her words reminded him of the terms of their agreement.

She turned back to the house. "Jill, come and meet everyone."

Jill hesitated a moment, then made her way slowly to Sawyer's side.

Carly introduced Jill, then began introducing their visitors. "These are all Marshall men, Annie's brothers." She went around the group, naming each one.

"Dawson and Isabelle and their daughter, Mattie, who is six years old. Logan and Sadie with their children. Beth, fourteen, Sammy, seven, and Jeannie who is three. Conner and Kate and their baby, Ellie." Each adult shook Sawyer's hand, welcomed him and congratulated him on his marriage to Carly. Then they extended a warm welcome to Jill.

He acknowledged each introduction and hoped he'd be able to remember them when he met them later.

The women returned to their wagons and lifted out baskets.

Annie explained. "We brought a party."

Carly pulled Sawyer to the side and waved the visitors in. Then she and Sawyer followed. Jill had joined the children, though he noticed she held back, taking her time. He could hardly blame her. So many strangers and all so enthusiastic. It was a bit overwhelming even for him. He expected it was the same, or worse, for his little sister.

Everyone greeted Mr. Morrison and inquired about his health. The old man beamed with pleasure. "This is just like when yer Mother and I married," he said to Carly.

"Not quite," she murmured to Sawyer.

He bent close to answer. "Let everyone have their party. Our agreement was between you and me. No need to share the details."

She met his gaze, her eyes dark and—why did he think she sought something from him? What could it be? If he knew, he would do his best to give it. She smiled. It ricocheted in his heart, setting free a dozen or more fluttering butterflies of awareness.

He smiled as the feelings flapped upward. Told himself it was only because he wished to offer her encouragement. Not because he couldn't keep his feelings stuffed away. He considered the last thought. That couldn't be right. After all, he had only met her this morning. Hardly time for anything to change…especially his long experience at not having feelings.

Since this morning, he'd met her, married her and now was about to celebrate their marriage with a host of friends. He promised himself he would do his utmost to make it a party she would remember. Seemed the least he could do, considering she had given up any hope of a romantic union.

Soon a feast of cakes and cookies and two pies filled the table. Chairs, a bench from under the hooks for the coats and a stool or two provided seating for all the adults. The children were content to sit on the floor as they enjoyed the repast. Jill joined them, though she sat at the edge of the gathering. He recognized the feeling because it was familiar. He distanced himself from people, too. With a start, he looked around the crowded table and realized that might no longer be possible. Or even desirable.

Dawson, the eldest Marshall brother, lifted his hand to get attention. "I'd like to hear more about Sawyer than what Annie told us."

Sawyer stiffened at the question. He sat next to Carly, pressed tight to her elbow. She must have felt his reaction for she laughed and answered in his stead. "Why not let the poor man enjoy an evening of peace before you all start on him?"

A chorus of protests greeted her request. "We haven't started anything," Dawson said above the uproar.

"Only because I stopped you." Carly's grin never faltered, yet he detected a fierce warning note and perhaps the others did, too.

"I expect we could tell him a little about you," Conner—the middle brother—said.

Carly groaned. "I don't think that's necessary."

Sawyer leaned forward. "I'm all ears."

He ignored the way Carly poked her finger into his ribs. When she did it a second time, he captured her hand and held it firmly enough she couldn't escape.

The others noticed and nudged one another. Annie whispered loudly, "She's already learning submission."

Carly jerked her hand free and scowled at them all, saving her fiercest scowl for Sawyer. "No one lords it over me."

"Now now, lassie," her father said. "Give the man a chance to show you how pleasant it can be to have someone to help you and take care of you."

"I don't need anyone to take care of me." She began to push to her feet but Annie, at her other side, pulled her down.

"Carly, sit down and enjoy the party." She leaned close to whisper. Sawyer heard her words. "Set a good example for the children."

They all glanced toward the youngsters. Several watched the adults with interest. Sawyer noticed that Jill seemed particularly drawn to the conversation.

He studied her, hoping beyond hope that she wasn't tucking Carly's words into that little brain of hers to throw back at one of them the next time someone asked something of her.

Carly sat back down and with a strained smile, asked for someone to pass the plate of cookies.

Sawyer thought it best to change the direction of the conversation. "Carly said something about the Marshalls being big around here."

The women all laughed. "It's because they are big." Pretty Isabelle held her hand above her head to indicate they were tall.

Carly held up her hand to get the attention of the others. "I meant because the Marshalls pretty much run the place."

The men protested. "Not all of us. Just Grandfather."

Mr. Morrison chuckled. "He is a fine man."

One by one, sometimes all speaking at once, Sawyer learned that Grandfather Marshall had come west, the first of the early ranchers. When gold was found nearby and a rough mining town, Wolf Hollow, sprang up, he saw the need for a gentler, kinder place and built the beginnings of Bella Creek.

"Over a year ago, in the dead of winter, a fire took out a block of buildings," said the youngest brother, Logan Marshall. "Among them the schoolhouse, the doctor's quarters, the barbershop, the lawyer's office and a store. They've all since been rebuilt."

Logan's wife, Sadie, took up the story. "They needed a new teacher and doctor. I came as the teacher."

Logan's grin was wide with pride. "I persuaded her she'd be a happier woman as my wife." The look he gave Sadie was so filled with love that Sawyer couldn't take his eyes off the pair. He would not admit that he had denied himself the one thing he longed for—love—even before entering into a loveless marriage. Something about losing his mother and brother and the many moves afterwards that he and his father had made caused him to close his heart to that emotion. And to every emotion. Seeing the open love between the couples at the table made him feel hollow inside.

"We adopted the three children."

He heard everyone's story of finding love and family. This was what he wanted—family for Jill. That's all that mattered.

He learned that Conner worked with wild horses, gentling them in a special way. "Like I saw an old man do years ago."

The stories grew wilder and funnier with lots of laughter to follow.

Baby Ellie had been put down to sleep on a blanket. But when Mr. Morrison roared with laughter, she jerked awake and cried.

Kate scooped her up and jostled her to calm her. "We need to get her home to bed."

Conner unwound from the table. "It's time to go home."

The others rose at his announcement. And in a flurry of activity, the women gathered up their things and organized children, and the men carried out dishes.

Carly had risen, too, as had Sawyer and together they went to the door to thank everyone and wave goodbye.

The wagons headed down the lane in the silvery light of night. Annie turned and rang her bell. A jangle of many bells accompanied the departing wagons.

Sawyer and Carly stood side by side, their elbows touching. Neither of them moved.

Carly let out a long sigh. "Well, that's that. I wonder if I should have said anything."

"About what?"

She faced him, her eyes catching the lamplight from inside. Her mouth worked back and forth as if she dealt with a bad taste. "About our marriage."

"What would you say? That I'm sleeping in the store-room?"

She shrugged. "Seems wrong to deceive them."

Not often something triggered a sense of frustration in him, but this did. "Carly, we signed papers making us man and wife. We each have our reasons for this marriage. We understand what we've done. Does it really matter what others know or think about it?"

She drew back slightly but did not tear her gaze from his. Nor did he tear his from hers as he continued, "I thought we were resolved on this matter." Was she having regrets? Would she change her mind?

She looked down, sucked in a deep breath and lifted her face again.

He saw the determination in her face and held his breath, fearing she had decided to end this pretend marriage.

"I have not changed my mind. Nor do I intend to. The ranch is far too important to me to risk having Father sell it simply because I'm not married."

His lungs emptied in a whoosh. "Good." On his part, it was all about a home for Jill. He had to keep believing that was the only reason…not secretly wishing for something he had lost when he was seven years old.

Carly edged away. "It's bedtime. Father, do you need help?"

The older man had watched them set up beds in the different rooms without making a comment. "I can manage on my own." He didn't move.

Carly waited. Seems the man wasn't going to be the first to retire.

"Fine. Jill, I made a bed for you in my room."

Jill's head jerked up. She'd been half asleep. She tried to look stubborn. Sawyer knew she wanted to argue. But was too tired. Instead she got to her feet. "Fine. It don't matter to me where I sleep." And she shuffled into the room.

Sawyer watched her go. This would be the first time she was out of his sight for more than a few minutes since he had found her. "Is it okay for her to go to sleep now? Didn't the nurse say to keep her awake twelve hours?"

"I'll check on her but I don't see any sign that she's got any ill effects from her accident."

He nodded. "I suppose you're right."

She patted his arm. "Don't worry. I'll take good care of her."

Mr. Morrison's attention followed Jill and then he studied Sawyer. "Yer gonna sleep there?" He tipped his head toward the small room.

Sawyer nodded.

Mr. Morrison turned to Carly. "How long do you plan for this to go on?"

"Pardon?" Carly did her best to look confused but Sawyer figured her father wasn't any more convinced she didn't know what he meant than Sawyer was.

"Dinnae toy with me, lass."

"Father, you'll have to be clearer about what you mean."

Sawyer wondered if she knew her attempt at innocent confusion wasn't working. The gal had a face that revealed far too much.

"I suppose it's understandable considering you're practically strangers." His eyes grew dark, filled with warning. "But I expect a real marriage."

Carly's chin went up. "You want to see the papers we signed?"

"Dinnae pretend that's what I meant, Carly Morrison, though I suppose 'tis now Carly Gallagher."

She turned away. "You get yourself to bed while I clean the kitchen."

Sawyer stood by the door, wondering which way to go to avoid the tension between the two. He made up his mind as Carly gathered the cups to wash. "I'll help."

"No need." She kept her attention fixed on the basin as she filled it with hot water.

"No bother." It triggered a memory. "I used to help my ma with dishes before she died. I enjoyed it." They talked as they worked, with her telling little things from her childhood and he about growing up in the city of Philadelphia.

Mr. Morrison got up from his chair and hobbled to his room, muttering under his breath about his daughter and her wily ways.

As soon as the door closed behind him, the air went out of Carly and she sagged over the dishpan.

Sawyer watched her. "He's upset you."

She attacked washing the cups and handed them to him to dry. "He'll get used to the way it is." She snuffled.

He bent his head to look at her. "Are you crying?" He didn't know how to handle a crying woman.

Chapter Eight

Carly swiped at her nose with her wet hand. "I'm not crying." She wouldn't. She quickly finished the last cup and carried the basin of water outside to toss on Mother's flower bed that Carly had kept alive and thriving since her mother's passing. The tulips had blossomed bright yellow and red. The lavender, peonies and other perennials were growing well. They would blossom when their time came.

She glanced up the hill even though she couldn't see the tiny graveyard in the dark. A cool breeze shivered across her and she wrapped her arms about her, the basin clutched to her side. Mother and the baby brothers lay up there.

A tear trickled down her nose. She blinked her eyes clear. She didn't need a man. She didn't need love but she couldn't help but be grateful her mother wasn't alive to witness this marriage.

Father had forced her to take this step and she wouldn't allow regrets.

She bent to wipe her eyes on her sleeve and tucked determination into her heart.

Before she could return indoors, a shadow fell from the open door. Sawyer waited and watched. At least he didn't say anything.

They stood a few feet apart. He blocked the light from the kitchen, leaving his face in the dark, though likely his expression would have been inscrutable even if she'd seen it. She could only hope her face was equally shadowed. Neither broke the silence.

Father's bed creaked as he lay down.

Big Harry snuffled as he readjusted his position.

An owl hooted from the nearby trees.

The scent of silver willows wafted from the river. Spicy as cinnamon.

Still Carly and Sawyer did not move, waiting, assessing. In the stillness, her decision grew firm. Her hopes and expectations adjusted. Some might have said she married in haste and would repent in leisure. Right here and now, with thoughts of Mother close and Sawyer waiting in the doorway, she vowed she would not repent. She would allow no regrets. Although neither of them expected a real marriage, they both had expectations that they discussed. Meeting those was enough for her.

She took a step forward. Sawyer moved back to allow her to enter the house.

"Is everything okay?" he asked.

"Everything is fine. Do you have what you need for the night?"

"I'm fine. Thank you."

His thanks eased her tension. They could both be polite and gentle with each other, thus making the agreement between them pleasant.

"Good night, then." She crossed to her room.

"Good night." Two doors closed quietly.

Carly lit the lamp on her bedside table and turned it down low. She sat on the side of her bed, facing Jill. Should she waken the child to make sure she was okay? She smiled as she thought of the foolishness of doing so but she had been instructed to make sure the child didn't slip into unconsciousness.

Jill's eyelids fluttered.

"You aren't sleeping, are you?"

Jill squeezed her eyes tightly.

Carly laughed. "That's not going to work."

Jill flipped over so Carly stared at her back.

"It's all right. You can take your time deciding what you want from your new life." Her heart went out to the child who had lost her parents, then been shuffled from home to home as if no one cared enough to keep her. "I remember something my own mother said. 'Carly, you can be about as happy as you decide to be. Or you can choose to be unhappy.' After she died, I needed to remind myself of those words over and over."

She quickly prepared for the night as she talked, leaving her trousers on top of her boots at the side of the bed. Thinking of her mother had triggered so many memories. "Mother used to read me stories at bedtime. And when I got older, she read to me from the Bible." She pulled her Bible from the nearby drawer. "Now when I read the Bible, I think of her."

Jill snorted. "Shouldn't you think of God?"

Carly laughed softly. "You're awfully smart. Yes, of course, I should think of God and I do. It's comforting to know my mother is with Him in heaven."

Jill switched to her back, her face shadowed so Carly couldn't read her expression. Though there might not have been anything to see, as the child was as good as

Sawyer at hiding her feelings. "You think you'll see your mama again?"

"Yes, I'll see her in heaven."

"Not me." She flipped to her side again, allowing Carly to see nothing but her back.

Carly went to the side of the bed, holding the lamp so she could see Jill's face. "Why do you think that?" But Jill buried her face in her pillow.

"Because I'm bad. Bad girls don't go to heaven." Her voice was muffled, perhaps explaining the heavy tone. Though Carly wasn't convinced.

"Who said you were a bad girl?"

Jill turned and stared at Carly, her eyes narrowed and her mouth tight. "People."

"What people?"

No answer.

"Sawyer?"

Jill shook her head.

Carly knew an unexpected and shuddering relief to hear that Sawyer had not condemned the girl. "I know it wasn't your mama and papa." She thought of all the child had been through. According to Sawyer, Jill had been moved from home to home. Was it because she had acted out? If someone had spoken such unkind words, Carly could understand why Jill would see no reason to being good. "I'm guessing it was some of the people who took you in." She perched on the side of Jill's bed, paying no mind when the child scooted as far away as possible.

"Jill, honey, those people were wrong. They didn't understand what it's like to lose both your mama and papa and feel alone and scared."

"I wasn't scared." The words were spoken bravely but Carly knew them to be untrue.

"Sometimes when we're hurting and afraid, we don't know how to act. We might even say and do unkind things. But listen to me. That doesn't mean we are bad people. And when we do bad things, all we need to do is confess them to Jesus. Let me read you a verse my mother taught me when I was about your age."

She still held her Bible and opened it to First John chapter one, verse nine. "'If we confess our sins, he is faithful and just to forgive us our sins, and to cleanse us from all unrighteousness.' That means because God always keeps His word and is fair, He forgives our sins. Don't you think what God says is more to be believed than what some people say?"

She longed to hug and kiss the child but Jill wasn't ready to accept such gestures. "You think about it. Good night now. If you need anything, don't be afraid to call."

The next morning, she glanced at Jill, sleeping soundly and so sweet and innocent looking. Poor child had lost so much.

Carly hurried from the room. She wanted to check on the cows this morning.

Sawyer came from his room, stretching and yawning as Carly prepared a bountiful breakfast.

"I trust you slept well." She was determined to be kind and polite from the beginning of each day to its end.

"Great. How about you?"

"Good."

"Jill?"

"Once she fell asleep, she didn't stir." She held up

a hand to stop his protest. "Don't worry. She's fine. I shook her once to check on her and she protested loudly at being wakened." She'd like to discuss with him what Jill had said. Perhaps tonight after Jill was in bed.

Jill came from the bedroom, rubbing sleep from her eyes just as Father joined them in the kitchen.

"Good morning to ye all," he said in his customary boisterous morning call.

Jill blinked and looked ready to flee.

"Father, you're frightening the child."

"Aye, little one, ye might as well get used to me. I can't help myself 'cause I love mornings so much. Now up to the table and let's enjoy the meal Carly has prepared."

She poured coffee for the men, milk for herself and Jill. She served toasted bread, fried eggs and bacon. It was plenty enough food for her and Father and likely for Jill. But maybe not for Sawyer. "Would you like griddle cakes as well with your breakfast?"

His eyes lit. "I love griddle cakes. But only if it's not too much work."

She chuckled. "I think I can manage to fry up a few. Starting tomorrow."

"I'd appreciate that." Their gazes held and Carly felt the pleasure of knowing she could please this man by preparing good meals.

Sawyer and Jill helped her do up the dishes.

"I'll run out and take care of the chickens," she said when they were done. She milked the cow and hurried through the rest of the morning chores. She gathered the eggs and took them to the house, pausing to toss some leftover biscuits into a sack to take with her. Jill sat at the table with Father, a checkerboard between them. Father would be pleased to teach another little girl to play the game.

She glanced about, didn't see Sawyer. Perhaps he was in his room. Or gone outside for something. "I'll be back later," she told Father and Jill. "There's bread and cheese for sandwiches if I don't get back by noon."

"Where are ye off to, lass?" Father asked.

"I need to check the north side of the ranch and push back any cows wandering too far."

"Aye, you do that."

She wondered at the amusement in his eyes. Then shrugged. Perhaps he was simply enjoying a little girl to keep him company. "How is your leg?"

"It gets better every day." He made a move in the game. "Your turn," he said to Jill.

Carly left the pair to their fun and headed for the barn. She was about to step inside to saddle Sunny when Sawyer led his saddled horse out.

"You aren't riding away, are you?" Did he intend to leave her alone with Jill to take care of?

His eyebrows did a little dance. "I'm a man of my word."

"Then where are you going?"

"To check the cows."

She couldn't have been more stunned if he had pulled a gun on her. "*I'm* going to check on the cows." How could he— "You don't even know where they are."

"Your father told me how to identify the boundaries and what cows were yours." He reached for the reins, intending to mount.

"Checking the cows is my job." She crowded his horse back into the barn, scooped up her saddle and blanket and tossed them on Sunny's back.

Sawyer left his horse and followed her. "What about Jill?"

She reached under for the cinch.

He persisted. "Our agreement was for you to provide a home for Jill."

She didn't even look at him to see if his expression had changed. She heard the warning note in his voice and that was enough.

He tried again. "She needs a real home."

Carly slowly straightened, keeping her back to Sawyer. She'd heard Jill cry out in her sleep last night. Had seen the almost hidden uncertainty in her face throughout the day.

More than that, she recalled the days after her own mother's death when she felt so alone and afraid. That's when she'd begun riding the range and soon after, began taking care of the cows. She'd found solace and purpose and so much else there. She loved the wide-open spaces, the heat of the sun and the scents on the breeze. She loved seeing the wild animals—big and small— and the birds.

She came round to face Sawyer. "I can't give it up."

He watched her calmly.

She had to make him understand. "The ranch is mine. You need only concern yourself with Big Harry. I could do that, too, but Father has made me promise not to. I believe in honoring my promises. From what you said, I thought you did, too."

He continued to watch her, revealing nothing of what he thought.

His steadfast indifference set off a reaction in her. "She has a home. Father is there. She doesn't need me."

"What about our agreement?" His words were soft

but she wasn't fooling herself into thinking they carried no weight.

She couldn't hold his challenging gaze and looked past him to the sunny, beckoning outdoors. "You need someone to show you around."

He recognized her stalling. "Jill will be home alone with your father."

"We could take her with us. Wait here." She rushed past him and out to the corral behind the barn to catch up Daisy, her gentle old roan-colored mare that she had learned to ride on. She led Daisy inside. "Meet Daisy. Jill can ride her."

Again that silent, steady challenge from him.

This time she held his gaze. "It's the perfect solution."

"Your father will be home alone."

"He often is. He can get around fine with his crutch."

"He must get lonely."

She thought of the pleasure she'd seen in his face as he entertained Jill. "You can't have it both ways. We can't leave her here for Father's company and take her with us. It's one or the other."

"Those are not the only options."

They were back to his demand that she stay home with Jill and Father.

"Look at me." She flipped her hand across the legs of her trousers and touched her battered cowboy hat. "Do I look like a homebody?" She would not give into him and stay at the house. Not that she minded cooking, cleaning and housework. The laundry was a different matter. It took far too long. But her mother had trained her well in all those chores. She'd enjoyed them when Mother was alive. Yes, she'd often ridden out with Father, but for the most part, she was content to help her mother. That had changed after Mother's death.

"I know what it's like to lose a mother when you're as young as Jill." He spoke as if that clinched the argument.

Carly considered his words. She'd been older, almost ready to leave home if she'd chosen to do so. Jill was so young, dependent on others to provide a home and care. And then someone had said such awful things to her. She felt sorry for the child and would stay with her except— "You heard her. She doesn't want me."

"What she wants and what she needs are two different things."

"Sawyer, I'm sorry you misunderstood the terms of our agreement. I never once thought you'd expect me to give up what I've been doing." She hated that she had to plead but he'd left her little choice. "Please don't ask me to do so."

His expression never changed yet somehow she knew she had disappointed him. She tried to tell herself that didn't bother her but it did. Seems she was always to be a disappointment to the men in her life. Father, who wanted and needed sons. Bart Connelly, who wanted her to be a pretty ornament and provide him with a ranch. And now Sawyer, who wanted—

She wasn't even sure what he wanted. A mother for his little sister? A wife who wasn't a wife? A family without love?

They both turned at the sound of a wagon driving into the yard and hurried to see who approached.

"It's Dawson," Carly said. "He has Grandfather Marshall with him. I better go see what he wants."

Sawyer stayed at her side as they hurried to the house.

Dawson jumped down before they got there. He reached up to help his grandfather down.

"Howdy," he called. "Grandfather wanted to see your father. I can leave him for a visit while I conduct my business in town."

"He'll like that." And it provided Carly with the perfect setup. She escorted them inside, and Sawyer followed her. She put the coffeepot on and put out a plate of cookies.

The two older men were eager for a chin-wag so Dawson drove away.

"Can I talk to you?" Carly asked Sawyer and they stepped outside. "Father has company. He doesn't need me to babysit him. He and Grandfather will visit and play checkers until Dawson comes back."

Sawyer said nothing. She could only conclude that he didn't see that this provided the answer for them.

"Jill will be okay here with them. But even better, she can come with us. It will give her a chance to see the rest of her new home."

This most certainly was not what Sawyer had expected. No. He'd thought to replace Jill's mom. Judith would be teaching Jill to bake cookies or sew a hem or make a cake or something. He recalled the times he'd visited and had seen Jill standing on a stool at the cupboard, helping her mother with whatever there was to do.

When he agreed to this marriage contract with Carly, he had no idea what she had in mind...and that it was vastly different from what was in his mind. Carly confused him. She was a good cook. The house was clean and tidy. But she was determined to run the ranch. It wasn't that he was opposed to a woman riding after cows. There had been a woman on one of the trail drives he was on—the trail boss's daughter. She was as good as any man on the outfit. No, what he was concerned about was what was best for Jill. He mulled over the question.

Jill had donned trousers again this morning, giving him a look of such defiance he had chomped off any comment. She seemed to like Mr. Morrison fine. And then it hit him. Jill would resent any attempt to make her think of Carly as a replacement for her mother. Perhaps seeing Carly out on the range would make it possible for her to accept friendship between them.

"Fine, if she wants to go with us she can."

Before he finished the sentence, Carly had gone to speak to Jill. "Jill, we're going to ride out and check on the cows. I have a horse for you if you want to join us."

Jill's eyes brightened and then she banked back her reaction and looked at Sawyer, perhaps wondering if he would contradict Carly.

"Do you want to come?" he asked.

She looked from the two old men at the table to Carly and then again to Sawyer. She rumbled her lips. "I suppose I might as well."

Carly chuckled. "Your enthusiasm is overwhelming, Jill. Come along. You can help me saddle up."

In the barn, Carly handed Jill a saddle blanket and took her to the little roan mare. "Meet Daisy. She was my horse before I trained Sunny. She'll be glad of someone to ride her again. I'll get a saddle while you put on the blanket."

Jill looked surprised. Sawyer guessed she'd never

before saddled her own mount but she sucked in air and hid her uncertainty. By the time she had adjusted the saddle blanket, Carly was back with a small saddle. As she put it in place, she talked, explaining to Jill how to do it.

Sawyer stood back and watched, enjoying the patient way Carly explained things and how Jill did her best to follow instructions. Perhaps taking the child away from the house might prove to be a good idea.

Carly reached for her horse, and Jill did the same with Daisy. Sawyer followed with his mount. After listening to Carly talk about Daisy, he felt he needed to introduce his horse. "This is Dusty. I've had him for three years."

Well, it wasn't much but he didn't feel like going into details about how he had chosen and bought the horse. Besides, it wasn't interesting. Just a careful business deal. He saw the dark bay horse, liked his size and he was for sale. The horse had proven to have heart. His head jerked back as he realized he'd never before admitted any sense of gratitude or appreciation of the horse. A horse was just a horse.

Seeing Carly's open affection for her animals made him want to tell Dusty what a fine and loyal friend the horse was to Sawyer. Sawyer shook his head. When had he ever been so…so…absurd?

Carly cupped her hands to help Jill mount.

Sawyer swung to his saddle and the three of them rode from the yard. Carly stayed close to Jill, quietly offering instructions. They kept to a walk as they rode north.

Carly indicated they should veer to the right and led them toward the river. She raised her voice, addressing both of them. "I like to go to the river. It changes every day. It should be flowing briskly now with the spring thaw. It will rise later when the snow in the mountains melts." She led the way through the cottonwoods, heavy with their white cotton. Jill followed with Sawyer at the rear.

They drew to a halt by the rumbling waters. The air was filled with the scent of fresh green on the trees and the mushroomy smell of old leaves on the ground.

He arrived to see a duck fly away, squawking protests over the intrusion. A ring of rocks and ashes indicated someone had camped there in the past. "You have people staying here often?"

She shifted to study the cold fire pit. "Annie and I used to camp here but now that she's married, she doesn't have time."

Jill eyed the place. "I could stay here."

Sawyer held his peace. An eight-year-old child could not stay out on her own.

Carly studied Jill. "You and I could spend a night here. I'd like that." She left it at that, not pushing Jill, but as they left the spot, Sawyer noticed that Jill looked back with longing in her face.

They rode onward, climbing rolling hills. Carly pointed out landmarks and gave a history of the area. Sawyer was fascinated with her enthusiasm. "You love the land," he pointed out after a bit.

She moved to his side. "I'll do anything to keep it." She reined away, urging her horse into a gallop. She didn't slow until she reached the top of the nearby hill, then she dismounted and waited for Sawyer and Jill to catch up.

He swung to the ground and helped Jill down. She

ran to examine the nearby rocks and pocketed a couple. Seeing her do something he'd also done as a child filled him with fondness for his little sister.

"From here, you can see the northern boundary of your land." Carly pointed it out. "You can see the river winding to the east." She sat down on the grassy slope.

Sawyer waited a moment, trying to gauge her feelings. When she showed neither welcome nor dismissal, he sat beside her. He had to make her understand something. "I don't want to take your land from you."

She turned to study him. "I'm sorry for being so prickly. It's just…."

Curious, he willed her to finish. "Just what? Tell me."

She nodded. "It no longer matters but I once had a beau."

"That doesn't surprise me. I would think you had them lined up waiting their turn."

She tipped her head back and laughed. Her eyes sparkled when she sobered enough to speak. "Sawyer Gallagher, who'd have guessed you were capable of sweet talk?"

"Just being honest." Yet it pleased him to know she'd liked his comment. A smile tugged his mouth upward.

Her eyes widened. "Why, look at you. A real smile. You ought to try one more often. It's quite—" Her cheeks turned rosy and she turned away, suddenly interested in the scene before them.

He didn't press her to finish, content to provide his own words. Quite handsome. Quite attractive. His smile widened. He wished for an excuse to take her hand and squeeze it but could find none. He waited for her to tell him about her beau but she turned back to the landscape.

"I never get tired of this view." Her voice had grown soft. "When I come here, I am reminded of my mother. She often came here with me. She loved nature and said it made her so aware of God. She sang a song. I always sing it when I'm here…sort of for her." She looked away and began to sing in a strong voice. "'I sing the mighty power of God, that made the mountains rise, That spread the flowing seas abroad….'"

He sat mesmerized. It was as if they had entered a holy place. Jill must have felt the same awe for she sat a few feet away, her attention riveted on Carly's face.

"'And everywhere that we can be, Thou, God are present there,'" she finished and sat quietly.

No one moved. Jill wore an expression that could be best described as peaceful. He had not seen that look since the last time he saw her with her parents. She sniffled and turned away. The moment was over but his heart lifted with hope that settling in this place would be good for her.

Something rose within Sawyer, a feeling of having found something he lost so long ago he couldn't remember when or where he'd last known it. A feeling that all was right with his world. Of course! The words of the song. They made a person feel that way.

Carly sighed. "I miss her. Guess I always will."

Jill again let her feelings show. Her mouth twisted with her own loss. Both parents. He longed to wrap his arms around her and assure her he would make sure she had a good home.

And love?

Perhaps she would get it from Carly and her father. Sawyer had closed his heart to that emotion.

Carly turned to him. "I know you must miss your

mother, too. And your brother." She tipped her head from side to side as she studied him.

He forced himself not to look away, even though he sensed she saw something about him that puzzled her. He resisted a derisive snort. No doubt there was much that did that.

"I keep thinking of how you blame yourself for not doing anything to help your mother and brother."

His insides soured. The pleasant feeling torn aside by her reminder.

She squeezed his hand. "Have you thought any more about what I said? That your mother would have been happy that you weren't trapped as well?"

Her touch seared a path straight to his heart. It was all he could do not to turn his palm to hers and hang on like a drowning man. Her words touched him, too.

"My ma loved me. She loved both her boys. I never doubted it. But why should I live while she and Johnny died? He was only five." Sixteen years since that dreadful fire and he'd never spoken of it to anyone. He'd tried to talk to his pa soon after the fire but Pa got so agitated that he stopped mentioning it. Once or twice, he'd approached the topic with people they stayed with. Had been told to forget the past. And he'd determined to do so.

Until now. He wished he'd never mentioned it to Carly. Seems she wasn't going to let it go until she thought he had overcome his feelings.

He slowed his breathing, fearing his feelings would erupt like a boiling pot. Out of control. Hurting everything in the way.

But instead, he discovered the sharp, ragged edges of that memory had grown smooth. Perhaps time had done that and he had been unware. Or maybe Carly's understanding and her words and touch had provided healing.

Somehow his hand had turned and he gripped her fingers. He forced his muscles to relax. As afraid of the feelings that blossomed inside him as he was of hurting her with his strength.

She withdrew her hand. A tender smile curved her mouth. "Shall we go see where the cows are?"

He nodded, his insides too tangled to allow him to speak.

She helped Jill mount again and they continued riding north. She seemed to know where the cows were and led them to a wide, green basin where they grazed placidly. Several spooked at the sight of three humans on horseback but for the most part, they ignored the intrusion.

Mr. Morrison had informed Sawyer that he would make Sawyer a partner in the business. Sawyer said it wasn't necessary. His needs were few. A token wage would suffice. But the older man said he thought it was necessary. "You and Carly—equal partners."

Sawyer wondered if Mr. Morrison had told Carly this news. Sawyer had no intention of being the one to inform her. But he studied the stock with a sense of pride. A mixed herd, mostly Texas longhorns, but according to Mr. Morrison, the man was trying to introduce some heavier English stock. Sawyer could see sign of his program in the new calves, the evidence of the bull Mr. Morrison had purchased.

"They'll stay here for a few weeks," Carly said. "Who's hungry?" She swung to the ground and pulled a sack from her saddlebags.

Jill didn't wait for help but climbed down on her own.

Sawyer hesitated. For a man who had learned not to feel anything, this rough ride of emotions left him anxious, afraid of where it would lead. But at the sight of Carly's tender biscuits, he pushed all that aside and joined the other two.

They sat on the verge of the hill, side by side. He was close enough to Carly for her arm to brush his as she moved. He could have shifted away but didn't. He kind of liked having her at his side, being able to feel her every breath and breathe in the scent of hay, baking and wildflowers.

They had three biscuits each. He passed around his canteen that he had filled with water before they left. When he thought he'd be riding alone. How had he gone from a loner to sharing the day with a girl and a woman?

"You're smiling again," Carly said.

"I didn't realize." He failed to make it end.

"Don't mind if you keep doing it." More pink in her cheeks and she lowered her eyes as if embarrassed.

Jill jumped up. "A baby rabbit." She dashed after it. It darted from side to side so when she thought she had it, she missed it. She started to giggle.

Carly laughed.

Sawyer's smile deepened, tickled something inside him and he chuckled.

Carly looked his direction. Laughter filled her eyes. Their gazes held, filled with amusement and something more. On his part, an awareness of something sweet and fragile hovering between them.

Is this what marriage did to him? He wasn't sure if he liked it. Wasn't certain he didn't, either. Suddenly he couldn't wait to see what the next few days held for him. For Jill. For all of them. A shiver crawled across his neck. The last time he had felt even remotely this content about his life had been before the fire.

Chapter Nine

As they rode toward home, Carly tried to sort out her feelings. Why had she been so embarrassed to see him smiling and laughing? So aware of the fact he was her husband? She'd almost blurted out how handsome he was. Today he'd donned a clean shirt, the dark green bringing out the color of his eyes. He'd shaved this morning, allowing her to see his strong jaw. But when he smiled, oh my, his eyes flashed the color of early morning sky with the remembrance of lingering stars.

"If I caught him, I would keep him as a pet," Jill said, referring to the rabbit.

"Good thing you didn't catch him," Carly said. "Wild animals don't make good pets."

Jill shot her a cross look. "You just don't want me to have it."

"That's not true." Carly rode a little ahead so she wouldn't have to see Jill's expression.

Sawyer pulled up beside her. "She wasn't always like that."

Carly nodded. "She's been told some cruel things." She relayed what Jill had said the night before.

Sawyer's jaw muscles bunched. He might think he had no feelings but when it came to his little sister, he felt plenty.

She wanted to encourage him so she told him of the Bible verse she'd read to Jill. "I'm convinced she will be okay. She's had to face a lot for one so young but I've seen glimpses of a happier child. She'll find her way back to that." She paused to think how else to reassure him. "Everyone has to deal with loss in their own way." She felt Sawyer watching her but didn't look at him. For some reason, although she'd started it, she didn't want to continue this discussion.

"Do you handle yours by trying to be the son your father never had?"

She pulled Sunny to a halt and came round to stare at the man. "How can you say such a thing? You've known me a day and you jump to this conclusion? Based on what? Your keen observation? Your awareness of how people feel?" She shook her head. "Are you insane?"

Jill gave them both a piercing look and rode on by them. Wise girl, wanting nothing to do with an argument between them.

She guessed Sawyer did his best to hide his reaction, pulling his face into the mask he normally wore. Disappointment at losing sight of his smile colored her thoughts but not enough to quench her anger.

"Forget I said it." His voice was so flat a marble wouldn't have moved off center.

"How can I forget when I know that's what you think? What have I done to give you that impression?"

"Nothing. Leave it be." He rode after Jill.

Carly went after him. "I deserve an explanation."

He pulled to a halt. "I suppose you do. Very well. I

heard you mention several times that you had lost brothers. And when your father insists on a man on the place and you marry a stranger, all the while telling him you are in charge…well, I guess I jumped to conclusions."

"I guess you did, all right. Best you disabuse yourself of that notion here and now." At least he hadn't mentioned her little slip of tongue while they sat at Annie's table.

"I'll do that."

They faced each other. Her insides curled with disappointment that the pleasant morning had turned bitter. Daisy snorted. Jill screamed. A tremor of fear ran down Carly's spine. Daisy was the most placid of animals unless….

She reined about to see Daisy rear and then gallop away in panic.

Carly forgot everything else and kicked Sunny into his top speed. "Hang on," she yelled to Jill, not knowing if her words carried that far. "Grab her mane. Grab the saddle horn." Grab anything to keep from falling off.

Sunny's hooves thundered. The wind tugged Carly's hat off and it strained at its strings. She leaned over her horse's neck as Sunny stretched out. It took only a few minutes to catch up to Jill…minutes that seemed an eternity. She guided Sunny close and reached out to grab Daisy's reins. "Whoa. Whoa, Daisy. You're okay."

The horse slowed and came to a panting halt.

Sawyer rode up on Jill's other side and snatched the girl from the saddle and held her against his chest. "I thought this was a gentle, old horse."

"Only one thing will make her do this. A snake. Jill, did you see a snake?"

Jill nodded, her eyes wide.

"Are you okay?"

Jill stared at her without giving any indication one way or the other.

Carly dismounted and went to Daisy. She rubbed her neck and soothed her. "You're okay, old girl. That mean old snake didn't stand a chance against you, did it?" She spent a few minutes calming the horse, then led her close to Sawyer. "It's okay now, Jill. She'll be fine. You can ride her home."

Sawyer's jaw clenched. "She can ride home with me."

When he would have ridden away, Carly blocked the horse. "That's not a good idea. A person should always get back on after a scare. It's the only way to overcome fear." She met his stubborn look with one equally stubborn.

Jill shoved from Sawyer's grasp. "I'm not afraid." When Carly would have assisted her to mount, she pushed her away. "I don't need help." She managed to climb into the saddle and gave both Carly and Sawyer a look of pure defiance as if to say she took pride in proving them wrong.

For her part, Carly was pleased to see her reaction. "Good for you. You're a little trooper."

A flash of acknowledgment sparked in Jill's eyes before she could think to hide it.

Smiling, Carly remounted and they resumed their journey with Sawyer staying close to Jill.

Carly spotted a patch of palest purple. "Crocuses. I'm going to pick some." She rode that direction and hurried to gather up a handful. She'd put them on her mother's grave when they got back. "Mother loved crocuses. She said they were so brave, pushing up through the snow, enduring the cold. She said we should strive to be like the flower, willing to overcome challenges and adversity." Remembering her mother's words renewed Carly's inner strength. She had willingly, knowingly entered into this marriage. Disagreements or difficulties would not deter her from the path she had chosen. She would make the arrangement work.

Feeling as if life would be all she wanted, she remounted and they continued homeward.

They reached the barn and led the horses inside. Jill dropped the reins and headed for the house.

Carly stopped her. "Father says the animals must be cared for first. You need to take off the saddle, brush Daisy down and make sure she has feed and water."

Jill crossed her arms and gave Carly a mutinous look. "I'm too tired."

"As long as you're able to walk, you aren't too tired." Father had drilled that into Carly. *The animal has carried you without complaint. The least you can do is treat him kindly.*

"I'll do it this time," Sawyer said.

Carly sensed the weariness in his voice as if arguing with this child took too much effort. Or perhaps he was tired of arguing with Carly. It didn't matter. "We can both help her, but she's old enough to be responsible for the animal she rides."

Neither of them spoke. Jill scowled at Carly. Carly didn't look at Sawyer. She didn't want to see his disapproval of how she dealt with Jill but Carly knew she must establish her role as an adult in charge or things could get difficult in the ensuing weeks.

"Oh, whatever you say." Jill flounced past Carly to take up Daisy's reins.

Carly was glad to see she didn't jerk the horse's head around.

She followed, instructing Jill on loosening the cinch. Carly lifted the saddle. "Always put it on the saddle rack so it stays in shape." Step by step, she talked Jill through the process. "You did a good job." She left the girl brushing Daisy to tend to her own horse.

Sawyer watched her. Did he disapprove of how she'd handled the situation or did he see the wisdom of what she'd done? She couldn't tell and wasn't about to ask because she didn't care to hear criticism of her actions.

But she decided one thing. Instead of taking the crocuses to the graveyard as she had intended, she'd put them in a bowl of water to place on the headstone later. She'd make supper right away. Poor Jill was probably hungry as well as tired.

Done taking care of their horses, the three of them went to the house. Grandfather Marshall was gone, Father sat in his big armchair, a stack of newspapers on the table beside him. He came to his feet, struggling with his crutch as they entered. "How did you find things?" He looked at Sawyer.

Carly pushed aside the bit of resentment that Father should seek the answer from Sawyer. And she didn't give the man a chance to answer. "The cows are in the hollow to the north. About thirty calves on the ground. Grass is looking good. Cows are looking good."

"Fine. Fine."

"What's new with the Marshalls?" Not that she expected there was anything. They'd seen them all just last night.

"No news. Just two lonely old men keeping each other company."

Deciding to ignore his sorrowful tone, she went to the stove. "I'll get supper on right away." She'd left meat stewing on the back of the stove. There were cooked potatoes to warm up.

As she prepared the food, Sawyer, without being asked, filled the wood box, brought in more water and carried out the ashes.

"Thank you," she said.

"Least I could do."

Hearing the strain in his voice, she faced him. "I was only doing what I thought best."

They studied each other. She wished she could erase the differences between them and have nothing but the pleasant hours they'd spent earlier in the day.

After a moment, he nodded. "I know. I'm sorry. I have no experience in this." He circled his hand.

She didn't know if he meant raising a child, being married or sharing duties on a ranch. She grinned. Likely all three. "It's all new to me, too, you know. We'll have to learn together."

His eyes changed first, growing less dark. And then the skin around them lifted. Then his mouth curved into a smile. And the weight of a thousand regrets slipped from her shoulders.

A few minutes later, she served the meal. At first, Jill ate slowly but as the food warmed her stomach, she perked up. "I almost got throwed," she told Father. "Daisy ran away."

"Daisy, you say. Nothing fazes her." Understanding came. "Except a snake."

"You should have seen her. She stood on her back legs like this." Jill illustrated. "Then she ran so fast I didn't think anyone could catch her."

"And Jill hung on and didn't panic." Carly smiled her approval. Jill ignored Carly and beamed at Father.

"Aye, child. You did good."

Jill practically glowed from the praise.

Carly looked at Sawyer. He met her look and raised his brows, nodding so slightly no one would notice if they hadn't been watching carefully. Carly understood he, too, saw Jill's reaction to Father. Carly felt that they shared something private and special in that moment, though the feeling fled as quickly as it had come.

There were no sweets in the house for dessert. Even the last of the fruit she'd canned last fall was gone. She promised herself she'd find time in the next day or two to make something special. After all, she had her reputation as a good cook to uphold.

Sawyer insisted he and Jill would help do dishes. Father said he'd like to help, too, but it was difficult with his bum leg.

"I'll bring you dishes to dry," Jill offered, seeming to think she did Father a favor.

Carly kept her back to the table so her father wouldn't see her amusement. He was firm about men's and women's roles. Women ran the house. Men did the *real* work. Her hands grew still and she stared out the window over the cupboard. Why did she fight him on this?

Sawyer seemed to think it was because she tried to be the son Father never had.

But that wasn't it. She simply did what she enjoyed. And what needed to be done. Good thing she had taken over the ranch work or where would they be with Father now crippled up?

She ignored the answer that blared through her head.

There was Sawyer, ready and able to do the work. If Sawyer hadn't been in the diner, looking for someone to care for Jill, there was the threat of selling the ranch.

At least her marriage had stopped that plan.

She finished the dishes, picked up the bowl of crocuses and left the house without a backward look.

Up on the hill, she stepped through the gate and carefully closed it behind her. She stopped momentarily before each of the tiny graves. Father had carved the names on the simple wooden crosses. Callum was the name on the oldest cross. Errol on the next one. After that, they hadn't named the babies. Simply put Baby Boy Morrison on two crosses.

She knelt at her mother's grave. Father had ordered a real headstone with an angel carved into it. Carly set the bowl of crocuses in front of the headstone and sat back on her heels.

"Mother," she whispered. "I need you." Why had God left her without a mother? Her heart went out to young Jill. Carly had agreed to provide a home for the pair but a home needed family. Sawyer and Jill needed family. She and Father provided that but they needed even more. "There's a little girl here who needs a mother." There was no mother. There was only Carly.

She sat upright on her knees and stared at the angel on the headstone. *There was only Carly.* Could she be a mother to Jill even though the child made it clear she didn't want it? "Mother, I wish you were here. You're not. That means things have to be different." She sat quietly, listening to her thoughts. Something Mother often said surfaced. "Things are not always what we want. Disappointments leave us staggering but in all things we can trust God to guide us through. Never forget what He says in His word. 'Thou art my hiding place. Thou shalt preserve me from trouble. Thou shalt compass me about with songs of deliverance. I will instruct thee and teach thee in the way which thou shalt go. I will guide thee with Mine eye.'"

Mother had suffered so many disappointments and yet she never stopped trusting God's goodness and guidance nor His sufficiency for her every need.

"Thank you for guiding me and teaching me." She would do her best to honor God in the life she had chosen—wife to Sawyer, mother to Jill.

The creak of the gate drew her attention. "Jill."

The child's mouth set into a stubborn line. "You said you would show me where your baby brothers were."

"I did. Come in." She rose and went to Jill, offered her hand.

Jill shook her head.

She wasn't going to make it easy but Carly, having made up her mind, wasn't going to let it deter her. "They're right there. Four little boys."

Jill studied the four little crosses. "Did you get to meet them?"

"Two of them I did." Callum had lived several hours. Errol just two. "Not the other two." They'd never drawn breath. She'd only seen their tiny bodies wrapped in white cotton before they were laid in the ground.

Her heart twisted at the pain of the loss. She knew her sorrow was but a drop of what Mother and Father felt. Mother, especially. But Mother had never let her sorrow quench her faith or her joy. She tried to find words to explain it to Jill. "I think the hardest thing for a mother is to lose a child. Mother said loss could turn us bitter or grow our roots deep. We get to choose."

"Like the crocuses?"

Surprised that Jill had listened to Carly's comment and then taken it and applied it to this situation, Carly answered, "That's right. And a very keen observation."

"My mama would say things like that, too." She looked into the distance. "One time I was angry because a trip to the store was canceled. Papa had promised to buy me a candy. Mama said I'd learn there were lots of things in life I could be upset about. Or I could learn to be happy anyway." She sighed deeply. Her shoulders rose. "Don't suppose she meant her and Papa dying." She turned to the headstone. "Is that where your mama is buried?"

"Yes." Carly led her to the foot of the grave.

"I like the angel."

"Me, too."

"Why do you bring her flowers? She doesn't know." When looking at the four little crosses, Jill had shown only curiosity but now her voice grew hard, her expression tightened.

"I do it for me. Because I wish I could really give her flowers and talk to her."

"That's stupid." She kicked at a clump of grass, sending a shower of dirt over Mother's grave. Then she dashed from the little plot, running full speed away from the house up the rise beyond the cemetery and stood staring into the distance.

"Oh God, how am I to show her love and care when she runs from it?"

The answer came into her silent heart. *Love one another. As I have loved you.* God loved her through good times and bad. Through mistakes, rebellion and disobedience. Because of His unfailing love, she could show love to this child whether or not she received it.

Sawyer trotted up to the gate. "Where's Jill? I thought she was with you?"

"She went that way." She blinked.

The child had disappeared.

Sawyer took in the little cemetery. Four wooden crosses and a granite marker with the bowl of flowers before it. Pain ripped through his heart. His mama and Johnny were buried far away. Pa and Judith lay at rest by the church in Libby, Kansas. He understood none of them were there. They had been taken into glory. But seeing these physical reminders of each of Carly's dead family members made him long to be able to visit the graves of his loved ones. He reached for something to hold on to. But changed his mind before he took Carly's hand and grabbed the top rail of the metal gate instead.

He'd been talking to Mr. Morrison after Carly left.

"Son, ye can't keep calling me Mister. It's much too formal. Either call me Father or Robert."

"Okay." He liked the old man. Wouldn't mind if he'd been his father but was he ready to put someone else in Pa's place? Course, no one had suggested Sawyer call him Pa. Father felt different. Comfortable even.

"And the little one can call me Granddad. That okay with you, Jill?"

Jill had nodded but didn't try out the word.

Sawyer had given his opinion on the calves showing the breeding of the English stock. Then the conversation had turned to the need to get the crop in the ground. When he next looked Jill's direction, she was gone.

He glanced out the door and saw she made her way

toward Carly so he wasn't concerned. But by the time he'd pulled on his boots and grabbed his hat, she had disappeared.

"I'll go find her," he said.

Carly touched his arm and pointed. "No need. Here she comes."

Jill's head appeared over the rise and then her body. Her hands were full of weeds. As she drew closer, he made out crocuses and little bluebells.

She stomped past them and went to the far corner of the yard where she knelt and arranged the flowers on the ground.

Carly leaned close to whisper in his ear. "I told her I bring flowers to my mother's grave because it makes me feel close to her."

"But her mother isn't buried here."

Carly shrugged. "Let her pretend. It doesn't hurt anything."

"I guess not." Carly surprised him. One minute insisting Jill ride the horse even after it had bolted and the next so aware of Jill's heart.

Jill sat back on her heels. She glanced to the headstone to her left. Then and there a plan was born in Sawyer's mind.

Carly took Sawyer's arms and led him through the gate. "Let's give her some time alone." They went as far as the barn where they could keep an eye on Jill without intruding on her moment.

"Your father would like me to get started on the planting."

She dropped his arm, leaving him cold and alone. "You met Big Harry. The harnessing is in the barn.

The plow is over there." She pointed. "What else do you need to know?"

"Your father said you would show me where the wheat is to be planted and the oats."

"Come along then." She strode away.

Jill left the graveyard and trotted down the hill. She sat on the step and pulled rocks from her pockets and was soon intent on some kind of play.

Sawyer followed Carly to the fenced plots. "Oats here. Wheat there."

He leaned against the fence post. This was what he'd signed on for, so her brisk attitude didn't bother him.

The next morning, he hurried out to do chores, meeting Carly as she returned to the house with a pail of milk.

"I'll feed the animals," he said.

She ground to a halt. "I do the chores."

"It will take less time if I help." *While you make breakfast.* But he kept the latter to himself. "Jill and your father are up. I made coffee but Jill is looking for something to eat. I told her to stay out of the cupboards and wait."

She shot a look toward the house. "I fed Tosser already."

"Tosser?"

She grinned. "The milk cow."

Her amusement tickled him and he smiled. Funny how it was getting easier and easier to see the humor in things. "Let me guess. She likes to kick the milk bucket, tossing it up."

"Nope."

He looked at her dancing eyes, her teasing expression and forgot every uncertainty, every disagreement between them. Marrying her had been a good idea. He promised himself he would never allow regrets. And if they crept in, he would remember the feeling of this moment. The pleasure of watching her humor. How she quickly forgot any discord. The way she seemed in tune to Jill's needs.

And his own?

That wasn't necessary. His needs were practically nonexistent.

He reminded himself they were talking about a cow. "So why did you name her Tosser?" Why did his tongue feel so floppy? It could not have anything to do with the way she made him smile.

She chuckled. "We bought her from a passing family on their way to the gold fields. They were getting short of funds so were willing to part with her. After we got her, we realized they were tired of her shenanigans. She seemed as placid as cream until someone sat beside her to milk her, then she turned, dropped her head and bunted that person off the stool. If cows could laugh, I'm sure she did."

His grin widened and laughter rumbled up his throat. "She still toss you off your stool?"

"Nope. Father bribed her with oats. If she tossed him, he took away the oats. Now, so long as she gets her oats, she's well behaved."

His feet grew roots as they shared amusement. His past disappeared in the flash of her smile.

Jill stood in the doorway. "I'm hungry."

Carly startled. "I better get this milk to the house and think about breakfast. I'll call when it's ready." She hurried away.

He stared after her a moment, then slowly made his way to the barn. As he gave Big Harry an extra ration of oats, he studied the horse. "I wonder why they named you Big Harry. I expect when she saw you she said, 'Look at those big hairy feet.'" He chuckled. His second day of marriage and he was already discovering unexpected joys.

His smile lingered as he took care of the other animals, making sure the water trough was full and checking the gates on the pasture where the other horses were corralled.

"Sawyer, breakfast is on." Carly's voice sailed across the yard and encircled him like a bit of shining dew.

"She's a good cook, too," he said to no one in particular, though Dusty lifted his head to see if Sawyer talked to him. Sawyer jogged across the yard, something more than hunger urging him to hurry. A trickle of concern reminded him how often he had let himself settle into a place only to move until he finally stopped letting himself care. He stepped inside to be greeted with enough pleasant smells to crowd out any thought of warning himself that he should guard his heart.

Like Gladys had said, he was a loner who didn't know how to be anything but.

This time, he had a marriage contract to ensure he had a permanent home.

Except the marriage wasn't real. What was to stop either of them from ending it?

Chapter Ten

Carly watched from the kitchen window as Sawyer drove Big Harry to the field. She'd watched him do so for three days now and discovered there was something strangely soothing about seeing him plowing in the nearby field as she went about her own work. She'd begun planting the garden, enlisting Jill's help. At first the child had resisted but Carly, following her mother's example, turned it into a game.

Intent on fulfilling her decision to provide more sweets, Carly had spent a few hours each day baking and discovered that Jill enjoyed helping. They'd made cookies and a yellow cake. They'd baked cinnamon rolls. They'd worked together on preparing meals.

Every evening, after Sawyer brought the horse to the barn, he washed at the pump before coming to the house. From her station in the kitchen, Carly could watch his every move. Every day, her pleasure grew at knowing this man was her husband.

After they had supper and the kitchen was cleaned up, they went for a walk. Carly told herself she was teaching Sawyer intimate details about the ranch—

where the boggy area would appear after a heavy rain, the place where she'd discovered a buffalo rub, the pine tree hidden among the cottonwoods along the river.

She shared the details of her day. "Jill talks about her mother as we work. I think it's getting easier for her to remember the good things and less painful to think of her being gone. Not that I expect that pain will ever leave. But I don't need to tell you that. I'm sure it's the same for you."

They had gone to the river where they walked along the shore. He stared ahead.

She waited, having discovered that he considered his words carefully before he answered.

"So much changed when Ma and Johnny perished."

"You lost your home, too." She pressed her hand to his arm. She'd grown more at ease with touching him and had discovered something reassuring and steadying about the strength beneath her hand as his muscles flexed.

"In a way I lost my pa, too. He stayed lost until he met Judith." A beat of consideration. "I guess if there's one thing to be grateful for, it's that he didn't survive without her. I don't think he would have—" He shrugged as if uncertain what he meant.

She understood that he didn't think his pa would be able to go on without Judith at his side. "Poor Jill. I can't imagine losing both parents."

"Even worse, she acted so badly that no one would keep her."

Carly chuckled. "She was hurt and fighting her pain. That little girl is a fighter."

"I can never hope to replace the home she's lost."

Carly tried to not let it bother her that he spoke as if

he were alone in this. She gently corrected him, wondering if he would even notice. "No, we can't. But we can give her something else. A new beginning. A chance to learn that love is still an option."

They had stopped walking and faced each other. He searched her gaze so intently that her eyes stung. She didn't look away. Didn't want to end this moment and prayed he would see that she included him in her hope of a happy future.

A smile began in his eyes and spread to his mouth. "Love is an option. That sounds very hopeful."

She sensed an unasked question. Did he wonder if love was available to him? She'd married a stranger. Their agreement was to remain businesslike. But did he sometimes want more? "I remember something my mother would say. Love is not a feeling. It's an action."

He studied her some more, then turned away. She couldn't tell whether or not he was disappointed with her answer. She wanted to explain what she meant… that feelings didn't need to exist in order for a person to show loving actions.

That was what she wanted to show when she baked treats for everyone. Partly because she'd entered into this arrangement with honorable intentions. But partly because she wanted them to know someone cared about them. It sprang from the decision she'd made at Mother's grave to be a mother to Jill. And a wife to Sawyer, though she wasn't sure what that would look like.

They returned home a short time later. It was Saturday and she'd left water heating for baths. She brought the washtub into the kitchen.

Sawyer, seeing her intent, looked startled.

"Tomorrow is Sunday and church. Tonight we bathe."

"Aye," Father said. "My own mother, God rest her soul, said washing the body reminded one that there should be a regular cleansing of the heart."

"I'd forgotten what day it was," Sawyer said. "I'll go to the river to wash." He grabbed a bar of soap and a towel and left before anyone could say anything.

"Jill, you can go first." She covered the windows. Father went outside to sit in the cool evening air.

"Get undressed and I'll wash your hair for you."

Jill stared at her. Her throat worked. Carly understood she struggled with some emotion and waited for the child to say something.

But Jill turned away and stripped off her clothing, then climbed into the tub.

Carly let her relax in the warm water for a few minutes and wash herself, then knelt beside her. "I loved it when my mother washed my hair." She lathered up Jill's hair as she talked and rinsed it well, then wrapped a towel around her head.

Jill sat up. Tears flooded her eyes.

"Did I get soap in your eyes? I'm sorry. Let me wash them out."

Jill rocked her head back and forth. "No soap." She sniffled. Finally, she spoke. "Nobody has washed my hair since Mama."

The child was finished bathing. Carly wrapped a towel about her and lifted her to her lap. She pressed Jill's head to her shoulder and rubbed her back. "I'm glad I could be the one to do it for you. You're a precious, sweet child and I'm honored to be part of your family now."

Jill's stiffness eased.

Carly continued talking. "We might not be the kind

of family each of us started out to be but that doesn't mean we can't be good. It's been so much fun having you help me with the baking. I can tell your mama has taught you many things. I think she'd be happy that you've remembered them."

Jill nodded.

"We'll keep learning together, doing the things we know our mothers would want us to. You know…" She leaned back so she could look into Jill's face. "I think both of our mamas would be pleased to see us working together to make a happy family."

Emotions raced across the child's face…hope, uncertainty and then the blank look that she used so often.

Carly pushed back her disappointment. It was early yet. In time, Jill would learn that they could be as happy as they chose to be. All of them. Together as a family.

"You think about it." She finished drying Jill and helped her into her nightgown. She dried Jill's hair in front of the stove and she braided it, still damp, to keep it tidy. "Do you want me to read you a story before you go to sleep?" She'd asked several times and always Jill had said no, thanks. She would keep asking until Jill agreed to let her.

Jill hesitated.

Carly waited, hoping for agreement. Then Jill shook her head.

"Fine. You get to bed. I'll come and tuck you in."

She let out a slow sigh when Jill didn't tell her not to. One step forward. She hung the wet towels as she gave Jill a few minutes to get into bed, then went to the bedroom.

Jill had the covers up to her chin.

Carly tucked them tight around her, then leaned over

and kissed her on the forehead. "Have a good sleep, sweet Jill." Seeing the wariness in the girl's eyes, she left the room before Jill could protest.

In the kitchen, she sucked in air. It was progress. *Thank You, God. Help me show love every day and in every way. And let that love help us build a new family.*

Sawyer and Father spoke outside.

Carly couldn't help but smile in anticipation of seeing Sawyer after a dip in the river. She shivered. She'd take warm water any day.

She added hot water to the tub, pulled a chair near and put the soap and towels close at hand.

"Father, would you like a bath now?" She allowed herself a quick glance at Sawyer. His hair sparkled with dampness. His skin glowed like freshly blossomed roses. Her 'quick glance' had become an all-out stare.

Father pushed to his feet. "I'll do me best."

Carly remembered to breathe as she brought her attention to her father.

Sawyer leaped forward. "Do you need help? I don't mind."

Father's face crinkled in appreciation. "Thank you for the offer, son, but I've been managing on my own."

"How does he do it?" Sawyer asked after Father went inside.

"He sits on a chair and leans over the tub. Seems to work for him." She chuckled. "He's particular about keeping his beard clean. He once told me a story about an old bachelor who didn't wash as often as he should. Claims the man found a mouse in his beard one day." She met Sawyer's surprised look. "Now I can't say if it's really true, I'm simply repeating what I heard."

Sawyer grinned. "I don't expect your father would spin a wild tale, would he?"

She lifted one shoulder. "Never known my father to tell a lie. Though I'm not saying he saw this first hand. I suspect it was a story told to him and he only relayed what he'd heard."

Sawyer's gaze held hers like a steel clamp. She couldn't have turned away if she wanted and she didn't want to. His smile gave way to a deep-throated laugh. Still their eyes remained locked.

They both sobered. Something sweet and eternal blossomed deep inside even as she tried to resist it. Yes, he was her husband but not in the real sense. Not in a way that included mutual fondness. Both of them had been clear that this would be strictly business.

Business could be pleasant and sweet, she reasoned. Like honey to the soul.

She sat on the outside chair where Father had been sitting and indicated the chair beside her.

Sawyer sat.

Neither spoke. The air between them was heavy with unspoken words.

Sawyer broke the silence. "I want to thank you."

She jerked about to face him. "For what?"

"For how you are with Jill." He grinned. "For being a better cook than me." His smile shifted into a considering look. "For everything."

She tried to think but her brain was stuck, frozen by the way his eyes shifted from one shade of blue-green to another as he spoke. As if they responded to something inside. If only she could know for certain what it was. She guessed it was surprise, even pleasure, at how well their first few days of marriage had gone. His gratitude left her dry mouthed. Finally she was able to get some words out. "I've only been doing what we agreed upon." She hoped he had accepted that she would be doing ranch work because she didn't want to upset this sense of accord by having to make it clear to him.

Sawyer sat on the wagon seat with Carly at his side. Father Morrison and Jill sat behind. He smiled inwardly. This would be his first appearance in public with a wife. He studied her out of the corner of his eyes. She wore a dark blue dress and had her hair done up in a loose roll about her head. It peeked out from under her Sunday bonnet.

His wife. It still felt strange to say that.

They arrived in Bella Creek and stopped at the church.

Annie ran out to greet Carly. "I still can't believe you're married."

Grandfather Marshall nodded from the step as Father Morrison hobbled toward him. The rest of the Marshall family waved a greeting as they entered the church. A murmur followed them as Carly led them down the aisle after her father. Jill sat beside him, leaving Carly and Sawyer to sit together. As well they should, he supposed. As man and wife.

Preacher Hugh welcomed the congregation. "I have a special announcement today. I'd like to introduce Mr. and Mrs. Sawyer Gallagher. Would you please stand?"

Carly frowned, then jerked to her feet. Sawyer stood as well. Carly's smile looked as plastered on as his. "Thank you," he murmured to the applause. He noticed many surprised looks.

Carly sat down and jerked his hand to sit as well.

He felt like the world suddenly moved through a dense fog. The preacher's words echoed. The songs the congregation sang seemed distant and he heard barely a word of the sermon. Their marriage was public knowledge now. Somehow that seemed to change things. People would have expectations of them as a couple. Could he live up to those expectations? It didn't seem likely, seeing as their marriage was a fraud.

But then, the only people who needed to be concerned about that were he and Carly and they had agreed on the matter.

What did it matter what others thought? He'd long ago decided not to let such things bother him.

He relaxed and sat back. So far, he had no reason to complain about the arrangement between himself and Carly. In fact, he'd enjoyed many parts of it.

He didn't realize he sat grinning to himself until the preacher said amen, and Carly whispered, "What's so amusing?"

"Later," he whispered back, then realized he couldn't tell Carly why he smiled. "Nothing."

Conner and Kate hurried toward them after the service. "Come to the ranch. We're all going to be there." They included Sawyer and Carly in their invitation.

He waited for Carly to choose.

She turned her face to him. "It's up to you. What do you want to do?"

His heart glowed that she had consulted him. "What would you do if I wasn't here?"

She gave a little shrug. "I used to always go to their place after church. But that kind of ended when Annie got married."

Annie crowded to her side. "Hugh and I are going, too. It will be like old times."

Carly continued to look at Sawyer, waiting for his answer. "I don't mind going if that's what you'd like," he said.

Her eyes smiled. "I'd like it."

"What about Jill and Father?"

Her eyebrows jerked upward and he realized it was the first time he had called Mr. Morrison *Father*.

"Oh, you must bring them as well," Kate said. "Everyone would be disappointed if they didn't come."

So a short time later, the four of them drove to the Marshall Five Ranch. He had never been there and looked about with interest. Two houses, a much bigger barn than the one at the Morrison Ranch and more outbuildings.

"They are a bigger operation," Carly said as if reading his mind. "There's Grandfather, Grandpa Bud and Annie's three brothers plus half a dozen cowboys on this place."

"Just you and me at the Morrison place."

She grinned. "That's right. Just Sawyer and Carly."

He looked at her, revealing nothing of the way his heart swelled at the way her smile acknowledged his statement.

"We've decided it's time for the first picnic of the season," Dawson said as they drew to a halt in the yard.

At the ranch house, the women all sprang into action, packing up food that had been prepared ahead of time.

Sawyer hung back with the men until everyone was ready and then helped carry the food, blankets and a few cushions. Father Morrison and Grandfather Marshall waved them off.

"They'll enjoy another visit," Carly assured him when he wondered if someone should stay with them. "There are men hanging about if they need anything."

In fact, a weathered old man watched them depart and the Marshalls waved goodbye to him, calling him Jimbo.

They traipsed to the nearby creek, a much gentler flow of water than the river running through the Morrison Ranch. A gentle grassy slope slanted toward the creek. The others seemed to know where they were going and continued on for a few yards.

The children ran ahead, Jill and Mattie side by side.

"It's good to see her making friends," Carly said.

"She's feeling safe enough to let herself start caring." He knew as soon as he said the words that it would spark interest.

They had fallen behind the others, so thankfully Carly was the only one who heard him. She slowed and turned and studied him. He pretended a great interest in the grassy field on which they walked.

"I'm glad to hear that."

He darted a glance at her. That was all?

Her study continued. "I see a difference in you, too. Does that mean you are starting to let yourself care?"

"Different? How?" He wouldn't admit he felt different. Nor could he explain in what way. Most certainly he was sure it didn't mean he cared. That was not part of the agreement.

"When I first met you a week ago—"

"Not a week yet."

She waved aside his protest. "Close enough. A week ago, you never showed any emotion in your face. Do you remember you told me you didn't feel anything?"

"I remember." It seemed a lifetime ago.

"Now you smile and laugh readily, though sometimes you wear that solid mask again." She grinned. "Like now. I haven't figured out if it's because you don't feel anything or if you are afraid to trust your feelings." They had stopped walking and considered each other. He couldn't say what she sought any more than he could say what he looked for in her eyes. Except he hoped she would say something that made him comfortable with his feelings.

"I believe, however, that it's the latter. You are afraid of your feelings. Or of trusting people to value you and your feelings." She nodded, satisfied with her conclusions.

He walked on. She kept pace with him.

"Are you going to admit it?"

"Sure, if that's what you want."

She gave him a playful shove. "I want honesty."

He stumbled away and faced her, doing his best to look stern while his insides bounced with an unfamiliar sense of adventure and play. He took a step toward her and another until she tipped her head back to meet his gaze. "Exactly how honest do you want me to be?"

She swallowed hard. "Completely."

He took in her wide, dark eyes, the way her tongue skimmed her lips, the beat of her pulse in the V of her neck. Complete honesty would mean confessing he found her attractive and appealing at that moment. Not just physically, though she was a beautiful woman, but he saw her caring heart, her commitment to doing what she thought was right.

His gaze lingered on her mouth.

She leaned closer.

He shook his head. "I don't think you want complete honesty." For certain, he wasn't ready for it.

She jammed her fists to her hips. "Of course I do."

"Well, you've had it. I've been totally honest with you from our first meeting." Except things had changed. He clamped down on his back teeth. He only wanted a home for Jill. Nothing more.

"Hey, you two," Hugh called. "Are you coming?"

Carly made a disapproving sound and hurried toward the others.

Sawyer lengthened his stride to keep pace with her. "Carly?" He didn't want her angry at him.

She glanced over her shoulder. "Never mind, Sawyer. We made an agreement and I mean to hold up my end of it."

"As do I." Which meant pushing back those fledgling, demanding feelings. It should be easy. He'd done it for years. Except it wasn't easy. And a part of him didn't want to dismiss them. He had made a deal, though, and his honor depended on keeping his word.

Yet a little thought refused to be silenced. What would Carly say if he admitted his changing feelings? Would she be displeased or otherwise?

Chapter Eleven

Carly kept her feelings stuffed back as she helped set out the picnic. They put the food on a tablecloth and spread blankets to sit on. She had noticed the many cushions the men carried.

"Here's one for you," Kate said. "You and Sawyer." Her eyes twinkled.

Carly dropped the cushion to the ground.

Hugh took off his hat. The other men followed his example. "I'll ask the blessing."

Carly bowed her head, grateful no one could see the tangle of her thoughts. She'd believed Sawyer meant to kiss her as they lingered behind the others. She'd leaned close, inviting it. But then he had stepped back. As he should have. Their agreement clearly left no room for kissing. She understood that. But it was getting hard to remember.

She realized Hugh had said amen, and the others had seated themselves on the blankets. The food was passed from hand to hand. The children sat in a group, eating with gusto. Conversation hummed around her. She was more than content to let it be so.

"Carly, how have you enjoyed your first week of married bliss?" If the question had come from anyone but Isabelle, Carly might have suspected she was being teased,

"We've been busy. Sawyer has started seeding. I've been planting the garden."

"I don't think she was asking about the work," Annie said, her eyes sparkling with amusement.

Carly's mouth opened but nothing came out.

Sawyer chuckled. "Seems she's speechless."

The others laughed.

Her cheeks grew warm. Let them think what they wanted. But did Sawyer have to give the impression that they had enjoyed a week of conjugal bliss?

"Relax," he murmured and patted the cushion on which he lounged on one arm.

She glanced about. All the other couples had finished eating and lingered over the coffee Annie served. Each pair leaned on a large cushion. Happily married couples, eager to share the same, intimate space.

Sawyer patted the cushion again.

She stared at the spot, studied his elbow which he'd bent to support his head. Slowly, wishing she could resist but acknowledging she couldn't, she lifted her gaze along his arm, taking in every detail. The crease of his shirtsleeve where his elbow bent, the strain of the material across his biceps, the darkness of the skin on his hands. And the blinding light from his eyes.

What was he thinking?

Surely not what she wished.

She blinked. She wished for nothing. She had what she wanted. A pretend marriage that protected the ranch.

He patted the cushion again, his eyes steady and the tiniest bit challenging.

She shook her head and fanned her skirt out before her.

"Chicken," he murmured so softly she knew no one else would hear.

She wasn't going to let him tease her into doing something she didn't want to. Because she wanted it so badly it frightened her.

Something tickled her neck and she swatted at what she thought was a spider.

Sawyer chuckled—a sound so sweet it rivaled the meadowlark on the nearby stump.

She grabbed the blade of grass he'd been tickling her with and tossed it aside. Would this picnic never end? If it didn't soon, she'd end up doing something she'd regret, though at the moment she couldn't say if she meant she'd give in to her urge to plant her elbow close to his and share a special moment.

Or if she meant she'd regret not doing it.

Determined to keep things between them as they had been and as they had agreed they would be, she turned her attention to the conversation around them.

"We're planning for the spring roundup," Dawson said.

That got Carly's attention. Their cattle, for the most part, were on their land, but she enjoyed the roundup even though Father absolutely forbade her to follow the crew. No, she had to wait until the animals were gathered and then join in identifying and branding the calves.

Sawyer sat up, pressing to her side, as he listened to the planning for the spring gathering.

Carly felt his interest and knew he'd want to go with the men. She refused to acknowledge that thinking of him being gone left her empty inside.

A scream rent the air, sending tension across Carly's neck.

The parents were on their feet in seconds. The children, except for Kate and Conner's baby, were playing nearby. All of them were used to playing outdoors and fourteen-year-old Beth, Logan and Sadie's oldest, was supervising.

Beth rushed toward the adults. "Jill's hurt. Come quick."

Sawyer and Carly bolted to their feet and raced after the girl. They ran down the slope toward the creek. Carly saw Jill, crumpled on the gravel and let out a cry.

Sawyer would have outdistanced her but fear gave her wings and she reached Jill at the same time as Sawyer. They both wrapped their arms about her and helped her sit up.

"Honey, what's wrong? Where are you hurt?"

Jill sobbed, unable to answer. She lifted her arm. A deep gash above her elbow bled. She lifted her right foot. The children had removed shoes and stockings to play in the water. The sole of Jill's foot bled.

"What happened?" Sawyer demanded.

Did he realize how thick his voice had become? He cared far more than he had ever admitted.

He scooped up his sister and stood. He looked around. "Did any of you see what happened?"

Carly kept her arm about Jill, needing to offer as much comfort as she could. Finding strength in contact with Sawyer.

Beth's brother, seven-year-old Sammy, stepped forward. "She stepped on that sharp rock." He pointed toward the offending item. Then he picked it up and threw it into the water. "There's lots of blood. Is she okay?"

The others had gathered round. Kate pushed forward. "Let me have a look." She examined both cuts. "There's gravel here." She held Jill's arm. "I need to wash it out."

Sawyer carried Jill to the edge of the water. Carly held out the injured arm and Kate washed away the debris.

Kate spoke to Jill. "Will you let me put your foot in the water? It's cold but that will help."

Jill looked at Carly, her eyes brimming with tears and fears.

"Do you want me to do it?" Carly asked.

Jill nodded.

Carly hunkered down beside Sawyer. Together they tended the child. Their gazes caught and held and a thousand thoughts raced through her mind. She cared about this little girl in a way that made her heart tremble. And perhaps cared just a little for a man who would hold his little sister so tenderly and murmur that everything would be okay. He would make sure it was.

Jill squirmed. "It's not hurting so much now."

"We need to get her home," Sawyer said.

Carly nodded agreement.

Sawyer carried his sister back to the picnic spot. The others began to gather up items.

"No need for the rest of you to end the outing."

Dawson, the eldest, looked about. "It's early yet. We can stay and let the children play."

The family gathered round them to say goodbye before Sawyer and Carly began the return trek to the ranch, Jill in his arms.

Carly stayed at his side, holding Jill's hand where it lay across her chest. Sawyer's hand covered them both. It made walking a little awkward but Carly wasn't about to end the connection between them.

In that moment, she knew they had become family.

Jill had been hurt. Sawyer had not known he could feel another person's pain until now. If not for Carly's steadying presence, he didn't know what he would do. He held her hand and Jill's as they hurried back to the Marshalls' ranch house.

"I'll get Father while you settle her in the wagon." Carly ducked into the house while Sawyer went to the wagon.

Two old men hobbled from the house.

"The wee lassie is hurt." Father Morrison hurried to the wagon and climbed into the back. "Ack, poor lassie."

"Is she okay?" Grandfather Marshall called from the doorway.

Jill poked her head over the edge of the wagon box. "I cut my arm and my foot on a rock."

"I'm sorry. You're in good hands, though. Robert, I'll take care of that business we discussed."

Sawyer would have helped Carly into the wagon but she was up before he could reach her. She sat beside him, leaning forward as if she could make the wagon go faster.

Sawyer was equally anxious to get home even though he knew there was no need for rush. Jill's cuts had stopped bleeding. Her injuries were not serious.

The way his heart ached was serious. It both alarmed him and enticed him.

His pulse settled to a normal pace as they made the journey.

By the time they reached home, he could speak without his words catching in his throat. "It scares me to think of her hurt."

"It didn't look serious to me and Kate didn't think it was." She shuddered a little. "I suppose I had cuts every bit as bad. Likely you did, too."

He understood she tried to reassure him with those words. "I was a boy. Boys get banged up lots. But Jill's just a little girl."

"I know." She put her hand over his.

He turned his palm to hers. His insides settled.

Back at the ranch, he carried Jill in and Carly arranged her in the armchair across from her father's. Father Morrison followed them and sat down facing Jill. "Aye, now ye'll be keeping me company, I think."

Jill nodded. "I can't walk."

Carly placed a pillow behind her and unearthed some children's books.

Then she and Sawyer stood side by side, watching the girl.

"Look, it's stopped bleeding." Jill held up her arm. Her foot had stopped bleeding after being placed in the cold water of the creek.

"I'll get a cloth and clean up the blood on your arm." Carly went to the cupboard.

Sawyer felt her departure like the blast of winter wind.

She returned and cleaned up Jill's arm.

Sawyer watched them, a feeling foreign, yet familiar tugging at him. How could he feel like he had seen this before? And then it hit him. A memory so full of emotion it left him breathless and confused. Made him want to reach out and pull Jill and Carly into his arms and never let them go. He allowed himself to place his hand on Carly's shoulder, needing the contact, hoping she wouldn't think it untoward.

The memory ballooned within him, threatening to choke off his breath.

He dropped his hand and rushed from the house. He didn't slow until he leaned against the fence beyond the barn and stared toward the horses, though he couldn't have said which animals were grazing before him.

He didn't know how long he stood there, his thoughts a whirlwind of hopelessness as he tried to push away the memory. He didn't move when Carly came to his side, standing shoulder to shoulder with him.

For several minutes, she didn't speak but her presence settled him like nothing else could have.

"Seeing Jill's injury reminded me of something." A beat of waiting. If she didn't want to hear this, she could change the subject or move away. She didn't and he continued.

"Johnny fell and cut his arm in almost the same place as Jill. It was my fault. We'd been out playing and I climbed a tree." His breath shuddered out and steadied again when Carly took his hand and squeezed.

"Johnny followed, always trying to keep up to his big brother. He slipped and fell against a stub of a branch. Tore his arm badly." He stopped as the memory of his little brother filled every pore of his body, then he forced himself to continue. "I carried my crying little brother home. Told Mama what happened. She cleaned up the cut and tied a bandage around it. When she was done, she sat in the big armchair where she often held us to read stories to us. She lifted Johnny to her lap and pulled me to her side." His throat thickened and for a moment he couldn't go on.

Carly waited, calm and accepting.

"She said, 'Sawyer, I'm proud of you for taking care of your little brother. Accidents happen and no one is to blame for them.' She took my chin and made me look at her. 'Promise me you will never forget that.' Of course I promised."

"Of course you did. But have you kept the promise?"

He heard the doubt in her voice. "I think so."

"Are you blaming yourself for Jill's accident?"

"I should have been watching her." He tried, and failed, to keep the harsh note of self-accusation from his voice.

"It was an accident. No one is to blame. Children get scrapes and bruises unless they are wrapped in cotton wool and never allowed to play."

"I suppose so."

"Do you blame yourself that Jill was alone after your parents died?"

"I stayed away longer than I should have." There, he'd admitted it. Confessed to a sense of blame. How would she answer that?

"But you didn't stay away forever."

"That's so." He met her look. Found sweet release in her words.

"I think you should stop blaming yourself for their deaths. Your mama wouldn't like it."

He wanted to dismiss the idea. But every time she said he wasn't to blame, he grew closer to believing it. "I'll try to stop blaming myself."

She chuckled. "It's hard to let go of an old belief, isn't it? Try putting a new one in its place."

"What are you suggesting?" He hoped she had a concrete idea.

"A Bible verse. 'Give thanks unto the Lord: for He is good: for His mercy endureth forever.'"

He breathed in the words, letting them sink into the depths of his being. Yes, God was good. Even when created mankind wasn't. "That's a good verse to remember."

She stepped away, heading for the barn. "I have something to do."

She'd changed from her dress to trousers and her wide-brimmed hat hung down her back.

"You're going riding?" It was as much statement as question.

"Kate said they had kittens ready to leave their mama. I'm going to bring one home for Jill. I think she'd like that."

He followed her and stayed nearby as she saddled Sunny. He couldn't explain to anyone, least of all himself, why he could barely restrain himself from reaching out and grabbing the bridle and begging her to stay.

She led the horse from the barn. "Make sure Jill is okay."

They stood inches apart. *Don't go*, his heart said. "Be careful," his mouth said.

She grinned and stretched up on tiptoe and planted a kiss on his cheek.

Before he could react, she swung into the saddle and called, "Never. I'll never be careful." She waved.

He lifted his hand in a farewell salute as he watched her ride away. After she was out of sight, he realized

his arm was still raised and he lowered it just enough
to touch the spot she'd kissed. He was grateful no one
could see him standing in the middle of the yard, grinning widely at nothing.

After a bit, he pulled himself together and returned
to the house where he had to explain that Carly had
gone for a ride. He didn't want to tell Jill about the kitten. Let it be a surprise.

Jill and Father Morrison had set up a checkers game
and played it.

Sawyer wandered from window to window.

"Son, it's too early for her to be back. You might
as well light somewhere before you wear a trench in
the floor."

He hadn't realized he had made so many trips. "I'll
do the chores."

"You do that." Father Morrison sounded relieved at
Sawyer's announcement and Jill giggled.

Out in the barn, he fed the animals, which didn't
take nearly long enough. He checked the harnessing.
All in good shape. He climbed the ladder to check on
the hayloft. And if he pushed open the doors, allowing
him a view of the trail that would bring Carly home, it
was purely coincidental. Wasn't it?

He was happy he didn't have anyone there with him
to demand an honest answer.

He sat in the doorway, his feet swinging until he
saw her coming. He stayed there until she was almost
close enough to see him watching and waiting before
he closed the doors and slipped down the ladder.

He was brushing Big Harry when she led her horse
into the barn.

"See what I have." She pulled a fluffy gray-and-white kitten from her shirt and held it close to her face. The kitten meowed and licked her cheek.

Carly laughed. "It's very affectionate. The friendliest one of the bunch. Do you want to hold her while I take care of Sunny?" She took his agreement for granted and handed him the little bundle of fur.

The kitten was soft and warm and purred. "I haven't had a cat since..." His voice trailed off.

She nodded. "Since your mama was alive. Right?"

"Couldn't have pets when we were always moving."

"Maybe I should have picked one for you, too."

He chuckled at the teasing note in her voice. "Maybe Jill will let me share her cat."

She unsaddled Sunny, brushed him, let him drink and made sure he had feed. "Shall we take the kitten to Jill?"

He held the little cat toward her but she had already stepped through the door and let him follow her.

"Yer back," Father Morrison said as they stepped inside.

"We're back and we brought something for Jill."

Jill turned around, a cautiously eager expression on her face. She searched Carly's hands and seeing nothing, showed her disappointment.

"Don't give up so soon," Carly said with a laugh and stepped aside so Jill could see the kitten in Sawyer's hands.

Jill came out of the chair, her sore foot completely forgotten and rushed to Sawyer's side. "Is it for me?"

Carly plucked the kitten from Sawyer's hands and handed it to Jill. "She's all yours."

Jill grinned so wide, Sawyer thought it must hurt.

She pressed the kitten to her cheek. "Thank you. I love her. What's her name?"

"That's up to you."

Jill returned to the chair, the kitten cupped in her hands. "It will have to be a special name." She giggled as the kitten squirmed. "She wants to explore." The kitten roamed the perimeter of the chair cushion, edging behind Jill and then it teetered at the front, falling to the floor. It skittered from corner to corner, jumping at imaginary dangers. Jill laughed at its antics.

"Her name is Skippy because she skips from place to place."

"Skippy?" Carly pretended to give the name serious consideration. Finally she nodded. "I like that. What do you think, Sawyer?"

He'd been so caught up in the moment, enjoying his little sister's happiness, silently thanking Carly for this kind gesture, that he startled at her question. He quickly recovered. "Skippy is a fine name."

Skippy sat and gave a plaintive meow.

"She wants me." Jill hurried to the kitten and retired to the chair. The little ball of fur was soon asleep on her lap. Jill looked at Sawyer. "Thank you."

Sawyer's heart swelled against his ribs. It was the first time he'd seen his little sister acting like the child he remembered before her parents died and his throat clogged with emotion.

"Thank Carly. She rode all the way back to the Marshalls' to get it for you."

Jill slowly turned her eyes to Carly. He saw in them a look he knew personally…resistance and caution.

Would she thank Carly? More important, would she accept Carly and the home she offered?

Chapter Twelve

Carly waited, her heart still and hopeful, to see if Jill would acknowledge the gift she'd brought her.

Jill's eyes were dark with a look she had borrowed from Sawyer. Both so guarded. So afraid to believe life could be as good as their past.

"Thank you," Jill murmured, ducking her head to hide her face.

"You're welcome." Carly barely stopped herself from reaching for Sawyer's hand and giving it a hard squeeze. It was getting harder and harder to remember their agreement. Or why she'd laid out the limitations.

That night as she lay in the darkness of her bedroom, Jill spoke softly. "Are you awake?"

"I am. Why aren't you sleeping?" She'd gone to bed an hour or more ago, the kitten curled up beside her. Carly had checked Jill's injuries at her bedtime and they were scabbing over.

"Can I take Skippy when we go?"

Carly's heart thudded. "Where are you going?"

"I dunno. But Sawyer goes. He always goes. Papa said he was like a rolling stone."

"But, honey, he isn't going to leave. We're married." Doubts flashed through her mind. Married in name only. And even if that wasn't the case, there was nothing to keep him from leaving if he chose. But she could offer Jill reassurance. "This is your home now. You don't ever have to leave." She wished she could see Jill's expression but that might not provide her any information. The child was good at hiding her feelings. She learned from her big brother. Or perhaps from the events of the past few months.

"You're not just saying that?" Jill's voice was thin, uncertain, yet full of hope.

"Nope. I've never had a little sister and now that I do, I'm not going to let her go."

"Okay." A moment later. "I'm glad."

"Me, too." She smiled into the dark and listened to Jill's breathing deepen.

A few days later, Carly glanced out the window at the sound of an approaching conveyance. "Doc Baker," she informed the others who lingered at the breakfast table. He'd said he'd be out this week to check on Father's leg. Hope and sorrow laced through Carly. She understood that Father's leg was not going to get completely better. But perhaps the doctor's predication had been wrong.

She opened the door to let Doc enter. "Would you care for coffee?"

"Wouldn't say no." He eyed the biscuits.

She offered them to him, knowing he must miss his daughter, Kate, now that she had married Conner Marshall and lived on the ranch.

Doc looked about at the little Morrison family. Or—Carly corrected herself—was it the Gallagher family?

"How are you all doing?" he asked.

"Fine," they answered in unison making Jill giggle.

Doc turned to Jill. "What's this I hear about you getting hurt again?"

Jill lifted her arm to show him the scrape on her elbow. "And my foot." She reached down to start taking off her shoe and sock.

Doc chuckled. "No need to show me. I'll take your word for it." He studied Jill. "That's two accidents in quick succession. Are you being careless?"

She returned his study with serious expression. "Sometimes I get in too big a hurry."

Doc nodded. "Then maybe you should slow down."

Carly and Sawyer exchanged a smile. She understood he thought the same as she—Jill wasn't likely going to slow down.

His coffee and plate of biscuits finished, Doc rubbed his hands together. "Robert, are you ready to have your leg checked out?"

Father nodded. "So long as you have good news for me."

"I can't promise."

Carly got to her feet. "We'll wait outside." The three of them exited.

Jill stopped two feet from the door. "Is he going to hurt Granddad?"

"I think his leg hurts much of the time," Carly said. "But he won't complain. Father never does." She picked weeds from the flower bed, enjoying the bright orange of the poppies that had blossomed in the last few days.

Sawyer leaned against the corner post of the veranda, his gaze on the closed door. "I hope he'll be okay."

"Me too, but—" Carly didn't finish. Doc had already warned them that Father's leg would never be the same.

Doc opened the door. "Can you all come back inside?"

They trooped in and sat down. Father's face was drawn but the splint was gone.

Doc spoke. "His leg is healed as well as it's going to. I regret that I wasn't able to set it better. Because of that, it will always be crooked."

"Can he walk on it?" Carly asked.

"I've told him to start using it as much as he can. The muscles will shrink if he doesn't. However, that leg will never be as strong as the other. Robert, you can use the cane or the crutch, whichever helps the most."

Up to this point, Father hadn't spoken. "I'll manage fine. Aye, I'll make the best of it."

Doc pushed from the table. "Then I'll be on my way."

Sawyer and Carly escorted him to the door and waved him off. They exchanged regretful looks.

"Granddad, are you okay?" Jill's voice jerked their attention to the pair.

Father stood, gingerly putting weight on his leg. His face was almost as white as his beard.

"Father!"

He lifted his hand to stall her. "I know my leg will never be the same but I'm not about to give up." With the aid of the cane Doc had provided, Father limped across the room. "I think I'll sit outside for a bit.

Tears flooded Jill's eyes. "Why can't the doctor make him better? What if he dies?"

Sawyer and Carly knelt on either side of the little girl. Sawyer spoke first. "He'll get stronger every day."

"Honey, do you think he'll let a sore leg defeat him?" Carly waited.

Jill met her eyes. After a moment's consideration, she shook her head.

Carly smiled. "Of course he won't. He's far too stubborn."

"Can I go see him?"

"I think he'd like that."

"I'll let him hold Skippy." Jill picked up her cat and headed outdoors. They heard her chattering away.

Sawyer and Carly stood. Carly lifted her gaze to his. Saw his concern. "It must be hard for him," Sawyer said.

"Yes, but it's the news he expected from the beginning. That's why he insisted I needed a man."

Sawyer blinked, pulled that inscrutable mask over his face. "That's why you married me."

"You know that." They both did. "I don't regret it."

They stared into each other's eyes. Neither blinking. She wished she would read his thoughts, know what he was thinking…feeling.

He gave a little nod. "Nor do I." And with that, he strode from the house.

She went to the window and watched as he went to the barn and brought out Big Harry.

He looked toward the house.

She raised her hand. Couldn't say if he saw her beyond the glass. But he touched the brim of his hat and went to hitch the horse to the seed drill. He then went to the field to resume planting.

Carly turned away from the window. No regrets. It was a pleasant thought.

Jill came back inside. "Granddad says he's got things to do."

Carly returned to the window and saw Father hobbling toward the barn. She knew better than to warn him to take it easy. He'd have to find his own pace and wouldn't welcome interference from her.

Over the next few days, life settled into a peaceful routine. Sawyer plowed and planted the crop. Carly finished planting the garden and baked up a storm—several varieties of cookies, an oatmeal-raisin cake that Father liked, bread and cinnamon rolls, enjoying Jill's company as she worked.

"You know how to make pie?" Jill asked as they finished breakfast dishes.

"Sure do. Why?"

"You should make some today. Like maybe raisin. That's Sawyer's favorite."

"I suppose we could make pies," Carly answered cautiously. Normally she found making pies, baking even, to be a waste of time…normally, she would be out riding the range…but Sawyer had shown appreciation of her efforts, causing her to take a great deal of pride in producing something special for every meal.

She blinked and stared out the window. She hadn't ridden out since last week. What if the cows had wandered? She'd have to check on them this afternoon. In the meantime, she and Jill prepared pie dough, rolled out the crusts and filled the pie tins with raisin filling that Jill had stirred as it cooked.

She roasted enough meat to give them ample leftovers for supper.

A little later, she sent Jill to call Sawyer from the field for dinner.

Carly went to the barn to call Father. He'd taken to sorting through the old harnesses and leather scraps. "Making something new out of the old," he'd explained. Carly was happy to see him occupied with something that gave him pleasure.

She hurried back to the house to set out the noon meal. Sawyer entered, water glistening in his hair. His sleeves rolled to his elbows to reveal muscular arms. He'd grown deeply tanned in the past few days.

He sniffed. "Smells good in here."

"Carly baked you a raisin pie," Jill said, looking pleased with herself.

"You did?" His eyes must have captured the sun and brought it indoors with him.

She had been about to say it wasn't just for Sawyer but the words stuck in the back of her mouth.

"Hope you don't mind sharing," Father said.

"Not at all." The men grinned at each other.

Somehow Carly managed to serve the meal without spilling anything even though her arms felt wobbly.

She cut the pie and gave each a piece, careful to make Father's and Sawyer's the same exact size. Her baking efforts were rewarded with sighs of appreciation from both men.

Sawyer returned to the field after the meal. As soon as she had cleaned the kitchen, she turned to Father. "I'm going to check on the cows." She spoke to Jill. "Do you want to come or stay with Skippy?"

The girl barely looked up from playing with the kitten. "I'll stay here."

A few minutes later, she rode Sunny from the yard,

her journey taking her past Sawyer. She slowed to study how the planting was going. And if she did not look at the field, but rather at Sawyer, admiring the way his muscles rippled with the effort of holding Big Harry, well, who was to know? She wasn't about to tell anyone.

Sawyer noticed her at the trail and pulled Big Harry to a halt. "Howdy," he called.

"Planting is going good."

"Yup. I'll soon be done."

"I'm going to check on the cows. Jill is staying with Father."

They stared at each other across the planted field. His hat shielded his eyes so she wouldn't have been able to see them even if they were close enough. As she watched, his expression never changed unless she counted the deepening of the grooves beside his mouth.

He touched the brim of his hat. "Be careful."

She lifted her hand in a tiny salute. "Never." She didn't mean it. She didn't take chances, just didn't hearken to silly rules of society—no trousers for a woman, women couldn't be cowboys, she should pretty up if she wanted a man. See, she'd gotten married without following those rules.

He tipped his head. "I know. That's what concerns me."

"I don't do dangerous things."

"I know."

A silent understanding formed between them. As if he accepted the way she dressed and acted. And as if she promised not to do foolish things. "Okay," she said, agreeing to the unspoken pact.

Her heart floated as she rode onward.

Not so long ago, she would have ridden the land alone

and thought nothing of it but now she remembered Sawyer and Jill accompanying her and saw dozens of things she would have liked to share with them…the billowing white clouds, the hawk diving for its prey, the antelope racing away and the profusion of wildflowers. She would pick some on her way home and put them on Mother's grave.

She found the cattle had moved to the west, grazing contentedly in a large, open pasture. Twenty more calves had been born. Well-fleshed in comparison to the longhorn stock. Father had done well to start the new breeding program.

She watched for a bit, but was anxious to get home and turned back. She picked flowers before she reached the homestead. Again she passed Sawyer. He was at the far corner, his back to her so he didn't notice her return. She rode by without stopping.

Her first thought was to take the flowers to the cemetery but she reconsidered and as soon as Sunny was taken care of, went to the house. Jill and Father were outside, entertained by the kitten. "I have flowers for Mother's grave. Does anyone want to come with me?"

"Aye," Father said.

"Can I come, too?" Jill asked.

"Of course." The trio climbed the hill, taking their time as Father hobbled along.

She let him go in first and stood back, letting him pay his respects in private. She looked at the grave markers. Something to the left of Mother's grave caught her eye. Four wooden crosses standing side by side. From where she stood, she could make out the names. John Gallagher. Sarah Gallagher. Judith Gallagher. Cecil Gallagher. Had Sawyer done this?

There was no other explanation.

"Jill, look." She pointed.

Jill gasped. "Mama and Papa." She tiptoed to the markers and sank down to her knees before them.

Carly followed slowly. She hunkered down beside the girl. "Would you like some flowers?"

Jill nodded, her eyes bright.

Carly divided her bouquet in half.

Jill placed a few flowers before her parents' markers. "Maybe I should give some to Sawyer's mama and brother."

"That would be nice." What a sweet thought to include the two she didn't know.

Jill drew in a shaky breath.

Uncertain how the child would react, Carly followed her heart and pulled Jill close. When Jill turned to Carly, clinging to her, Carly hugged her, making soothing noises as Jill cried.

After a bit, the tears were spent but Jill remained in Carly's embrace. Carly was not the least bit anxious to end the moment. A bond had been forged from her heart to Jill's. Love had sealed the bond.

"I'm going back to the house," Father said.

"I better go, too," Jill said. "Skippy might be missing me."

"I'll be along shortly." She waited until they were down the hill before she went to Mother's grave. She placed the flowers near the headstone, then sat back.

What would her mother say if Carly could tell her about the confusion and uncertainty in her heart? How her feelings toward Sawyer were changing so that she wasn't sure how to handle them.

"It isn't what we agreed on. But I can't help but admire him for so many things. His steadfastness, his tenderness toward Jill, his acceptance of me, his respect for Father." She stopped talking. Bringing the words out in the open gave them too much power, made them too real.

You should never be embarrassed to tell someone how you feel.

Her mother had said those words when Carly spoke of her admiration for a teacher but confessed she didn't feel she could tell the woman.

Sometimes, she silently argued, it was more than embarrassment that kept her from saying what she felt. Sometimes it was that she had given her word and meant to fulfill her promise.

She spent some time praying for strength and wisdom before she returned to the house to make supper.

"Carly," Jill said at bedtime. "Can you read to me?"

It was the first time Jill had taken advantage of Carly's offer and Carly couldn't decide if she wanted to laugh or cry. She would have liked to share the moment with Sawyer but he had gone to take care of Big Harry. "I'd love to read to you."

Jill climbed into bed, Skippy in the crook of her arm. She moved to the far edge of the bed. "There's room for you beside me."

Her heart so full it felt like it might burst, Carly lay down beside the child and drew her close, pleased when Jill snuggled against her. "I'm going to read from the Bible storybook my mama read to me when I was your age."

Jill nodded. "Okay."

Opening the book to the first story, Carly read about

creation. Finished, she closed the book. "God made a beautiful world," she said. "And it's still beautiful."

"I know. Like the flowers and Skippy."

"Like you." Carly planted a kiss on Jill's forehead.

Jill looked up at her. "And Sawyer?"

Carly's cheeks grew hot but she hoped Jill wouldn't notice. "I don't think he'd like to be called beautiful."

"Well, he's handsome."

"I suppose he is. Now, do you want me to hear your prayers?"

Jill nodded and scampered from under the covers to kneel at her bedside.

Carly knelt beside her. This was so much like it had been with her mother that her throat tightened.

Jill said a child's prayer and then added her own thoughts. "Help us be able to stay here forever. Help Sawyer and Carly to be in love. Amen."

The words slammed into Carly and she remained on her knees as Jill climbed back into bed. How was she to tell the child that her prayer must be refused? "Jill, honey, people can live together and be happy without being in love."

Jill studied her with wide-eyed innocence. "Then you aren't really married."

She had a point. "That's between Sawyer and me."

"And God." Jill burrowed deeper under the covers, closed her eyes and gave a satisfied sigh as if she'd spoken the final word on the matter.

If only life could be that simple. "Good night." Carly placed another kiss on Jill's forehead and left the room.

Father lay back in his armchair, snoring softly.

Carly tiptoed out to find Sawyer, determined not to let the reasoning of a little girl affect her. She was halfway to the barn when she saw him standing at the fence that enclosed the seeded wheat field and went to join him.

"I finished the oats today," he said.

"You'll be glad to be done with farming, I expect." Most cowboys resisted any sort of farming, even though hay must be cut and feed had to be grown.

"I kind of enjoyed it. There's something satisfying about turning up the soil and then planting seed and knowing it will supply the winter's need."

Carly chuckled. "That sounds like something Father would say."

He turned to study her, a smile creasing his face. "I consider that a fine compliment."

"Now then, wouldn't Father be pleased to hear it."

They smiled at each other. She had no thought in her head, just the heartfelt enjoyment of the moment that hovered motionlessly between them.

He shifted his gaze to her right and then brought it back to her. "How did you find the cows?"

"They've moved west a mile or so. About twenty more calves."

He took her hand and pulled it through his arm and they walked along the path toward the river. "I am impressed with the look of those calves."

For a while, they discussed the cows and Father's breeding program. They reached the trees along the river and he took her hand to lead her down the path, keeping her fingers wrapped in his when they reached the edge of the water. He crossed his arms, still holding her hand, pressing it to his chest. "Tomorrow is Saturday. We should do something special now that the crop and garden are in the ground."

Her heart picked up speed. "Special? Us?" Who exactly did he mean and what did he have in mind?

"You and me and Jill if she wants to come. I'd include Father but he can't ride anymore. Poor man." He paused. She waited. "As I worked, I've been eyeing that hill past the barn. Been wondering what's beyond the top of it."

She could tell him but she'd far sooner show him. "We could ride out and see."

His fingers tightened around hers. "Kind of what I thought."

"Let's do it."

"Yes, let's."

The next morning, Carly wakened early, an eager smile on her lips. It didn't make sense to be so excited about a ride across familiar land and yet she was. She sprang from her bed and rushed to the kitchen to make breakfast.

Jill followed to let Skippy outside.

Sawyer came from his room, looking as pleased about the day as Carly felt.

"Jill," Sawyer said. "We're going for a ride today to see what's west of the hill behind the barn."

"Aye, I can tell you," Father began.

"Let them see for themselves," Carly said.

He nodded, a twinkle in his eyes. "'Twill be for them to discover."

"Can I take Skippy?"

"Ye can leave the kitten with me," Father said. "She'll like that better than being carried on the back of a horse."

Jill considered her options, looking from one adult to another and then whispering something in Skippy's

ear. She handed Skippy to Father and went to Sawyer's
side. "Okay. I'll go with you."

Because of all the baking she'd done over the last
week, there was plenty of food to take with them so
they could spend the day out if they wanted. She made
sandwiches using the roast meat she'd cooked the day
before and packed the food in saddlebags. They were
soon on their way.

Carly and Sawyer rode side by side. Jill sometimes
rode beside them but more often ventured ahead or fell
behind and seemed lost in her own thoughts, leaving
Carly and Sawyer to visit with each other.

Sawyer asked about who lived in every direction and
she told him about the distant neighbors. She told him
more about the Marshall family and how Annie and
her brothers had all married in the last few months. She
told him of adventures she and Annie had experienced.

He listened with a thoughtful look and she grew silent. Then asked, "Do you disapprove of how I've conducted myself?"

He chuckled. "Not at all. If you weren't a daring
young lady, you would have never agreed to my suggestion of marriage. No, I was thinking how nice it is
that you have friends you share the past with."

At the lonely note in his voice, she reached out to
touch his arm. "You can have that from now on."

Their gazes found each other and stayed there while
their horses moved restlessly.

Her heart flooded with a foreign feeling of longing
and warmth as they continued onward.

Knowing the way, she led them round the hillside to
another and another, always climbing. The vegetation
thickened. Ragged pine and spruce were more abun-

dant. They scrambled up another hill and before them lay a tiny, blue-green lake, not dissimilar to the color of Sawyer's eyes, Carly thought with a start and couldn't stop staring at the water.

Sawyer chuckled. "So this is your little secret? I like it."

Jill rode to his side. "Are we going to have a picnic here?"

He slanted a questioning look at Carly. "What do you think?"

She studied the position of the sun and pretended to be quite concerned. "It's early yet."

"But I'm hungry," Jill pleaded.

Carly laughed. "Me, too. So let's eat." They left their horses to graze and Sawyer spread a groundsheet for them to sit on.

Carly put the food out.

Sawyer tossed his hat to one side. "I'll ask the blessing."

Knowing she had more to be grateful for than the food, Carly offered her own silent thanks for the many things God had sent her way. And if she thought of Sawyer and Jill, she expected God wasn't surprised.

As they ate, a doe tiptoed from the trees with two spotted fawns at her side and went to the water to drink. She slipped away as quietly as she'd arrived.

They finished and Sawyer leaned back on one elbow. Carly wished they had cushions as they had when picnicking with the Marshalls. She might have been tempted to lean back, using the pillow as an excuse to be close to him.

Instead she sat with her arms wrapped about her drawn-up knees and watched Jill playing nearby.

She recalled her mother's admonition to not let embarrassment—and surely she also meant fear—stop her from acting but when she turned to rest her elbow close to Sawyer's, he had fallen asleep.

Poor man had worked hard for the past two weeks, putting in the crop. He deserved a rest. And she didn't mind the opportunity to watch him unobserved and edged back so she didn't have to turn to see him.

He looked younger with his worries and caution gone from his face. Lines fanned out from his eyes from squinting into the sun. He wasn't as big as the Marshall men and yet he gave off an aura of strength and determination even in his sleep.

She was still studying him, memorizing every detail of his features, when he snored and jerked to a sitting position looking startled and defensive.

Seeing her beside him, he relaxed and stretched. "I think I fell asleep."

She grinned. "You surely did."

He studied her teasing smile. "Did I snore?"

"Loud enough to wake yourself up."

"Sorry. I didn't mean to."

"Fall asleep or snore?"

"Both, and you're teasing me." He grabbed her and pulled her down.

She lay in his arms looking into his eyes as they darkened to piney green. His breath fanned her cheeks. She lifted a hand and touched his strong promising lips.

He captured her hand and pressed it to his chest. "Carly." His voice sound deep and distant or was it that her ears heard differently?

Time waited as they studied each other, the moment heavy with indecision. She wanted him to kiss her. Didn't want him to kiss her.

His gaze lingered on her mouth. Was he as undecided as she? Was he willing to break their agreement?

"Carly, Sawyer, look what I found." Jill's voice called Carly back to reality and she sat up, edging over a foot and a half so he wouldn't think she wanted more.

He pushed to his feet. "Let's see what you have." He took a step away, stopped and returned to hold out a hand to Carly.

She knew she should refuse. She didn't need help to get to her feet, but it wasn't help she wanted and she took his hand, didn't pull away when he retained it as they went to see the rock Jill had found.

"I'm sure it's gold," she said, pointing to the golden-colored fragments. "Carly, maybe there is gold on your land."

"It's likely fool's gold. See how sharp the edges are and it shines when the sun hits it. That proves it."

"Oh." She quickly swallowed her disappointment. "I 'spect there's gold around here. I just have to find it." Jill pocked the rock and went in search of gold.

Carly shuddered. "I wouldn't want gold found here. Miners would destroy the land."

"This is good cattle country. Let's hope it stays that way."

They watched Jill examining rock after rock. Tossing away one after another with a grunt of disappointment.

Sawyer laughed. "It doesn't look like gold is here for the picking."

Sawyer watched his sister and thought what he said was true on so many levels. Most things weren't as easy as stooping down and plucking them from the ground. Or even as easy as reaching out and pulling Carly into his arms. Though it had felt so right when he'd held her. He'd ached to kiss her. He had the right as her husband. But their marriage was not real. Their agreement was. And he was a man of his word, though he had to remind himself of such with increasing frequency.

Even so, he wasn't eager to return to the ranch and Carly seemed happy enough to walk around the lake and look for birds' nests and watch the geese and ducks on the water. Jill followed them, still looking for gold.

A few hours later, they returned to the horses. There seemed no reason not to go back to the ranch so they mounted up and rode home.

If only he could change their agreement. But did he really want that? Was he willing to take the risk of opening up his heart? To do so held the allure of love and acceptance but also the possibility of disappointment. Hadn't he long ago decided to guard his heart against that risk?

Chapter Thirteen

Sunday morning was sunny and bright, a reflection of Carly's thoughts. She'd enjoyed the Saturday outing far more than she had a right to. But she could no more stop the joy and hope that rushed through her heart than she could stop the rising of the sun.

She sat beside Sawyer on the wagon seat as they drove to church. She noticed a long table set up in the yard behind the church. Was some special event planned? She searched her thoughts for a forgotten announcement but could find nothing. Though it wouldn't surprise her if it had slipped her mind. It seemed she was easily distracted of late. How many times had she found herself staring out the window—generally in the direction that would allow her to see Sawyer—the task she'd set out to do completely forgotten?

She let out a little sigh. Whatever the occasion, she'd find out soon enough. She waited for Sawyer to help her down from the wagon, ignoring the knowledge that not many days past, she would have jumped down on her own and scoffed at needing assistance.

She glanced up at him, tucking away a little joy at

the way he smiled at her before he placed her hand in the crook of his arm. They followed Father and Jill inside and settled into a pew.

The service began and they shared the hymnal. Carly's heart thrilled to join her voice to his as they sang the familiar songs. Hugh preached a sermon that seemed to hold Sawyer's attention. Carly struggled to concentrate. When had she ever had so much trouble listening to Hugh? Never, she admitted. From his arrival a year ago, his deep voice had pulled her into his sermons.

Hugh closed the service. Then he said something that had Carly's complete attention.

"Folks, we haven't properly welcomed Carly and Sawyer as newlyweds, so several of the ladies have organized a potluck. There's plenty of food for those who weren't aware of the plans. Please join us in celebrating the union of these two fine people."

Sawyer stared straight ahead, as surprised by this turn of events as was Carly. Slowly he brought his gaze to her, his look inscrutable. She leaned close to whisper, "I didn't know anything about this."

His eyes smiled as he whispered back, "I'm not about to turn down a church potluck."

They laughed a little and then allowed themselves to be escorted to the yard where the table was now filled with a variety of dishes.

Hugh called everyone to attention. "I'll ask the blessing but before that, there is someone we've neglected to introduce. Jill is Sawyer's sister. Jill, welcome to our community."

Jill ducked her head but not before Carly saw both surprise and pleasure in her face.

As the honored guests, Carly, Sawyer and Jill filled their plates first from the bounty…potato salads, baked beans, hot pots and fried chicken. Carly knew that Annie, Sadie and the town ladies had kept the food hot in their ovens.

Makeshift benches had been set up for those who wanted to sit on them. Jill sat on the ground, surrounded by the Marshall children and a host of other youngsters.

"She fits in well," Annie said, sitting beside Carly.

Dawson sat beside Sawyer. "Guess we managed to surprise the pair of you."

Sawyer chuckled. "You did that, all right."

Others came to them to wish them well and welcome them, then Annie and Sadie brought a big cake from the parsonage and placed it at the end of the table.

"Time for you two to cut the cake," Annie announced.

Carly and Sawyer stood in front of the cake. Annie handed Carly a knife. "Put your hand over hers," she told Sawyer and he did so.

Together they cut the first piece of cake, his hand firm on hers. Tears clogged the back of Carly's throat. This simple act made her feel more married than signing the papers in Hugh's office had. This was public. Their hands were joined. And her heart had undergone a change.

"Give each other a bite of cake," someone called. Annie put a piece of the white cake on a small plate and handed them each a fork.

Carly filled her lungs. She could do this. She could go through the motions.

They both held the plate. She cut off a bit as he did the same. His steady hand gave her strength. She lifted the fork to his mouth. He lifted his fork to her mouth. They met each other's eyes…his reflecting the sky. She opened her mouth and took the cake as did he. She could not swallow. Could not think. All that mattered was the promising look in his eyes. Promising what? She couldn't say. Didn't want to analyze the thought. The moment had taken her away to hope of a shared future. Sharing more than a name.

Clapping and cheering jerked her back to reality.

"Kiss, kiss." People tinkled their silverware against their plates.

Annie took the plate and the two forks from Carly and Sawyer.

"Kiss. Kiss." The chanting and tinkling increased in volume.

Sawyer raised his eyebrows, silently asking her opinion.

She shrugged. She had no objection to a little kiss, though she would have preferred it to be in private and have it given without urging from an outside force.

He caught her shoulders and leaned close. His breath, sweet with sugar, fanned her face and then he caught her lips in a gentle kiss. He tasted of icing. She leaned into him, wanting more. So much more.

It was only for show, she firmly told herself. No reason why it should send a bolt of longing clear through to her toes.

He lifted his head and grinned, his eyes flashing such a rich blue-green she knew she'd never before seen that particular color.

The crowd seemed satisfied. Carly was not. But she would never admit it.

Annie cut the cake and invited everyone to come and

get a piece. There was tea and coffee. Sadie led Sawyer and Carly to two chairs that someone had set near the table. Carly finally began to relax. All she had to do was enjoy the cake and coffee.

But then Sammy and Jeannie, Sadie and Logan's two youngest children, appeared pulling a wagon full of gifts toward them.

Tears stung Carly's eyes. How could she open presents when her marriage was such a fake?

Sawyer squeezed her hand.

She stiffened her resolve. Her marriage was real enough. They had papers to prove it. And a kiss to seal the deal.

She opened the first gift from Annie and her sisters-in-law. A quilt with the wedding ring pattern. "It's lovely. But how did you have time?"

Annie chuckled. "We enjoyed spending a few afternoons together."

There were gifts of fancy dishes, embroidered tea towels and a recipe book from Mary Marshall whose husband, George, ran the general store.

The gifts all open, Carly and Sawyer rose to express their thanks. It was all Carly could do to get the words past the lump in her throat. She felt so dishonest, letting these people believe she and Sawyer loved each other and had a real marriage.

People began to collect their dishes and their children to depart.

Dawson, Logan and Conner helped Sawyer put the gifts in the back of their wagon. Jill excitedly offered her assistance, exclaiming over and over, "It's better'n Christmas 'cause it's a surprise."

Sawyer joined Carly as she went round the circle of

Marshalls and extended her thanks. Then they were on their way home.

Up until now, Father had said little. Now he leaned over the back of the seat. "'Tis time you two took this marriage business seriously." He waited.

"Yes, Father," she said meekly, even though she knew there would be no changes.

"Sawyer?"

"Yes, Father." His tone conveyed the same resignation Carly felt.

She kept her gaze straight ahead, unwilling to take the risk of looking at Sawyer. If he seemed determined that things should continue as they were, she would know sharp, searing disappointment. If he revealed regret, suggesting he would like to change their agreement, she wasn't sure what she'd do. Things were so confused.

At home, they unloaded the gifts.

"Where do you want me to put everything?" Sawyer asked.

"Should I even use them?" They were alone and she could finally confess her uncertainty.

He stood with the quilt in his arms. His eyebrows drew together, the only indication that he didn't like her question. "What are you saying?"

"I hate fooling everyone."

"We're married." His eyes grew icy. "Unless you've a mind to change that."

She didn't address his latter statement but rather continued her train of thought. "Not in the usual sense."

They studied each other, wary and uncertain.

"That's our business and not anyone else's."

"I suppose that's true." But it felt wrong. "I didn't mean to anger you."

"You didn't." He took the quilt to her room and laid it on the bed, still folded neatly.

He said he wasn't angry but something sweet and promising between them was gone. She felt it keenly the next day and the next. If only there was something she could do to bring back that feeling. But she could think of nothing.

Sawyer knew better than to let his feelings have their way. Over and over, he'd warned himself not to count on things becoming what he wanted. But at the little party in the churchyard, he'd forgotten all his hard-learned lessons. Forgotten to guard his heart. When he'd kissed her, with her full consent, his heart had burst open.

He'd thought she felt the same.

She didn't and had firmly reminded him that theirs was not a real marriage.

He wished he could be behind Big Harry, putting seed in the ground. There had been something calming about that work but the planting was done, so he passed his time by repairing the fence around the cropland. Though if he had any sense at all, he would spend his days far from the house.

For some reason that he refused to admit, he didn't want to be away.

He looked up from his task as a rider approached and made his way to the house.

Carly stepped outside. He realized she had been sticking close to home, too. Though likely not for the same reasons.

He went to her side.

"It's one of the Marshall cowboys," she said. "I wonder what he wants."

The man rode closer. He touched the brim of his hat in greeting as Father Morrison came from the barn to see who had ridden up.

The rider turned that direction and handed Father a bundle of harnesses. They spoke for several minutes.

"Let's go see what's going on." Carly headed for the barn.

"Thank you," Father said and the man rode away. Father held up the harnesses. "When Annie's father, Bud, heard I was fixing old harnesses, he said there was a pile at his place that he'd like fixed." He began to turn away, then stopped. "Aye, he brought a message, too. I bought three more Hereford bulls. They're ready. You two will bring them home."

"Bring them from where?" Carly demanded, her voice thin with suspicion.

Sawyer had his own qualms about what her father was up to.

"Why, at the Bar None Ranch. Where else would they be?"

"Father, that's two days' ride away."

"Only one if you're in a hurry. But I don't want those bulls pushed hard. Take your time bringing them home. You can leave tomorrow morning."

"Sir, what about Jill?" Sawyer asked.

"Dinnae I tell you? Logan has agreed young Beth can come over. She's fourteen and capable of taking care of us."

Carly sputtered her protest.

Sawyer wasn't happy about the arrangement either. "It will be just the two of us?"

Father came round to face them. "I expect the pair of you can handle three animals."

Neither Carly nor Sawyer spoke, though she practically vibrated with her upset.

Father nodded. "Then that's how it's to be. Might be good for the two of you to work together." He limped back into the barn, his attention already on the harnesses he held.

Sawyer understood then that the old man knew exactly what he was doing and what he hoped to gain and it wasn't solely the safe delivery of three bulls. What he didn't know was both Sawyer and Carly had given their word that their marriage would be a business arrangement only.

How was Sawyer to remember that if they were to be alone day and night for probably three days?

He prepared provisions and a bedroll that night. Carly did the same, muttering under her breath comments directed at her father.

They left early the next morning as soon as Logan brought Beth over.

They rode in a silence broken only by the thud of horses' hooves and the call of the birds. They kept up a steady, mile-eating pace, heading to the northwest over rolling hills, keeping to the eastern slopes.

Sawyer had things he wished he could say. Such as, *could we change the agreement we made regarding our marriage?* But pride and fear stopped him. They'd been gone about two hours when the humor of the situation hit him and he started to laugh.

Dusty perked up his ears at the sound.

Carly gave him a confused look. When he didn't stop, she rode closer. "What's so funny?"

He stopped laughing but kept smiling. "You're father fancies himself a matchmaker. I'm surprised he didn't send someone along to keep an eye on us."

She harrumphed. "I suppose he thought if we were alone, we'd do what he considers the right thing."

"Maybe we should tell him about our agreement." He had no doubt how Father Morrison would react to the information. The man's voice echoed through his head. *Ack. Now wasn't that a foolish thing to agree to? So why don't we all just forget about it? You and Carly are married. Time ye acted like it.*

Carly shook her head. "He'd say we aren't married at all and then what would happen to the ranch?" She let that soak in. "And a home for Jill? She's really settling in, don't you think?"

"Aye, and I believe you've learned a few tricks from your father to bring Jill into the discussion."

Carly grinned. "Aye, and maybe I have. But seriously, I don't see we have any choice but to honor our agreement."

He slouched in his saddle. Why had he even allowed the thought to take root that she might be willing to reconsider that agreement? Obviously she wasn't.

They rode on, silence again their companion.

As the sun reached its zenith, he began to look about, hoping to see a place where he could suggest they rest the horses for a bit.

"There's a place over there where we can stop." It was as if she read his mind. And the idea did nothing to make him forget how much he wanted to change their agreement.

They turned aside to a grove of trees along a little stream and let the horses rest, eat and drink. She pulled biscuits and cookies from her saddlebag and shared them with him. They sank to the cool grass to eat.

"Do you like this country?" she asked.

"It's good cow country."

"You said that before."

"Yup." Why did he get the feeling she wanted something more than his opinion about the land?

"So you can see yourself happily settled here?" She paid a whole lot more attention to the biscuit she held than it required.

He sat up. So that was her concern. "I want a home for Jill. She's happy here. But more than that, I said I would stay. And I keep my word." Even when it was hard.

Carly nodded. "Just checking to see if anything has changed." She lifted her head then and her brown eyes were dark and unreadable. Yet he sensed more questions.

"Has anything changed for you?" Sawyer asked.

"I'm committed to our agreement." Her look went on and on, searching, probing.

It was not the answer he'd hoped for. Yet it was the one he expected. He finished his lunch, went for the horses and they resumed their journey.

They rode hard all afternoon. As the shadows lengthened, he asked, "How much farther?"

She pulled up and seemed to consider the question. Finally she spoke. "If we rode hard until dark, we could get there but I'm not sure what we'd find."

He had no idea what she meant. "Your father wouldn't send you into a dangerous situation."

She sighed. "We're supposed to be man and wife. Will they want us to sleep in their guest room?"

He grinned. Quite the quandary for her to consider.

"I think we'll put up until morning, then pick up the animals and return home."

Sawyer could not deny that the prospect pleased him very much. A night out under the stars with her. He could foresee all sorts of pleasant moments.

"There's a good camping spot not too far ahead." They rode on until she guided them to a quiet stream. Within minutes, he had a fire going. He'd brought cans of food and opened them and set them to heat. Meanwhile, Carly took care of the horses and tossed the bedrolls to the ground.

He eyed their placement. Hers to the left of the fire, his to the right. Anyone coming along would think they weren't man and wife.

Well, they were. And they weren't. And they had one, possibly two, more nights on the trail. He allowed himself to think things might change in his favor.

It was almost dark by the time they finished eating but neither of them made a move toward crawling into their bedrolls.

"The stars will soon be out," Carly said.

He shifted his thoughts back to the night sky. "Do you know the constellations?"

"Just the Big and Little Dipper."

He jumped to his feet. "Come on over here away from the fire and I will introduce them to you." He lay on the grassy slope.

Without hesitation, she lay beside him, which set his hope soaring. Maybe this would be the time and place to talk about changing their agreement.

"It's a perfect night for stargazing." And the perfect companion but he kept that observation to himself.

"There's The Maiden. She's carrying a grain of wheat and a staff." He pointed and edged closer to guide her until she made out the stars forming the constellation. "There's Leo the Lion."

"I see it. It makes sense."

He pointed out several more.

She propped up on one elbow to look at him. "How do you know all this?"

"My pa taught me. Wherever we went, he would go outside and find the stars. He said, 'The stars don't change. Just like God.' He'd take a big sigh. 'I guess it's me that's changed.'"

"What did he mean by that?"

Sawyer could not make out her expression, so hung on to the gentle tone of her voice. "He changed when Ma and Johnny died. Seemed like a stranger to me." He lay back and looked at the sky. "Except when he took me to look at the stars. Then I felt like he was my father and he cared about me."

"Thank you for showing them to me." She lay down against his side. "It's nice you have this good memory of him."

"And now I have another good memory of looking at the stars." He took her hand.

She stiffened. But she didn't shift away. "Me, too." Her voice was as soft as the evening breeze.

Neither of them moved. He wished he knew what she thought.

"I could look at the stars all night," she said. And even though he'd just talked himself into settling for their pretend marriage, he hoped she meant she enjoyed more than the stars. That she enjoyed his company, too.

"We have lots of riding to do tomorrow, so I'm going to bed down." She rose and went to her bedroll.

"Yeah, me, too." He crawled into his bedroll and lay staring at the stars as his mind struggled with wishes.

He wished he had the courage to speak of his growing feelings toward her but he couldn't take the risk that she would say he hadn't lived up to their agreement, so it was null and void.

Better to accept things the way they were.

Better to harbor a secret fondness than to end up with nothing.

Jill had a home now. That made any risk even more unappealing.

He only wished it was enough for him.

Chapter Fourteen

Carly stared at the night sky. She'd enjoyed seeing the constellations and having them explained to her. Never again would she view the stars the same way…but not because she now knew the names and locations of several groups of stars. No, what she'd remember would be the eager note in Sawyer's voice, the way his arm brushed hers as he pointed upward, the longing that threatened to choke her as they lay side by side, touching but with an invisible wall between them.

She tried unsuccessfully to push away the thoughts, to dismiss the yearnings. They had a long two days ahead of them. She must sleep. But her thoughts went round and round, churning up more and more frustration.

Across the embers of the fire, she watched Sawyer's bulk to see if he was as restless as she, but the blankets didn't move, and she shifted to her side, her back to him. If only he felt as she did, if only they could mutually decide to change their agreement.

Fatigue overtook her and she slept, wakening to the smell of wood smoke and coffee.

"Good morning," Sawyer said as she sat up. "Did you sleep well?"

"Reasonably." She yawned and then sprang from the covers. "You?"

"Fine, thanks. Coffee's about ready." He poured two cups as she rolled up her bedding.

She hunkered down by the fire. "We could make breakfast here or, if we hurry, we could eat at the Bar None." A hot breakfast served at a table appealed.

He drained his coffee cup. "Let's do it." Seems he shared her opinion.

The fire was quenched, the horses saddled and the pair on the trail in minutes. Their destination lay over the next hill.

Sawyer laughed when he saw how close it was. "They must have seen the smoke from our campfire."

"I saw someone ride out to check on us last evening." The cowboy had recognized her and turned back to the ranch. She led the way to the main house.

Mike Day, owner, stepped from the house. "Howdy, I've been expecting you. Come right in." He turned and called over his shoulder. "Ma, put two more places on the table."

Carly climbed the steps, Sawyer at her heels, and introduced the two men.

"Your husband, you say?" Mike, short and stocky, built like a barrel, studied Sawyer from head to toe.

Carly waited, secretly smiling. Mike might be short but he exuded power and authority.

To his credit, Sawyer met the man look for look, seemingly unimpressed by the examination.

Mike grinned and gripped Sawyer's arm. "About

time someone took this young lady in hand and you look like you're capable of the task."

"Thank you, sir." Sawyer grinned and leaned closer to Mike as if to share a secret. "I'm afraid it will take two or more of me to rein her in."

Mike slapped Sawyer on the back and the pair laughed together like coconspirators.

Carly jammed her fists to her hips. "I'm not sure I like that."

Mike chuckled some more. "Come on in for breakfast."

Sawyer took Carly's hand, draped it around his elbow and escorted her through the door, his steps light as if he looked forward to this visit.

In the kitchen, Mike introduced his wife, Ethel. She was as tall and thin as he was short and stocky and she hugged them both, wiping her eyes at the news Carly was married.

"Tell us all about it," Ethel said in her booming voice.

"Let them eat first." Mike waved them to the table and Ethel served up fried pork, fried potatoes and a heap of eggs.

"Thanks. This sure beats dry biscuits," Carly said.

Ethel waved away her comment. "I want all the details. How did you two meet? When did you marry? No one mentioned it to us." She shot Mike a look. "Don't tell me you knew and didn't say."

The man held up his hands in a protective gesture. "No, darling, I didn't know."

Ethel smiled her affection before she turned back to Carly.

"We've been married…" Carly pretended to count on her fingers and muse about the answer.

"Seventeen days as of midmorning today," Sawyer said, his eyes steady and challenging.

"Ah, so still on your honeymoon." Mike reached across the table for his wife's hand and they beamed at each other. "That would be why your father sent the pair of you to get the bulls. So you could enjoy some time alone."

Ethel's cheeks reddened at the look in Mike's eyes and Mike chuckled. For a moment, Carly wondered if they remembered there were two others at the table and then Ethel pulled her hand to her lap, cleared her throat and asked, "And how did you meet?"

Carly looked at Sawyer, hoping he would answer.

He gave a grin that made her heart jerk, then turned his attention to their hosts. "I saw her in the restaurant. I could immediately tell she was a determined young woman and a beautiful one as well."

Carly's cheeks burned like she stood too close to an open flame.

"I overheard her tell her friend she needed someone to help on the ranch."

Carly coughed at the way he made it sound so reasonable.

He continued. "I have an orphaned little sister and I saw that we could all benefit from throwing in together." He shrugged but when he turned toward Carly, she saw a depth of emotion, an openness that she'd never seen before. And something more. She couldn't believe it was invitation.

Invitation to what?

All she could think was he wanted her to remember their reasons for marrying. It wasn't as if she could ever forget. Their agreement dogged her every thought.

Ethel sighed. "It sounds so romantic. I so enjoy a good love story." She sighed again.

Mike chuckled. "She reads those dime-store romances every chance she gets." His adoring look said he didn't mind. He leaned closer to Sawyer. "I think it makes her more affectionate so I buy them for her."

Ethel again blossomed pink and Mike grinned.

Carly envied them their marital happiness. Seventeen days ago, she had thought she didn't care for any of that—the affection, the touches, the mutual concern—but now she longed for it. Longed for the impossible.

"Father sends his greetings." Her comment turned the conversation to other things until she knew they must leave. "Thanks for breakfast. I've enjoyed the visit but we need to be on our way."

Sawyer stood. "It's been nice to meet you."

Ethel grabbed his hand. "Please come again. I've enjoyed this so much." She sighed. "So romantic."

Carly resisted an impulse to roll her eyes. Romantic it had not been. Practical and perhaps, in hindsight, a little foolish. She meant their agreement, not their marriage.

Mike accompanied them out to the barn. "These are the bulls your father bought."

Carly studied the three animals. "They're magnificent."

Sawyer pressed to her side. "They'll throw more of those fleshy calves showing up in the herd."

"I'm right proud of the critters," Mike said. "They're gentle and will drive easy."

"Gentle? How will they compete in the herd? I sure would hate to see them all busted up."

"Don't you worry, darling. They outweigh the longhorns and will soon establish themselves."

"That's reassuring."

Carly and Sawyer mounted up and Mike opened the gate. The massive animals plodded along as directed.

"Mike was right about them being cooperative," she commented as they hit the trail.

"I like Mike and Ethel," Sawyer said. "Their love for each other is so open and honest."

Carly didn't respond immediately. Dare she be honest and admit she had changed her mind about their marriage agreement? That she wanted…?

She didn't know what she wanted. Nor did she have the courage to express her thoughts. "Should I have told Ethel that it wasn't romantic?" Let him say something if he had any of the same feelings as Carly did.

"Why ruin it for her?"

Disappointment sank into her bones. "That's what I thought." She reined aside as if to herd the bulls more closely. Not that they needed it.

She kept her distance from Sawyer throughout the morning. If he noticed, he gave no indication.

The bulls had begun to lag when she pointed toward the nearby creek and they turned aside to let them rest awhile.

She and Sawyer dismounted. Ethel had given them a sack full of sandwiches and cookies and they sat beside the cheerful stream to eat their lunch.

Sawyer didn't immediately begin to eat but studied her. "Have I done something to make you angry?"

"What makes you think I'm angry?"

His eyebrows headed for his hairline. "I don't know. Maybe the way you stayed off to the side all morning."

"Not all morning." Just most of it.

"And the scowl that darkened your face."

"I was squinting against the sun."

"Did I?"

"I didn't look but I suppose you squinted, too."

"That's not what I meant and I think you know it."

She did know but intended to pretend otherwise and might have if his gaze hadn't been so demanding. "I'm not angry. At least not at you." Any anger she felt was directed at her. Why was she always wanting impossible things? Always? This one time hardly constituted *always* and yet the word had a ring of truth to them.

"I see. Tell me, what did you do to deserve a morning of anger?" His words were soft, inviting. Almost making her forget she couldn't tell him.

"Nothing that would make sense to anyone but me."

He leaned closer. "Try me."

"Why can't you let this go?" If he continued, she would blurt out the truth and ruin everything. If she suggested changing their agreement, would he see it as reason to abandon his end of it? It wasn't a chance she was prepared to take.

"Because I miss your company. I might as well be here by myself for all I've seen of you this morning."

"I was never out of sight."

"You know that isn't what I mean."

She looked to her left. Looked into the distance. Looked at the sandwich in her hand.

His gaze stuck to her like a burr.

She gave a long sigh. "Let's eat." But when she would have lifted her sandwich to her mouth, his hand stopped her. His touch threatened every bit of control she had on her thoughts.

"Not until you tell me."

"I can't even remember what your question was."

Partly true, as she didn't know if he wanted to know why she was angry or why she'd been avoiding him.

He held her hands loosely. She could have pulled away without effort but she didn't even try, even knowing it would make it easier to keep her longings under control.

"Why have you avoided me all morning?" Did she imagine a hint of hurt in his tone?

"Very well. If you must know. I find it difficult to continually deceive my friends."

"About what?"

She faced him full on. "About our marriage. It isn't romantic. It isn't even real." She had said too much and waited, unable to breathe, for him to respond.

He removed his hand from hers and stared across the creek. "If I remember correctly, it's what you wanted." He fell silent but she refused to be the one to speak first. After a bit, he rumbled his lips. "Have you changed your mind?"

Yes. But she couldn't confess it. Better what they had now then nothing, she reminded herself. "Of course not."

"Then I don't see a problem. Let others think what they will. You aren't responsible for that." He bit into his sandwich.

"I suppose not." She bit her own sandwich, surprised at how dry and tasteless it was. Ethel was a fine cook. She looked at the bread and meat and saw no reason for her disappointment. She admitted it wasn't the food but the situation that was at fault.

They allowed the animals to rest a bit. It would have been a perfect opportunity to share secrets and hopes. Ethel would have considered it a romantic interlude. But it wasn't that for Sawyer and Carly. Sawyer lay back, covered his face with his hat and, for all she knew, had a nap while she stared at the water rippling past. The sound normally would have calmed her but this time it utterly failed to do so.

In fact, she couldn't sit there any longer with Sawyer nearby, oblivious to her state of mind and she bolted to her feet.

"What's wrong?" Sawyer asked from beneath his hat.

"I'll be right back." Let him think she needed a moment of privacy. She ducked behind some bushes and stopped, pressing her fingers to her forehead.

How was she to live up to her end of their agreement?

That afternoon, Sawyer rode a little to the left and slightly behind Carly. She didn't put as much distance between them as she had in the morning and yet it seemed there was a mile-wide canyon separating them. What had happened to make her so aloof? He reviewed the events of last night and this morning before they left the Bar None and could think of nothing.

His worst fear was that she had changed her mind about their marriage. He was not so naive that he didn't know she could easily have it annulled. When he'd asked if she'd changed her mind, his brain had hammered from lack of oxygen as he waited for her to answer.

His relief when she said she hadn't was intermingled with longing for what he witnessed between Mike and Ethel. Loving. Caring. Understanding.

He mused on the idea as they rode along. The bulls moved so easily that all that was required of Sawyer and Carly was to guide them in the right direction. It left plenty of time for thinking.

Loving, caring, understanding. The words rolled over and over in his mind until he came to a firm conclusion. He could give those under their agreement.

Sweetness filled his being as he realized it was the first time since Mama and Johnny died that he was willing to let such feelings live in his heart.

He settled back in his saddle. *I think Mama would approve.* In fact, he could almost feel her breath as she leaned over him to kiss him on the forehead. It was a sweet memory from many years ago. One that warmed him clear through.

No time like the present to offer those things.

He rode close to Carly. "How long have you known Mike and Ethel?"

She startled as if her thoughts had been a thousand miles away and he wondered if she had felt that wide canyon between them as well. "Father met Mike years ago before he married Ethel. They're both cattlemen, so it's not surprising they ran into each other. One winter, Mike went east. Told us he was going to find a wife." She stared off into the distance. "I suppose we all thought he'd advertise and come back with a sort of mail-order bride. He's never said how he met Ethel, although a few people have enquired. But it's obvious to anyone with eyes that theirs is a love match." She grinned at him. "They can hardly keep their eyes off each other."

"It's so romantic." He pressed his hand to his chest and sighed, earning him a laugh from Carly. He felt his lungs swell to capacity at the way she grinned at him.

To his right, a flash of yellow color caught his eyes.

"I'll be right back." He rode toward the spot and dismounted. Strange-looking flowers with yellow petals hanging downward and brown centers pointing toward the sun. With his knife, he cut half a dozen of the flowers and rode back to Carly. "Flowers for you."

She stared at him, her eyes wide, then looked at the flowers in her hands. "Thank you." The words seemed strained.

He knew it was because he had surprised her.

"Why?" she asked.

He considered his answer carefully before he spoke. "You said you hated deceiving your friends, so I thought I would do something romantic so it isn't a deception when people make comments like Ethel did." Pleased with himself for the reasonable answer, he grinned. His pleasure went to the core of his heart when she ducked her head. He knew his little gesture had pleased her. He began to plan other surprises.

They pushed on slowly. He opened his canteen and offered her a drink before he quenched his own thirst. She reached into her saddlebags and brought out a sack of cookies and passed half to him.

The bulls began to weary. "We need to stop soon." They'd spend the night. Like Ethel had said, it was romantic to be alone under the stars. But how best to make the most of it?

"Let's stop over there." She pointed toward a nearby creek where trees would provide shelter. They turned aside. The animals drank eagerly while he and Carly made a temporary rope corral.

"I think they'll be happy enough to rest that they won't wander away," she said. "All the same, we need to take turns watching them."

He had to agree. His own plans would have to take second place to the necessity of making sure the bulls got home safely.

They ate a simple supper of beans and biscuits with more of Ethel's baking for dessert. The sun dipped toward the mountains in the west. Carly yawned.

They were both weary. "I'll take the first watch. You get some rest." He moved closer to where the bulls were corralled and sat down, his back to a tree.

"Wake me in a few hours." She removed her boots and crawled into her bedroll. Within minutes, she breathed deeply.

He would have no trouble staying awake as his thoughts churned in endless circles. Despite his decision to show Carly he cared, a portion of him wondered at the wisdom of that decision. Fear and uncertainty tangled within him. He recalled the moment he had learned not to let himself care. He groaned. Didn't realize how loud the sound was in the dark until Carly threw back the covers. "What's wrong?"

"Just thinking."

She pulled on her boots and joined him by the corral. The tree was small so her shoulder pressed against his as she sat beside him. "What kind of thinking makes a man groan as if he'd been punched?"

The moon shining on the water of the creek provided a silvery, wobbly light. A mesmerizing light that unlocked a door within him. "It was a sad memory."

She squeezed his hand, her arm resting across his. "Would you tell me about it?"

"It was shortly after Mama and Johnny died. Can't say for sure how long. Time didn't mean anything then. Pa couldn't seem to settle down. We'd go from place to

place to place. He'd start a job and then leave. Always
on the move. I guess it was his way of fleeing the pain
of what happened." He closed his eyes as the memory
gained speed. "Then a couple of years down the road,
he found a job on a ranch in the Dakotas. We had a little cabin to ourselves and ate in the cookhouse with the
other men. The boss man was really nice to us and his
wife kind of took me under her wing."

He told of getting special treats, being invited into
the house to test fresh cookies. Sitting next to the boss
lady on the sofa as she read to him and taught him
school lessons. "She was a schoolteacher before she
married the boss man."

They had stayed throughout the summer. "The cabin
was warm and comfortable. I spent time every day at
the main house. The missus took care of me in many
ways. I think she saw how hurt and lonely I was and
went out of her way to help me. She doled out hugs
freely." He paused as his throat tightened. "It was the
longest we stayed in one place and I let myself think
Pa had decided to settle down."

It took a moment before he could go on and Carly
waited, letting him take all the time he needed, draw-
ing strength from her touch.

"Then one morning he said we were moving on.
I'll never forget the day. There was a cold wind carrying pellets of snow. They stung my skin. I turned
my face into the wind, welcoming the discomfort. 'I'm
not going,' I said. 'I'll stay here.' I ran up to the house
and barged in. The missus looked up as I ran into the
kitchen. 'Pa's leaving and I don't want to go,' I blurted
out. 'Can I stay with you?' She gave a sad look. 'I wish

you could but you must go with your father.' When she tried to hug me goodbye, I pushed her away."

He relived that moment. The bitter disappointment. "That's when I promised myself I would never let myself care about anyone." He'd kept that vow until now. Maybe he should continue to keep it.

But it was too late for that decision. He'd already begun to care.

Did he want to retract his earlier decision to show his feelings toward her? Could he if he tried?

Chapter Fifteen

Carly withdrew her hand from Sawyer's. She eased around the tree trunk until cool air drifted between them. She'd almost convinced herself that he had changed. That he might be willing to reconsider their arrangement and allow it to be more than a business deal.

"I promise I will never turn Jill away," she said. It seemed to be the most she could offer to a man who admitted he would never care.

"It will keep her from feeling the same way I did."

"What about you?" She hoped her tone conveyed only mild interest when she ached beyond hope for so much more for him and from him.

"I have a partnership in the Morrison Ranch. That means I have a reason to belong."

"A partnership?"

"Yes, your father said I was a partner. I assumed you knew."

"Of course he did." It was news to her. News that made it so very clear that she would never be seen as good as a son. Even a son-in-law Father barely knew earned more respect from him than she did, even after years of hard work trying to prove herself.

She pushed to her feet, her limbs barely under control. "Wake me when it's time for me to take over." She made her shaky way to her bedroll, knowing she would spend the next few hours staring into the dark trying to pretend this news didn't upset her.

She took over her watch when Sawyer called her. She walked around the corral enclosure. Not because she felt she needed to check anything but because her insides were too restless to allow her to sit.

By dawn, she was weary but anxious to be moving.

Sawyer scrambled from his bedroll and hurriedly made coffee. Seemed he was anxious to get back to *his* ranch. His and Father's.

Neither of them had much to say as they ate a quick breakfast and got the animals on the move again.

The bulls were a little cantankerous, not wanting to be pushed onward. Several times, they turned back, wanting to return to their stable. It kept Carly and Sawyer both busy, guiding them in the right direction. Carly welcomed the diversion as it made conversation almost impossible.

If only it would make thinking impossible, too.

They paused briefly around noon, thinking the bulls would welcome a break but one raced away. Sawyer was in his saddle in moments, herding the animal back. Meanwhile, the two others took off in the opposite direction and Carly went after them.

"We better keep them moving," Sawyer called as he brought the stray back.

"Yup."

The sun was an orange ball on the peaks of the

mountains when they turned the bulls into the corrals at the Morrison Ranch. Carly refused to think it might soon be known as the Gallagher Ranch.

The animals looked about, saw the fences and knew they didn't have to go anywhere for the rest of the day. They leaned into the shelter of the fence, prepared to enjoy their new home.

Father and the girls came over to admire the animals. "Ye made good time," he said.

"Had to keep them moving," Carly said, struggling to keep sharpness from her tone. She loved her father but he had betrayed her. She glanced toward the hill where the five graves stood behind a wooden fence. Would she never count as much as a son would have?

No point in worrying about what might have been.

Sawyer and Carly took care of their horses, then they went to the house.

"I made supper, thinking you might be back tonight," Beth said.

Carly gave her a one-armed hug. The child had lost both parents, been treated poorly by a so-called stepfather, had taken care of her two younger siblings until Logan and Sadie rescued them and yet she remained cheerful and sweet.

Carly knew she must do the same and she could with God's help. Like Mother used to say, 'Disappointments can make us better or we can allow them to make us bitter.' To honor her mother, she would not be bitter.

The girls set the table while Carly washed off the dust of the trail.

Beth had made a meatloaf, carrots and mashed potatoes.

"This is excellent. Thank you." Carly said.

"It certainly is," Sawyer added.

"Aye, I've been well taken care of while you were away." Father's smile of approval brought a pink stain to Beth's cheeks.

"Jill helped me."

The child beamed with adoration for the older girl.

As soon as the dishes were done, Carly said, "Good night. I'm tired." Then she remembered Beth had been sleeping in her bed. "One of you girls can bunk with me."

"I will," Jill said. The girls followed her to the room and Jill crawled in beside Carly, snuggling close. It left Beth crammed into the shorter bed but she insisted she didn't mind.

"Did you miss me?" Carly asked in a teasing tone.

"Granddad said things would change when you got back."

"Change? How?" Did he intend to put Sawyer in charge and confine Carly to the house?

"He said you and Sawyer would be different after spending time together." She giggled a little. "Said you'd be really truly married."

It wasn't about the ranch. But was his opinion about their marriage any more welcome? She took slow, deep breaths. Like Sawyer said, other people's opinions didn't matter.

Except this was Father and his opinion mattered a great deal.

The next day, she said she was going to check on the cows. They'd let the bulls rest a few days, then take them out to the herd.

Sawyer said he'd accompany her.

"I've been doing this without an escort for a long time."

"But now you don't have to."

"Ack, daughter, let the man go with ye."

She scowled at them both.

Sawyer simply smiled as if unconcerned with her attitude. He kept up the same cheerful spirit as they rode to the northwest in search of the cows. "'Tis a bonny day." He imitated Father's accent so well Carly laughed in spite of herself.

Sawyer continued to imitate Father, pointing out the 'fair meadows,' the 'fine cattle,' until Carly's bad mood entirely vanished.

They found the cattle grazing near the creek. Sawyer glanced over them, then turned away. But he didn't head toward home.

Carly followed. "Where are you going?"

"Come and see." They passed through the band of trees and reached the edge of the creek. Sawyer swung down from his horse and gave her an are-you-coming look.

Curious, she followed. The banks of the creek rose, growing more rugged. He reached back and offered her his hand to help her. She took it even though a tiny, nagging portion of her brain warned her she couldn't hold hands and remain annoyed.

But then, she did not want to remain annoyed.

He kept her hand in his as they reached a wider spot. Ahead lay a small waterfall.

"How did you know about this?" she asked.

"I could hear it. Plus Logan told me about it. He said there was a really big waterfall on Wolf River toward the town of Wolf Hollow."

"There is." Did he know that she and Annie had visited the rough mining town of Wolf Hollow a few times before their fathers had forbid it? What would he think if he knew?

"We should go see it sometime."

She almost protested. They'd found the town dirty. The occupants, for the most part, rude. Then she realized he meant the waterfall. "It's certainly worth a visit. Jill would enjoy it."

"I suppose she would, though I wasn't thinking of her."

She met his gaze, the water reflecting in his irises turning them more blue than green and she had the feeling of falling. No floating. On a soft cloud. Speech had abandoned her.

He smiled gently and took her hand to lead her closer to the falls. They stood watching the tumbling water, listening to the gurgle and feeling the spray on their cheeks.

He sank down on a damp rock and pulled her down beside him.

She did not resist.

Neither of them spoke. There didn't seem any need. Peace settled into her soul.

He picked up a handful of rocks and tossed them, one by one in the creek.

She did the same.

He threw one across the stream.

She threw hers across. "Mine went farther."

"We'll see about that." He stood and released a rock that went into the trees on the far side.

She stood and threw hers as hard as she could. It went into the trees.

They took turns throwing rocks, each crowing that theirs had gone the greatest distance until they finally collapsed in a fit of laughter.

After a bit, they made their way back to the horses and headed home.

Carly's insides ached. If only they could be like this all the time. The ranch forgotten. The terms of their marriage forgotten.

Sawyer had hoped that the few pleasant hours spent at the waterfall would mark a change in their relationship. He couldn't explain how he thought that would look but one thing was clear over the passing days. Nothing had changed.

He and Carly worked together amicably enough. They laughed about things. They talked about their pasts. His admiration and affection grew as he came to understand how difficult it had been for her at times as she took over much of the ranch work and tried to be both son and daughter to her father. But if he mentioned that topic, she closed up immediately and the conversation went no further.

They attended church together. Sat together. Heard the same sermons delivered by Hugh. They ate meals around the same table and spent most of every day together or at least in close proximity. And yet the mile-wide canyon had grown deeper.

He had taken to going for an early morning walk while Carly, with Jill's eager help, prepared breakfast. His steps often took him to the river where he sat on a fallen log to think and pray. Daily he asked God to lead him and guide him.

I don't want to fail to keep my word. But, Lord, I care

*about her in a way that frightens me and I don't know
what to do.* He smiled as he realized Carly's faith and
her oft-quoted comments from her mother had brought
him back to the trust in God he had as a child.

Mostly he decided to let things go along as they were.
Safe and uncomplicated.

He returned to the house at Jill's call, determined to
continue along the same route.

Father Morrison said grace. "I'll be going to town
today."

He got immediate attention from both Carly and
Sawyer.

"Who goes to town on a Tuesday unless there's an
urgent need?" Carly asked.

"Aye, my need 'tis urgent." The man continued to
eat as if he hadn't just made an announcement that
made no sense.

Jill looked from one adult to another, the news
equally confusing to her.

Carly stared at her father, then shifted her gaze to
Sawyer. Would he ever meet those brown eyes without
his heart giving an extra-hard beat?

"You know anything about this?" she asked.

"I'm unaware of any pressing need to go to town."

Father Morrison made a deep-throated sound. "Aye,
and is that not the trouble with ye both? You are so unaware."

Sawyer studied the older man. "What are you saying?"

Father Morrison cleaned his plate, wiped it with his
piece of bread and sucked back more coffee, keeping his
curious audience waiting. "Very well, I might as well

tell you I have business to conduct in town. Now, who is going to give me a ride or do I have to take meself?"

"I'll take you." Sawyer hoped he'd learn what the old man was up to by taking him.

"I'm going, too." Carly likely shared the same desire.

"Good. I can go, too. Can I buy a candy stick?" Jill ate the last of her breakfast in two bites.

"Yes," Sawyer and Carly answered in unison. He guessed Carly was as distracted by this news as he.

The kitchen was clean and the others ready to depart by the time Sawyer drove the wagon to the door and then they were on their way.

Carly sat in the back with Jill while her father sat beside Sawyer. Which made any private conversation between Carly and Sawyer impossible. They'd have to wait until town to speculate what her father was up to.

"I'll go to the Marshalls' store," he announced and climbed slowly down. His steps were slow as he favored his injured leg.

Jill hurried ahead to choose her candy.

Carly and Sawyer followed her father. He went directly to the counter. George Marshall joined him.

"What can I do for you, Robert?"

"I want to post an ad here and place one in the paper. It's ready. I just need postage." He handed over a sealed envelope and Mr. Marshall got a stamp, glued it and put it on. Only then, did he open the sheet of paper that held the ad Father wanted to post.

He looked up at Carly and Sawyer. "Did you know about this?"

They shook their heads.

Mr. Marshall handed the paper to them.

Sawyer took it and Carly read it as he did.

For sale. One ranch near Bella Creek, Montana. Good grass. Good cattle. Imported Hereford Bulls. Oats and wheat seeded.

The skin on Sawyer's face tightened. He'd worried about Carly changing her mind but he'd never considered her father would.

Carly's cheeks blanched and she stared at the words as if doubting what they said. Then she spun around and strode from the store. He watched through the window as she hurried down the street and out of sight. Where was she going?

What were he and Jill going to do for a home? What about Carly? What was going to happen to her? To them?

Chapter Sixteen

Sawyer hurried toward the door and then paused to consider Jill and his father-in-law both standing at the counter. Jill drooled over the candy selection. Mr. Morrison tacked the notice to the bulletin board. Sawyer resisted an urge to snatch it off and toss it into the garbage.

"I'm going to catch up to Carly." He tossed a penny on the counter for Jill's candy. "Come on, little sister."

Mr. Morrison limped after them. "Wait for me. I'm done here."

Feeling less than charitable to the old man, Sawyer nevertheless waited for him to get up on the seat, then turned the wagon in the direction he'd last seen Carly.

Jill leaned over his shoulder. "Where'd she go? Why'd she go without waiting for us?"

He leaned forward, anxious for a glimpse of Carly but all he saw were the benches of the town square and the trees, leafed out in fresh green, which surrounded the square. "I guess she was upset about something." Thankfully, Jill had not read the notice so did not know what was planned.

"Oh." She considered the news. "Did you do something?"

"Me?" He looked over his shoulder at his sister, her face wreathed in worry and accusation. "Why would you think that?"

She got a stubborn look on her face. "'Cause you aren't nice to her."

"What? When have I ever been unkind to her?" The announcements of the day got stranger and stranger.

"You treat her like a man."

Mr. Morrison chuckled.

Sawyer resisted an urge to jump from the wagon and join Carly in marching away.

"I do not." He certainly never thought of her as a man. Not even for a second. They reached the intersection of the streets. He slowed the wagon to a crawl. "Does anyone see her?"

The three of them craned their necks.

He caught a movement to the south. "There she is." Seems she was headed home. Perhaps to pack. If her father succeeded in his plan, they would all be packing.

He overtook her. "Want a ride home?"

She shook her head and kept marching. "What home?"

"Girl, get in the wagon. 'Tis home until otherwise."

She stopped and faced her father. "I'm not sure I care to ride with you."

The man had the audacity to laugh.

Sawyer decided to try another way of appealing to her. "Get in. When we get back—" He no longer felt free to say home. "We can discuss this."

She glanced up at Sawyer. "My father is not known for being reasonable."

He guessed she meant being forced into a marriage agreement to save the ranch. Which didn't seem to satisfy her father.

Carly continued her journey, her feet pounding on the grass at the side of the road. Sawyer slowed the wagon so it kept abreast of Carly. She stopped walking, took a deep breath. "Very well." And climbed into the back with Jill.

Jill sidled close. "Why're you mad?"

"Because someone didn't keep his word." The words should have left bruises on her father but again, Mr. Morrison chuckled. He was getting far too much enjoyment out of the turmoil he'd created.

"Was it Sawyer?" Jill asked, still determined to blame her brother for Carly's anger.

Carly must have heard the confusion and fear in the child's voice for she wrapped an arm about her and her voice softened as she answered. "It wasn't Sawyer."

"Good." It didn't seem to cross her mind that it might be Carly's father.

They returned to the ranch in silence. Sawyer stopped at the house to let the others off, though he didn't much care for leaving Carly to deal with her father alone.

He continued to the barn to take care of the horse and wagon. As he turned to put away the harness, Carly joined him.

"Did you know he was going to do this?" Her words were little bullets looking for a place to explode.

"I'm as surprised as you." He met her look, saw the anger but also saw the hurting.

"I thought he would have discussed this with you."

"No. Why would he? That man does what he wants."

She nodded. "Is there any point in talking to him about it?" Defeat deadened her voice.

"I think, at the very least, we deserve an explanation." He pulled her arm through his. At first, she stiffened and he thought she might pull away and stomp off. "Come on. Let's confront the tiger."

She gave a half-amused, half-bitter laugh and allowed him to draw her back to the house and her father.

Back at the house, he asked Jill to take her kitten outside and play. "I'll let you know when you can come back."

Cradling the cat in her arms as she went to the door, she said, "I hope you work things out the right way."

He wasn't sure what she meant. But he hoped so, too.

Mr. Morrison sat at the table, looking through the mail he'd brought home. He didn't even bother to glance up though he most certainly had heard them enter and had to be aware of the tension in the air.

"Sir, can we talk?"

Mr. Morrison shoved aside the mail and planted his fists on the tabletop. Not a good sign in Sawyer's opinion. "Say what you have to say."

Carly and Sawyer sat side by side across from the older man. She perched on the front of her chair and looked mad enough to chew the cup her father held, so Sawyer spoke before her anger could erupt.

"We'd like to know why you did this." He congratulated himself on keeping his tone even while all the time his insides twisted and turned.

"Father, you said if I married you wouldn't sell the ranch. I never thought you'd be one not to keep your word."

"Aye, and what kind of marriage is it when he sleeps in the storeroom? 'Tis not a marriage at all, methinks."

Sawyer heard her little gasp. "You wouldn't do this to me if I was a son," she said.

"But you're not."

Knowing how much those words would hurt, Sawyer reached for her hand but she jerked to her feet, tipping the chair. He grabbed it to steady it.

"I'm tired of trying to be the son you always wanted." She fled out the door.

Sawyer studied the man across the table from him. "She is better to you than most sons would be."

"'Tis true but she needs a man."

"She has a man. Me."

"What's to keep you if you don't have a real marriage? If you don't love her? My daughter deserves to be loved."

"The details of our marriage are not your business." He pushed away from the table and headed for the door, his fists curled in anger.

"That's where we disagree," Mr. Morrison said just before Sawyer pulled the door closed quietly.

He glanced around, saw Carly in the little graveyard, kneeling before her mother's grave. She deserved some time alone and he needed to get his feelings reined in, so he headed for the barn where he saddled Dusty.

Jill stood near the fence as he mounted his horse. She held Skippy so tight to her chest he wondered the cat didn't try to squirm away. "Can I go in the house now?"

"Go ahead."

"Are you leaving?" His little sister tried to sound brave but he caught the tremor in her voice. At the moment, he was powerless to say anything to soothe her fears. What could he say when things were so unsettled?

"Going to make sure the bulls are okay." They'd turned them out with the herd.

"You're coming back?"

"I'll be back." He paused, understanding her uncertainty, and swallowed back his own fears. "Jill, I will never leave you."

She nodded.

He rode away in the general direction of the cows. The bulls really didn't need checking but he needed time to think.

Was he truly going to have to leave the only place that had felt like home since his ma died? Or was there a way to change the old man's mind?

Was he willing to take what seemed the obvious… the only way…to keep his home?

Carly knelt before her mother's headstone, her heart leaking blood with every beat. She brushed a bit of dust from the granite. "I've tried to please Father but he won't be satisfied."

The sound of a trotting horse drew her attention back to the yard. Sawyer riding away. Would he return? She wouldn't blame him if he didn't, especially when her father had made him a partner, then snatched it away.

Just as he'd snatched away the promise to keep the ranch if she married.

Her father's words echoed inside her head. *'Tis not a marriage at all.*

Was there a way she could convince Father to change his mind? She sat back, her legs crossed in front of her. She had to think this through.

The sun rose higher in the sky as she sat and considered what to do next.

It was Sawyer sleeping in the little storeroom that convinced Father their marriage wasn't real. So if he slept in her room, would he believe otherwise? Her cheeks burned at the idea of sharing a room with him.

But if it made it possible for her to keep the ranch…

All because she wasn't a son. She stared at the four little crosses. "If one of you had lived and grown to adulthood, this wouldn't be happening."

She didn't realize how long she'd sat there trying to persuade herself of what she must do, if he would agree, until she heard him return. She tried to get up but discovered her legs had fallen asleep and she was still sitting in front of Mother's grave when Sawyer strode up the hill and joined her.

He sat beside her, his legs folded in half. "I've been doing a lot of thinking."

"Me, too." She wondered what conclusion he'd reached. Could hardly blame him if he decided he'd been hoodwinked and wanted to annul their marriage.

"You go first."

"No, you." *After all*, she thought mockingly, *you're a man and as such your opinions matter so much more.* She knew her bitterness was uncalled for. He didn't deserve that judgment. He'd treated her fairly and didn't even complain about her wearing trousers.

"Very well. You might not like what I'm about to suggest."

So he was going to say their agreement was over. She marshaled up every bit of mental strength she could find.

"Your father wants you truly married."

"Yes."

"He does not know the terms of our marriage nor does he need to, but perhaps we can ease his concerns by sharing the same room."

"Not the same bed?" What did Sawyer truly want?

"I agreed I wouldn't expect that and I'm a man of my word."

You could change your word. Change your mind. Offer to agree to a new arrangement. But he didn't. "I was thinking along the same lines."

"Then I'll move into your room. Is that agreeable?"

"It is."

"Good." He sounded less than enthusiastic, which stung her to the core. It wasn't as if she was so undesirable. She recalled Bart's words. *Pretty up.* Perhaps if she didn't wear trousers and didn't ride like a man, he'd see her as a woman.

But she dismissed the idea. Seems she couldn't satisfy the men in her life. Father wanted her to be a son. Bart had wanted her to be a pretty little woman. She didn't know what Sawyer wanted. She was weary with trying and failing. From now on, she would be who she wanted to be.

If she even knew. All her life, she'd tried to please her father.

And she'd failed. "If only I had been a son."

He took her hand and gently squeezed it.

"You are who God made you to be and I don't see that anyone has a right to complain about that. Including you."

Despite her recent promise to herself to need no man and be who she wanted to be, she clung to the comfort of his words. The truth of them sank deep into her heart where they rooted and blossomed.

"You're right." Did he think she was fine as she was? "My mother used to quote a verse. 'I will praise thee, for I am fearfully and wonderfully made. Marvelous are Thy works, and that my soul knoweth right well.' She said the most marvelous of His words is mankind." Carly smiled as she recalled how her mother had hugged her and said Carly was the most marvelous of God's works.

What did it matter how her father viewed her? And yet it did.

Even more, it mattered how Sawyer viewed her. She wanted to be more than part of a contract.

She stared at her mother's headstone and brought her thoughts back to her father's latest trick. No longer would she be controlled by his opinion. But she cared about keeping the ranch and her home. She'd do what she must to achieve that.

Feeling had returned to her legs and she got to her feet and reached down to offer a hand to Sawyer. "Let's go do it."

They called Jill to join them as they returned to the house.

Father had retired to his big chair, his head tipped back as he slept. How could he sleep so easily after such a despicable deed?

Ignoring him, they told Jill she and Sawyer were changing rooms.

"I like sleeping with Carly."

Carly hugged the child. "I like sharing a room with you, too, but I'm married to Sawyer."

Jill's mouth formed an O. "You're gonna sleep with him?"

Father jerked awake in time to hear Jill's words. "About time," he muttered.

Carly's face burned and she dared not look at Sawyer. Instead, she hurried to her room to collect Jill's things and carry them to the smaller room. She and Sawyer passed each other, his arms full of his things.

"Where shall I put my stuff?" he asked.

"I left the drawers open that held Jill's things and there are hooks to hang stuff on."

"Can I take my bed?" Jill asked. "I like it."

"Of course. We'll exchange beds." She counted on doing so. Jill's bed was too short for her. Had been since she was twelve. Two beds would mean they didn't have to share.

"I dinnae think so," Father said. "Leave the little bed in your room."

"Don't you feel guilty at what you're doing?"

"Nay, daughter. Sometimes a little push is necessary."

A little push? Is that what he called this manipulation?

Too upset to deal with her father, she continued to the small room and quickly arranged Jill's things. She took longer at the task than it required, even after Jill decided it was okay and left.

Sawyer came to the doorway. "Are you all right?"

"Father is playing games with us." She kept her back to him, afraid he would read far more in her expression than she cared for him to see.

"We don't have to play along."

"Seems we do."

"Except we decide the rules of the game."

She nodded. Stiffened when he crossed the room. Fought an urge to turn into his embrace when he planted his hands on her shoulders.

"Carly, I will never expect more from you than you want to give. You can trust me."

She trusted him. Knew he would keep his word even when she wished otherwise. Her heart echoed with impossible longing. "You can trust me, too." She slipped away and returned to the kitchen. It was past time to make dinner.

The rest of the day she kept busy, weeding the garden, mending the chicken-yard fence, fixing a tear in the trousers Jill wore. But avoiding her bedroom and the evidence of Sawyer's presence in it were impossible no matter how frantically she worked.

How were they going to handle this situation and remain true to their promises?

You can trust me. She wasn't sure she meant his words or hers.

After supper, Sawyer disappeared outside. She watched out the window as he traipsed toward the river. She longed to join him...to ask what he really thought of sharing her room. But he seemed to prefer his solitude, so she and Jill cleaned up the kitchen together.

"Beth said I did almost as good as she does," Jill said.

Carly smiled at the sweet child, recognizing her yearning for approval. "Jill, honey, you are so helpful. I don't know what I'd do without you."

Jill beamed. "Mama would be proud, don't you think?"

Glad that her father had retired to the other room so

Carly could relax, she hugged the child. "She would be so proud."

Would Carly's mother be proud of her?

She straightened and looked out the window. Mother had always praised her, always told her how much she was loved. Now she saw something she had not been aware of before. Not until Mother died had Carly tried to be a son to her father.

Why did it matter so much at that point?

She found the answer. Because she missed her mother's approval and sought her father's instead.

"It's time for bed," she told Jill a short time later.

"Are you still going to read to me?"

"Of course I am. You get washed up and into your nightie while I get the book from my room." She retrieved the storybook and joined Jill in the little room. It still held hints of Sawyer's presence—a worn brown shirt he'd overlooked hung on a hook behind the door and most telling of all, his scent. She tried to ignore it as she lay beside Jill and read her a story. The kitten lay in the crook of Jill's arm. At least it was content with the arrangement.

Jill said her prayers, then crawled into bed. Carly pulled the light covers up to Jill's chin and bent to kiss her.

Jill wrapped her arms about Carly's neck and held her. "I liked being in your room."

"I liked it, too. I'm going to miss you close to me."

"Granddad said this is the way it should be."

"I know." She kissed the child again. "You have a good sleep." She petted the kitten. "You, too, Skippy."

Jill giggled. "She'll crawl up to my neck as soon as you're gone."

"Just make sure she doesn't eat you alive." She tick-led Jill and laughed.

Jill grew serious. "She would never hurt me."

"I know. Now you go to sleep. I'll see you in the morning."

She returned to the kitchen. Father sat in his big chair watching her. She sat at the table with her back to him.

"Where's Sawyer?" he asked.

"Outside."

"Aye, and why? Are you cold toward him?"

"Father, don't be blaming me for something you started." Next he'd be telling her she should get pret-tied up for her man.

"Me?"

Sawyer banged into the house.

She was inordinately pleased to see him. It would put a stop to Father's meddling. She sprang to her feet. "Would you like tea or coffee or something to eat?" They'd never bothered with a bedtime snack before but now seemed a good time to start doing so.

"No, thanks." He didn't sit.

His hovering presence unnerved her and she stood, too, and met his gaze. Saw so many things. Or imag-ined she did. Regret perhaps. Or simply acceptance. If only she could believe she saw longing.

He looked past her to Father, watching and waiting, brought his gaze back to her and smiled, a gentle com-forting smile. "You go ahead and get ready for bed. I'll come in a few minutes."

"Thank you," she murmured. This might not be dif-ficult if Sawyer was understanding about it.

She hurriedly prepared for bed, hesitating about slipping into her nightgown. She couldn't sleep in her clothes and she pulled the night garment over her head as quickly as she could. With a grimace, she lay on the child-sized bed. She'd be unable to straighten her legs unless she lowered them to the ground. But she wasn't about to complain.

Sawyer tapped lightly to warn her that he was entering and slipped in. "Your father is watching to make sure I don't sneak out and sleep in the barn."

She groaned.

In the dim light coming through the curtains, he studied her. "That isn't going to be very comfortable."

She shifted to her side and drew her knees to her chest. "I'll be fine."

"No, you won't. You sleep in the bed and I'll sleep on the floor."

"I can't do that to you. After all, it's my father who is forcing us to do this." She tried not to shuffle in an attempt to get more comfortable.

"Sorry, but I absolutely refuse to allow this." He grabbed a pillow and the quilt folded at the bottom of the bed. His boots thudded off. The rustle of material suggested he'd removed his jeans and shirt. With a sigh, he settled on the floor on the far side. "You might as well take advantage of the bed." His disembodied voice came to her.

"This is silly." She waited for him to change his mind but he remained on the floor and she knew he would. He was a man who meant what he said. Something she both respected and regretted from time to time. "If you insist." She scrambled into the bed and stretched out with a sigh. "It's lovely. Thank you. But now I feel bad that you're on the floor."

"Don't. I've slept on harder ground as you might recall."

"I suppose you have." She stared at the ceiling, so aware of him on the floor beside her that she could hardly breathe. "That trip to the Bar None seems like a lifetime ago."

"The bulls have settled in with the herd. Your father was right about bringing them in."

"Yeah, he's a canny cattleman." She waited a second to continue. "Too bad he doesn't understand people as well."

Sawyer chuckled. "Especially his own daughter."

"Aye," she said with a great deal of dismay. "'Tis the truth."

He chuckled. "It's been a long, trying day. Try and get some sleep."

"Good night." She shifted to her side.

"Good night." His voice sounded more distant and she guessed he had rolled away from the bed.

She didn't expect to sleep a wink but drifted off almost at once and wakened as Sawyer tiptoed from the room in the morning. She sprang up, dressed and hurried out.

Father limped from his room and sat down to wait for coffee. Sawyer had gone out to tend to the chores.

She felt Father's eyes on her as she made breakfast. The coffee boiled and she poured a cup. When she turned to hand it to him, his eyes twinkled. "So now you're well and truly a married woman."

Her cheeks stung but she stared at him without letting him guess at the truth. It was necessary for him to believe what he wanted to believe in order to save the ranch.

The day went smoothly. She went about her work. Sawyer kept busy with Big Harry. He said the horse needed his hooves tended to.

That night, she again went to bed while he waited in the kitchen.

She grabbed the pillow and quilt and curled up on the floor, getting as comfortable as possible.

He tapped and entered. He looked down at her, his hands on his hips. "What are you doing there?"

"We'll take turns. If you recall, I have slept on the ground a few times, too."

"Carly, it isn't necessary. I don't mind."

"I do. So leave it be."

"I don't want to argue. Can you imagine your father's reaction if he heard us?" He chuckled softly.

She laughed, too. "Sure don't want him barging in to straighten us out."

The springs sighed as Sawyer crawled into bed.

All she could see of him was his elbow crooked as if he clasped his hands behind his head. He was her husband and now he lay within touching distance. Yet there was so much she didn't know about him. "Sawyer, did you never have a lady you were interested in?"

"Once or twice. There was a young lady I thought I cared for. Gladys Berry."

"What happened?"

"She wanted what I couldn't give her."

Carly sat up so she could see him. Even in the dim light, she could tell he seemed unconcerned about the fact. "What couldn't you give her?"

Sawyer tipped his head so he could see her. "According to her, I wasn't capable of feelings."

"That's what you told me that first day." She grinned at the memory. How wrong he'd been.

"I felt I had to be honest."

"It isn't true, you know."

They studied each other across the narrow space. She wished she had lit a lamp so she could see him better but nevertheless she felt his surprise.

"Why do you say that?"

"Because I know you feel things deeply. I've seen you laugh. I've seen concern in your face when you talk about Jill and I've seen sorrow when you talk about your ma and Johnny. Which reminds me, thank you for making those markers for your family. It means a lot to Jill."

He lay back. For a moment, she thought he'd gone to sleep, then he turned to her. "Your turn."

"For what?"

"Tell me about your beaus."

She gave a mocking laugh. "That won't take long. I think men are afraid of me because I do a man's work."

He made a scoffing noise.

Somewhat eased by his response, she continued. "There was Bart Connelly. I thought he cared about me."

"Didn't he?"

"I think he saw me as a shortcut to a ranch. He thought I would turn into his idea of a regular lady and he would run the ranch."

"I expect you corrected him of that idea."

The amusement in his voice sang along her veins. "Guess I did."

Another pause. She was about to settle back down on the hard floor when he said, "Did you care for him a lot?"

"I suppose I thought I did. Father rather liked him."

"Was that the only reason you cared for him? Because your father approved?"

"Why am I always doing what Father would like? What's the point?"

"Maybe he's happy enough to have you as his loving daughter. Perhaps you don't need to try and be anything else."

She lay back on her pillow. Was Sawyer right? Was being his daughter enough? What would it take to discover the answer to her questions?

Would pretending she and Sawyer were well and truly man and wife suffice for her father?

Sometimes she wondered if anything would satisfy him. She reminded herself she wasn't going to seek his approval any more. But without it, he would sell the ranch.

Was her love of the ranch influencing her decisions more than she wanted?

Chapter Seventeen

Sawyer had worried about sharing the bedroom with Carly. How was he to keep his feelings hidden? But he found they settled into a comfortable enough routine alternating nights on the floor. And talking quietly as darkness settled over the land. Both of them seemed freer in the privacy of the room and he liked learning more about her.

It was his turn to sleep on the floor. There were so many things he longed to discover about her. "What was your happiest memory?"

She shifted to her side and peered at him over the side of the bed. "I'll have to think about that for a moment." She considered her answer. "I think I'd have to say it was the Christmas I was thirteen and a half. I remember Mother braiding my hair. She had made me a new dress and said I was so pretty. Father gave me a pocketknife." Her voice deepened. "I think he'd been saving it for a son but that was the year the fourth baby boy had died." Her voice brightened. "That was the year Mother gave me the little china shepherdess. I said I couldn't take it. I knew how fond Mother was of it. She told me it had served her well and she wanted me to take it and remember what it stood for. The Shepherd's Psalm. 'The Lord is my shepherd… He leadeth me—"

Her voice grew deep and she stopped speaking. "Mother died that spring."

How it must have hurt her to lose the figurine. He felt responsible. "I'm sorry about the shepherdess getting broken. I wish I could replace it."

"I just realized something. Mother would not let the breakage upset her because the words of the psalm were in her heart." She smiled. "They're there for me too."

He studied her, wishing he could see her better. "That's good to hear."

"It's your turn."

He knew what she meant. They had played this game every evening. "My happiest memory was the year Johnny was born. I remember how Ma placed him in my arms. She said he was my baby and I should always look after him. I failed to do so." He couldn't go on.

She reached over and found his hand. "You did for five years."

"I wish he was still alive."

"So many deaths. Your mother. My mother. Your brother. My baby brothers. Now your father and Jill's mother. It's overwhelming at times."

He longed for a way to comfort her and grabbed at another sweet memory. "My ma used to read to me at bedtime."

"Mine, too. When I grew too old for the Bible story-book, she read from the Bible."

He sat up, her hand still in his. "We could do that." He released her hand, shuffled toward the bedside table and lit the lamp. "Where's your Bible?"

She opened the drawer of the little table and pulled it out.

He took it. "What shall I read?"

"A psalm?"

He found the place and read the first psalm, closed the Bible and returned it to the drawer. He lay down.

"That was nice. Thank you."

He squirmed about, trying to settle himself so none of his bones protested about the hard floor. He could feel her eyes on him. "What?"

"You don't look very comfortable."

"I'm comfortable on the inside." He smiled at her.

"What do you mean?"

"My ma used to read to me from the Bible, too. This is like having a bit of her back."

"I know. I miss my mother."

"Me, too."

"Poor Jill," they said in unison and turned to each other.

He reached for her hand. "We must do what we can to make up for her loss."

"Agreed."

At that moment, something as solid as rock bound them together.

Later, after the lamp was out and they had settled down for the night, he realized it wasn't just that moment that had forged the bond…it was the accumulation of nights they'd spent together, talking and sharing.

Carly lay in the darkness of her bedroom. Sawyer's deep breathing indicated he had fallen asleep. She felt close to him, and she didn't mean because he lay on the floor inches from the side of the bed. It was far more than that. Over the past few days, or rather nights, he had allowed her to see into his heart and she liked what she saw. A man with many sorrows counterbalanced by his strength and kindness. A man worthy of her admiration.

And her love? She shifted about carefully so as not to waken him.

Love was not part of their agreement.

She stiffened as he moaned. She lay tense, listening for an indication that she might have disturbed his sleep.

He moaned again and mumbled.

"Sawyer?" No response. Perhaps he was dreaming. She flipped to her side, close enough to the edge of the bed she could see him. In the thick darkness, she could barely make out his form. One of his arms hit the bed and caused her to jump. "Sawyer?" she said again in a hoarse whisper.

He muttered something. She couldn't make it out but his tone sounded troubled, afraid even. From a nightmare?

She patted his shoulder. "Sawyer, wake up."

He thrashed about.

She shook him and spoke louder. "Sawyer, wake up."

He startled, drew in a shuddering breath. "I was dreaming."

"I thought so."

A shiver shook his body. "It was awful. I dreamed I was trying to rescue Johnny. I fought my way through flames only to discover he'd moved and I had to go through more flames."

She patted his shoulder. "It was just a dream. It meant nothing. Johnny is safe with your mama. You don't have to look for him in a fire. Now go back to sleep."

His hand cupped hers, claimed it. "Thank you."

She didn't ask for what because she preferred to fill in the blanks herself. He was grateful she was close by, grateful she'd wakened him and grateful even for her words of comfort.

He held her hand until he fell back asleep and his fingers relaxed. Only then did she pull her arm back to the bed and under the covers to warm it.

As usual, he was gone the next morning when she slipped from the bed. In a state half asleep, half awake, she'd been aware of him rising, pulling on his clothes and tiptoeing away. She knew he paused before he opened the door and tried but failed to force her eyes open to see why. He whispered something, then stepped from the room. She tried to make out what he had said, but again failed.

Later, she pushed aside the last of her sleep and dressed. She paused to make her bed and put the pillow and quilt back in place, leaving no evidence that Sawyer slept on the floor. Father would object if he knew. Perhaps continue with his threat to sell the ranch.

When he'd first forced her into this position, she had resented his manipulation but now she thanked him for it. She enjoyed having Sawyer close and being able to talk to him in the intimacy of the bedroom.

She didn't realize she smiled as she made breakfast until Father spoke.

"Looks to me like you two are enjoying each other. Aye?"

"You could say so." She knew they talked about different things but her words were true.

Over breakfast, Father said. "There's rain comin'. 'Tis a good day to burn that dry grass along the trail."

The track leading from the main road to the house had to be burnt off every year to eliminate a fire hazard. They would have normally done it soon after the snow melted but this year there had been Father's injuries and her marriage to distract them from the task.

He continued. "There isn't much danger with everything so green. All the same, I dinnae like to take chances, so ye'll all come help keep an eye on things."

"Me, too?" Jill seemed to think it an exciting prospect.

The skin on Sawyer's face grew taut but before he could protest, Father spoke.

"Aye, I think you better stay in the house and keep little Skippy with you so she doesn't get in the way."

As soon as the kitchen had been cleaned up and meat set to stew, Carly went out to join Father and Sawyer. She'd told Jill she could watch from the window but to keep the door closed so Skippy wouldn't get out.

Father saw her approach them. "Aye, and then let's get at it." He held a torch of twigs he had bundled together. He lit it and walked along the trail, using it to light the dry grass. Carly followed him, Sawyer behind, both of them armed with damp gunnysacks to put out any little fires that got away from the intended area.

The seedpods of some plant exploded, sending sparks toward the barn. A bit of dry hay caught the sparks and a flame quickly flared. She stomped it out. Sawyer stomped out another flame near the corrals.

"I don't like this," he muttered.

"We do it every spring."

"I know it's necessary but I still don't like it."

She rubbed his arm. "I can manage if you want to go back to the house."

"And leave you out here dealing with this? No indeed." He grabbed her hand and hurried her back to the trail. "Go ahead. I'll follow."

It was comforting to have him behind her, knowing he would come to her rescue if she needed it. Of course she wouldn't. Like she said, they'd done this every year with only her to help Father.

Still, it was nice to have him with her.

They finished one side as far as the road.

Father limped back to the house. "We'll start here. 'Tis most important to get the grass burned off close to the house." He glanced at the sky. "'Twill be good if the rain holds off until we finish." He began the process again.

Carly checked on Jill and found her playing with the kitten. She returned to the task, following Father while Sawyer brought up the rear. Twice she stomped out little flames near the buildings and once brushed a glowing ember off her skirts.

The wind picked up, tugging her skirts to the side. She smelled the approaching rain and lifted her face to the sky, her eyes closed as she reveled in the scents— dampness and smoke. An odd contrast.

Acrid smoke blew toward him. Flames danced and cavorted, orange and yellow bits of insanity. Sawyer shuddered and turned to watch Carly, smiling at the way she moved so gracefully along the road, pausing here to kick at a rock, there to smile at a flower, chasing after the fires that caught in areas they weren't planning to burn.

He was grateful for the enjoyment she provided. It helped him ignore the fear that coiled around his heart every time he saw flames racing in a line. Such a sight always brought the memory of flames licking up the wall of their house, the sound of his pa's cries echoing in his ears.

The wind jerked at his hat and he pulled it tighter to his head. He turned his attention back to the fire crackling at his side. He knew this had to be done but wished it could be otherwise. An ember caught in the wind and flew toward the barn. He chased it and stomped it out, made sure there were no other areas catching fire before he left.

Carly's skirts billowed out, fanned toward the fire, the hem of her garment waving over the orange flames. His lungs spasmed. It was only an illusion that made him think the skirts engulfed the fire.

The wind shifted. Her dress fell around her legs. The orange still clung to the hem. He shook his head. Blinked his eyes. Willed away the sight.

But it would not be dismissed. It wasn't his imagination. She was on fire.

He couldn't move. It was just like the day his ma and Johnny died and he stood rooted to the spot. Doing nothing.

The flames spread up the fabric. She strode forward, oblivious to her danger.

He would not lose her. He would not stand by and do nothing. His legs felt like thick posts but he forced them to move. He broke into a run. *Don't call her name. Don't make her turn.* The movement would swirl her skirts around her, spreading the flames.

He jumped over the charred grass and caught her around the middle, slapping the damp gunnysack against her skirts.

"Sawyer, what are you doing?" She tried to squirm around.

"Don't move. Your skirt is on fire." The orange turned to black. Still he beat at her skirt. Spent at last, he sank to the ground, pulling her down with him, holding her on his lap, his arms around her, his face pressed to the side of her head.

She touched his cheek. "Thank you. I didn't notice."

He leaned back and stared at her. "Why are you wearing a dress?" She always wore trousers when she was outdoors. But not today. Why not today? "Trousers wouldn't have blown into the flames." Why? Why?

She ducked her head so he couldn't see her face. "I thought if I prettied up you might notice me."

Notice her? If she only knew. But why did she seek his attention? He caught her chin and tipped her head toward him so he could see her expression.

She kept her eyelids lowered, hiding her eyes.

"Why would you think such a thing?"

Her eyes came to his. Wide, full of uncertainty. "Father says I should dress like a woman." She made a dismissive sound. "Yet he wants me to work like a son."

"There's more to it than that." She'd dealt with her father's demands for years.

"Well, if you must know, Bart said I should pretty up."

Her old beau who only wanted the ranch? Why would Bart's opinion matter so much? "I think we both know he isn't worth your consideration."

She nodded, studied the front of his shirt.

"Wait. You did this so *I* would notice you?"

She nodded again.

He tipped her head up and peered at her as if he'd

misheard her. "You think I would see you differently if you wore a dress?"

"I hoped so."

He considered her words as their gazes connected, found it hard to think clearly with her intently watching. He knew she wanted him to understand something of enough importance to her that she exchanged trousers for a dress. Poor choice, considering it almost cost her—

He shuddered and pulled her tightly to him. "You could have burned to death."

"I didn't." Her voice was muffled against his chest.

"I suggest you go back to wearing trousers."

She pulled away, turned her face toward the trail so he couldn't see her eyes.

He knew his comment had upset her. Why? He wasn't good at dealing with feelings but he had to figure this out. Only one conclusion made sense to him. "You wanted me to notice you as a woman?" He spoke cautiously, fearing he might offend her, send her running and disappoint her by going beyond their agreement.

She nodded. Faced him. "As a wife."

Her words hung between them, sweet and inviting. At the same time, fearful.

Did she really mean she wished to change their agreement? His heart tugged at its moorings, seeking release.

He dare not jump to conclusions. Yet her gaze held his, steady and challenging. And hopeful? Or was it only his own desires that provided the evidence of hope?

"You want—" His throat closed off and he couldn't finish. Couldn't even allow himself to complete the question inside his head. He must be dreaming. Perhaps his brain imagined things because of the shock of seeing her dress on fire.

"I want—" She blinked. Lowered her gaze.

He stared. His mind full of possibilities. And warnings. But had she not issued an invitation? And he meant to accept it. "Carly, are you saying—?"

"Company coming," Father Morrison yelled. He turned, saw Carly and Sawyer together on the ground. "Aye, and is this the way you watch the fire?" He tsked. "Get up now. Make sure the fire is out while I see who has come to visit." He tented a hand over his eyes and squinted toward the approaching buggy. "Dinnae think I know them."

Carly and Sawyer struggled to their feet. His thoughts were too tangled to make sense. He'd been about to ask her the most important questions he could think of. Did she have a fondness for him? Was she wanting to change the agreement between them? Now his questions would have to wait until the company had been dealt with.

He helped Carly dust herself off.

"How bad is it?" She peered around, trying to see how much damage had been done to her dress.

"Just the hem. Thank the good Lord above." He barely managed to stifle a shudder. "If I hadn't been watching…."

She touched his cheek. "But you were and you saved me. Thank you."

"You recognize them?" her father asked.

Carly and Sawyer both watched the approaching conveyance. A man with a woman beside him. She had an infant in her arms. A small boy peeked out between the adults.

"I don't know them." Carly gripped Sawyer's hand and murmured. "I wonder what they want." Her voice seemed strained, causing tension to knot in his neck.

Why should the approach of strangers fill him with foreboding?

Chapter Eighteen

Carly watched the buggy approach and told herself there was no reason to be upset. The occupants were just a young family out for a drive. Perhaps they'd seen the smoke and come to investigate. Yes, that had to be it. She said so to Sawyer.

"I suppose that could be why they are coming."

"But you don't think so?"

"They can see that the fire is out and there is no danger, yet they keep coming. And they look as if they have a purpose in mind."

She studied the couple and had to agree. Father stood at the bottom of the lane but she remained a hundred feet back and didn't go forward. For all her reassuring assessment, she couldn't ignore the eager look on the young man's face and it made her nervous even though she could not think why it should.

The buggy stopped in front of Father.

Clinging to Sawyer's hand, Carly edged closer so she could hear every word.

"Hello, is this the Morrison place?" the man called, ending Carly's hope that they were out for a little drive.

"Aye, 'tis. What can I do for you?" Father answered.

"I'm Art Jacobs." The man was shockingly blond and from what she could tell, of average build. "This is my wife, Elsie." She, too, was blonde with thick braids coiled about her head. A dainty woman. "Our two little boys, Neil and Ernst." A boy ducked down behind his mother.

Father waited for the man to state his business.

Mr. Jacobs pulled a piece of newspaper from his breast pocket and held it toward Father. "I saw your ad. My grandfather died not long ago and left me money. He knew of my desire to have my own ranch, so when we saw your ad, we knew it was a sign from God. We'd like to look around and if we like what we see, we'd like to buy your place." He reached over and rested his hand over his wife's. "So far we're favorably impressed."

Carly swayed.

Sawyer's arm slipped around her waist. "Are you okay?" he murmured,

"I will be when he tells them the ranch is no longer for sale."

Father limped closer to the buggy. "Two sons, you say? Which is which?"

"Neil is the older. He's eight. Ernst is four months old."

Mrs. Jacobs sat the baby up so Father could see him.

"Aye, both are handsome lads."

Carly's heart thudded reluctantly. "Sons." She hissed the word. "How can I compete with that?"

"They aren't his sons," Sawyer said, his tone suggesting Father would surely understand that.

Carly rolled her head back and forth. No one knew

how important male children were in Father's opinion. She'd never been able to fill that need in his life.

Father seemed to remember Carly and Sawyer standing behind him and introduced them.

"Hello," Carly murmured, but neither she nor Sawyer stepped forward to shake hands.

"Step down," Father invited. "My daughter will make tea and we'll talk about things."

She glowered at the back of her father's head, then steamed toward the house, Sawyer keeping in step.

"Why is he inviting them in? Why isn't he telling them they'll have to find another ranch to buy? Why is he such a stubborn old man?"

Sawyer caught her hand and stopped her headlong flight. He faced her. "I'm certain he can't be seriously entertaining their interest."

"No? Then why is he inviting them in?"

Sawyer wagged his head back and forth. "I wish I knew." His smile was regretful. "I wish we'd had a chance to finish our conversation. We'll make time later."

Carly had finally summoned the courage to speak to him of the changes in her feelings. She'd said she wanted him to see her as his wife. Had been about to say she cared for him when this intrusion was thrust upon her.

She sucked in air until her insides felt steady. "I'll make tea because it's the hospitable thing to do but I'm not feeling very welcoming toward them."

Jill waited at the doorway, Skippy in her arms. "Who are they?"

Carly provided the names. "They have an eight-year-old boy you can play with." No point in passing her resentment on to the child.

Jill pulled Skippy closer. "I don't like boys. They're mean."

Sawyer ruffled his sister's hair. "Not all of them are."

Jill ducked away and watched the company walk toward the house, their pace slow as Carly's father led the way.

Carly rushed to make tea. She'd serve cookies, too. The sooner they had tea, the sooner they'd depart.

They entered. Sawyer hurriedly put more chairs and stools around the table while Carly served the tea. All the while, Father kept up a running commentary. "The town is nice. Has everything a man or woman could want."

"There's a school and a church."

"Our land borders Wolf River to the east." On and on he went.

Why are you telling these people all this? You can't seriously be thinking of selling the ranch? After all I did.

The visitors finished their tea, complimented Carly on the delicious cookies and grew restless.

"Carly will show you around." Father turned to her. "Show them the buildings and yard first, then take them out to see the land."

She stared at him. Who was this man? He surely couldn't be her father and treat her like this. What if she wasn't his child? Maybe she was a foundling. Had been left on their doorstep. Or perhaps Mother had rescued her from a dying mother. That would explain why Father could do this to her.

Even so, she owed him for providing her a home.

But she would not have any part in encouraging this

young couple to buy the ranch. "Father, I am unable to show them around."

Father looked ready to sputter a protest. Then his expression hardened. She half expected him to order her to comply.

Instead he turned to Sawyer. "Will you—?"

"Sir, I'm sorry but I, too, am unable to show them around."

Father gave them both a stinging look.

Jill eased forward, a shy look on her face. "I'll take them."

Father patted Jill's head and sent Carly an accusing look. "Child, 'tis very kind of you. Let's do it together."

Young Mrs. Jacobs clutched the baby to her chest and sent her husband a worried look.

Mr. Jacobs cleared his throat. "Is there a problem?"

Father's look challenged Carly to say anything. "Nothing that concerns you."

"If you're sure."

Father grimaced as he got to his feet, doing nothing to hide his pain. In fact, if Carly wasn't mistaken, he wanted her to see how badly it hurt him to move.

Carly's conscience smote her but she didn't change her mind. Not even when Father moaned as he grabbed his cane and made his way to the door.

He waved for the Jacobses to join him. "Come then, we'll have a look around."

Mr. Jacobs looked from Father to Carly to Sawyer. Hesitated, then gave a dismissive shrug. "Thank you, sir."

Jill stayed at Father's side.

Carly waited until they headed toward the barn, then

spun about to face Sawyer. "I can't believe he is doing this."

"Nor can I."

"He's been toying with us this whole time." Letting them believe if she did certain things, he wouldn't sell the ranch.

An uncertain smile lifted Sawyer's lips. "Not that it's been so bad though."

Their gazes held.

She allowed a little smile. "There are parts I don't regret. But—" How could she ignore the fact her father was this very minute planning to sell the place? After pushing her into marriage? After forcing her to invite Sawyer into her room? But like he said, it wasn't all bad and she certainly didn't regret that he was her husband.

In name only. She went to the window and watched their progress. Her stomach burning. She'd hoped to find the courage to tell Sawyer of her changing feelings and now this. Prospective buyers. Father showing them around when he should be telling them the place was no longer for sale.

She stayed at the window, Sawyer by her side, until the little group made its way back to the house.

Rather than come inside, the Jacobses returned to their buggy.

Good. They were leaving.

Father stepped inside. Jill sat down on the grass to play with the kitten.

"They changed their mind?"

"Not at all. They are going to see as much of the land as they can. Someone should show them around, but I cannae." He gave Carly and Sawyer dark looks. "Aye, and it appears I'll get no help here."

"I can't believe—" What was the use? He'd never seen her for who she was. Why should she expect he would now?

"I invited them to join us for dinner."

She stuffed back all the angry words rushing to her mind.

"Aye, but they refused. I dinnae doubt they felt the lack of hospitality." He plunked down at the table. "Wouldn't yer mother be dismayed?"

"Aye, and now wouldn't she be?" Likely as much at father as at daughter. "Mother would never go back on her word."

"Aye," he said but he didn't change his mind.

It was past dinnertime and she was hungry, so she served the meal. Despite her hunger, she found it difficult to swallow and finally scraped most of her food to the cat dish. As soon as she had the dishes done, she hurried to her room to change into trousers.

She sat on the edge of the bed and let the memories of Sawyer rushing to rescue her from the flames drown out the bitter taste of her father's treachery. She'd seen the fear in Sawyer's eyes, had an inkling of how he must have felt to see flames catching on her skirt. He'd demanded to know why she wasn't wearing trousers. The question brought a sweet smile to her lips. So unlike Bart wanting her to pretty up. It seemed Sawyer accepted her the way she was.

She didn't need to put on a dress to please him or to gain his attention.

I want to be your wife.

She'd almost said how she felt. And then the Jacobses had come along, upsetting everything.

She pulled her dress off and jerked on her trousers

and strode from the room. "I'm going for a ride." The freedom of the open spaces, the wind tugging at her hair, the thrill of being at one with her horse would go a long way to easing her tangled thoughts. She saddled Sunny and galloped from the yard. Just before she disappeared around the barn, she caught a glimpse of Sawyer and Jill standing in the doorway, watching.

This isn't about you, she wanted to shout. But they wouldn't hear her. She rode hard over the hills until she reached the secret little lake. She walked Sunny to cool him, then flung herself to the ground. She walked back and forth along the verge of the lake. She kicked at clumps of grass and tossed twigs into the water. Finally, her anger mostly spent, she sat down and stared at the water. What would she do if Father sold the ranch? What would happen to Sawyer and Jill?

There would be no reason to continue their marriage agreement.

She sat with her legs drawn up, her chin propped on her knees and let her sorrow and sadness consume her. After a bit, her feelings abated and she was able to take each thought out and examine it, trying to find a way to deal with it.

Would she have to say goodbye to the land she'd loved since she was a child?

More than that, she would have nothing to offer Sawyer. Would he decide he was done with their agreement?

She moaned as pain seared through her. With surprising clarity, she realized the source of her pain. It wasn't the thought of losing the ranch—as much as that would hurt. It was knowing she could lose Sawyer and Jill.

Oh God, help me. I don't know if I can bear it if they leave.

The Lord is my shepherd. She focused on the promise. For Mother's sake, she would be strong, she would cling to her faith.

The thud of approaching hooves brought her to her feet. She grabbed Sunny's reins, ready to ride away if the sound brought trouble.

Her breath eased out when Sawyer came into sight. She waited for him to ride closer.

He dismounted several yards away and closed the distance separating them. He faced her, saying nothing but searching her with his eyes.

Neither of them spoke. She couldn't bring herself to address the issue that hung between them like a wall.

If Father sold the ranch, would she and Sawyer go their separate ways?

Sawyer wanted to soothe away the pain in Carly's eyes. Wanted to assure her everything would be okay. But he couldn't promise her that.

If her father sold the ranch, her need for a marriage would be gone.

Was that what she wanted? Not many hours ago, she had said she wanted him to see her as his wife. What did she mean? He hoped it meant she had started to care about him and perhaps even wanted to change the terms they had agreed to.

But had this latest development made her change her mind?

He told himself he would hold back until she made her wishes clear, but he saw the pain in her eyes and couldn't stand idly by. He pulled her against his chest and held her close.

"I'm sorry about the way your father is acting." So many other things crowded his mind—how hard Carly tried to please her father, to gain his approval and how oblivious her father was to her efforts, how much she loved the land and how intimately she knew it. She'd been willing to marry a stranger in order to keep the ranch. A needless sacrifice it would seem.

He had no choice but to release her from their agreement.

His arms tightened about her as his heart warred with what he must do.

"Carly." His voice grated like a rusty hinge. "If your father sells the ranch, our agreement is no longer necessary."

She'd been soft and close against his chest. At his words, she stiffened. Slowly, she eased from his arms. "You want to end our marriage?"

He could tell nothing from her expression or her tone of voice. Couldn't guess if she was pleased with his offer. Somehow he forced words from his reluctant throat. "We married so you could keep the ranch."

"And so you and Jill could have a home."

They stood inches apart but it might as well have been miles.

She nodded. "I understand." She walked slowly back to the edge of the water and stood looking out at the lake.

Was she finding peace? Relief?

The words she'd spoken along the trail burned through his brain. She wanted him to see her as his wife. She'd never explained and before he let her go, he had to know what she meant. He closed the distance between them and stood at her side, careful to leave space between them. He, too, looked at the water, hoping he could find strength and courage there.

He needed God's help to get through this. *Yea, though I walk through the valley of death. God, be my rod and staff.*

"This morning, you said something that I didn't understand. I'm hoping you'll explain yourself."

They both shifted so they faced each other.

Her eyes were watchful, guarded. If only he could see past the wall she'd set up and know what she wanted. His shoulders sank as his lungs emptied. He knew what she wanted—the ranch. He'd been the means to that end. But was he more?

"Carly, you said you wanted me to see you as my wife. What did you mean?"

Her gaze flickered. Did he see hope? Longing? Or was it regret? He couldn't allow himself to think so. And then her eyes darkened and he thought he saw resolve and something more. Something that caused him to tense with a mixture of fear and anticipation.

"I meant exactly what I said."

"I guess I don't understand. You *are* my wife."

"In name only. We both know it would take nothing to annul the contract between us." Challenge flared in her gaze.

"You want more than that?"

She nodded. "Do you?"

Yes. Yes. A thousand times, yes. "You only married me to save the ranch. Our marriage isn't necessary if your father plans to sell it anyway."

She lifted one shoulder as if that didn't matter and his heart swelled with hope.

"Do you want to stay married even if your father sells out?" There, he'd laid it on the line, risked everything to know the truth. And if she said no, well, he'd lived with disappointment before and survived. His insides quivered. Surviving this time might prove more of a challenge.

"Do you?"

He closed his eyes. She was forcing him to take the first step. He dug deep for the strength to open his heart and let her see to the darkest corners. He opened his eyes and fell into her gaze. For this woman, he would risk everything—even his carefully constructed security. For her, he'd knock down the walls surrounding his heart.

"Carly, I don't want to end our marriage. In fact—" He drew in a breath for courage. "I want it to be real."

She studied him as if waiting for more. Finally asked a question. "Why?"

He smiled. He should have guessed she'd want more. "I don't know. It just seems right. Like we fit."

She nodded. "I know. So we'll continue our agreement even if Father decides to sell?"

"Agreed."

She waited. "But—" Shook her head. "Never mind. Shall we go back and see what he's decided?"

As they rode back to the house, he knew he had missed something but couldn't say what it was. He was grateful she had agreed to continue their marriage.

But neither of them had discussed changing the terms. Or had she when she said she wanted to be his wife?

Had he missed an opportunity to tell her how he felt? All because of his habit of protecting his heart?

If he continued in this direction, he would protect his heart from everything he yearned for. She galloped homeward, making it impossible to say anything now.

Would he ever get another chance to say what he felt?

Chapter Nineteen

Carly tried to convince herself she wasn't disappointed with the decision she and Sawyer had made to continue their marriage. Except she was. How much plainer could she be that she wanted more than a contract between them? She'd practically spelled it out. She wanted to be his wife. She wanted him to love her as she loved him. There, she'd come right out and said it. Just not out loud. The next move was up to him.

They crested the last hill before the house. The Jacobses' buggy headed toward town. Good. Maybe they'd changed their mind.

If only she could believe that was so.

They took care of their horses before they went to the house. One minute, Carly wanted to rush the task and the next, she wanted it to last forever.

Sawyer finished first and leaned against the door-jamb, watching her delay. He chuckled. "Better to know the truth than to imagine the worst, wouldn't you say?"

"True." But she wasn't thinking solely of the ranch. Seems the words applied equally to their marriage. *Better to know the truth.* Unless it was a truth she didn't want to hear. "I'm done." Together they crossed the yard.

"They're gone," Jill said from the end of the porch where she played with Skippy. "Granddad is inside. He said he wanted to talk to you without little girls listening." She sighed. "He could have said me but he was trying to be nice."

Carly wished her father would try to be nice to her. They entered the house and stood facing him.

"Sit," he said.

They sat side by side across from Father and waited. She squeezed her intertwined fingers so hard they hurt.

Sawyer must have noticed for he wrapped a hand around hers. She untangled her fingers and turned her palm to his, cupping his hand between hers. No matter what happened, she and Sawyer would stick together. Her heart lightened.

"Father, what have you decided?"

"They're very interested in buying the place," Father said.

She wasn't surprised that he seemed set on choosing this route. "So you're going to sell?"

"I have yet to make up my mind." His eyes narrowed as he looked at her. "I dinnae like to sell without your agreement."

He didn't need her approval. Nor would he likely take it into account. "I have tried to make up for you not having any sons. I've done my best to handle the ranch work." She didn't think he had any reason to complain at her efforts.

Sawyer squeezed her hand a little as if to signal his sympathy.

"I'm sorry it hasn't been enough for you," she added.

Anger intermingled with resignation. "Father, you know what? It no longer matters because I love Sawyer and we'll make a new home elsewhere if you sell this place."

Sawyer tugged her hand and she looked at him, saw surprise in his face. Oh no, she'd blurted out her real feelings. Would her confession frighten him off?

"You love me?" he asked.

In for a penny, in for a dime, she decided. "That's what I've been trying to tell you."

He smiled so wide and bright she blinked. He pulled her hands to his chest and faced her father. "Father Morrison, I respect you as a man and a rancher, but you've been unfair to Carly. She's poured her heart and life into this ranch and you refuse to recognize her efforts solely because your sons have not lived."

Father stared from one to the other, then his gaze rested on Carly. "Aye, child, I only wanted you to be happy as my daughter. Not always trying to be a son. I have no son." He bestowed an approving smile on Sawyer. "But I now have a son-in-law. Thanks to you." He chuckled as if the whole situation amused him. "Could be I'll be blessed with grandsons."

He struggled to his feet. "I'll be informing the Jacobses that the land is no longer for sale. I have a daughter and her husband to run the place." He limped toward the door where he paused. "I already made Sawyer your partner. I'll let you two iron out the details regarding that. By the by, I've always believed you could run the ranch single-handedly. Always have. But I wanted more for you. Aye, I wanted you to have what your mother and me shared." The door closed quietly behind him.

Sawyer got to his feet, pulling Carly up with him. He still held her hands.

She couldn't look at him, afraid she had said too much. Afraid of all that was in her heart. "My father just wants me to be a daughter to him. Not a son. I always thought quite the opposite. Guess I misunderstood his comments to be criticisms of me."

"He seems pleased that you're his daughter." He drew her closer. "You love me?"

She nodded.

"Why didn't you say so sooner?"

Her head jerked up. "I've been trying to. But I was afraid you'd think I had failed to honor the terms of our agreement."

He chuckled. "Do you know how often I've longed to ask you if you'd be willing to change those terms?"

Hope blossomed in her heart. "Change them in what way?"

He tipped her chin up so he could smile into her face. "You heard your father. He's making us equal partners."

"Oh." Was that all?

He trailed his finger along her jawline, sending such sweet sensations through her that her knees grew weak. "I can only agree to being equal partners with you if…"

She held her breath, waiting for his conditions. Ready to accept almost anything.

He caught her chin. "Carly, I love you with my whole heart and everything in it. I don't just want to be partners, nor man and wife on paper. I want to share every bit of my life with you. Every moment, every thought, every feeling. Can you live with that?"

She crossed her arms behind his neck and drew him closer. "I do believe I'd enjoy that very much."

"Me, too." He lowered his head and claimed her mouth in a kiss so sweet she thought she might be floating.

They reluctantly ended the kiss. "I suppose nothing changes on the surface," she said. "Though it seems impossible when everything has changed inside." She pressed her hand to his chest.

"For the better, too." He kissed her nose, then lowered his head and caught her lips.

Jill barged in. "Yeww. You're kissing." But she grinned from ear to ear.

Sawyer caught his little sister around the waist and hugged her. He opened his other arm and pulled Carly into a three-person hug. The kitten wound around their ankles.

Jill patted his cheek, bringing a sting of tears to Carly's eyes at how much this pair loved each other and how they were learning to show it. "Is Granddad selling the ranch?" Jill's voice thinned with worry.

"Nope. You and me and Carly are going to stay here with Granddad. What do you think of that?"

"I think it's the best news ever." She laughed and wrapped her arms about both Carly and Sawyer's necks.

Carly had to agree. They were together and loving each other. She could ask for nothing more.

Epilogue

Carly stood in the circle of Sawyer's arms, her head tipped back against his chest, his chin resting on her head. "It's been lovely," she said. Five days alone in the secluded line cabin. Time to enjoy their love without dealing with family.

"I'm grateful Kate agreed to let Beth stay with Jill and Father while we were away."

Sawyer made a rumbling sound. "I'm grateful for so many things I can't begin to name them."

She turned to face him. "I'd like to hear some of them."

He kissed the tip of her nose. "You are the first and most important. You have made my life complete."

She rewarded him with a kiss.

"Then there's Jill and your father and the ranch and—" His voice deepened as emotions filled his heart. "And there is the life we will build together. A family where there is love and shelter and hope."

She sighed. "We are so blessed." She rested in his embrace a bit longer. "I suppose we should be going." It was time to return to the ranch and to their responsibilities. Though sharing her work and life with Sawyer would make every chore a joy.

They returned to the cabin and gathered together their belongings. She lingered in the doorway. "I will cherish the memory of the time we spent here."

"Me, too." He brought the horses forward and they rode toward home.

Jill must have been watching for them for she stood on the hill by the barn, waving a welcome.

They dismounted when they reached her and hugged her.

"Did you miss us?" Carly asked.

"I had fun with Beth." Jill tried to sound like that was enough but then she sniffled. "But I missed you both." They hugged her again.

"We will always come back," Sawyer assured her.

"I know."

They walked to the barn and took care of the horses, then Jill pulled them toward the house. "I have a surprise for you."

They stepped into the house. Father sat at the table, looking pleased with himself. Beth stood in the background and then Carly saw it.

"My shepherdess." She picked it off the table. "You can hardly tell it was broken."

"Granddad and Beth and I fixed it for you," Jill said. "I'm sorry I broke it."

Her eyes wet with tears, Carly hugged Jill. "I long ago forgave you." She set the figurine in the middle of the table. "I'm going to leave her where we can all see her and remember how much God loves us."

Sawyer caught her to him and, ignoring the others,

kissed her gently. He lifted his head, his glance circling their family.

"Love," he said, "will always be present in our home."

* * * * *

If you enjoyed this story, pick up the previous
BIG SKY COUNTRY *books:*

MONTANA COWBOY DADDY
MONTANA COWBOY FAMILY
MONTANA COWBOY'S BABY
MONTANA BRIDE BY CHRISTMAS

and these other stories from
Linda Ford:

A DADDY FOR CHRISTMAS
A BABY FOR CHRISTMAS
A HOME FOR CHRISTMAS
THE COWBOY'S READY-MADE FAMILY
THE COWBOY'S BABY BOND
THE COWBOY'S CITY GIRL
Available now from Love Inspired Historical!

Find more great reads at www.LoveInspired.com

Dear Reader,

I loved writing the story of these three wary people. I believe that losing one's mother is one of the hardest things to deal with in life, no matter what your age. Sawyer, Jill and Carly have all lost their mothers and deal with their loss in their own way. Helping them find healing and teaching them that they could live with their hearts open to receive love was such a fun journey.

I pray that my readers will also find the courage and healing to live with their hearts open to love.

I love to hear from readers. Contact me through email at linda@lindaford.org. Feel free to check on updates and bits about my research at my website www.lindaford.org.

God bless,

Linda Ford

COMING NEXT MONTH FROM
Love Inspired® Historical

Available February 6, 2018

SUDDENLY A FRONTIER FATHER
Wilderness Brides • by Lyn Cote

Mail-order bride turned schoolteacher Emma Jones no longer wants a husband. But when the man she planned to marry returns to town after being called away for a family emergency, can she resist falling for Mason Chandler and the two little girls he's adopted?

THE RANCHER'S TEMPORARY ENGAGEMENT
by Stacy Henrie

When he hires a Pinkerton agent to investigate sabotage on his horse ranch, Edward Kent doesn't expect the agency to send a female detective. Even more surprising is Maggy Worthing's suggestion for her cover story: a fake engagement to Edward.

HONOR-BOUND LAWMAN
by Danica Favorite

When Laura Booth's ex-husband escapes from prison with the intention of coming after her, former lawman Owen Hamilton must come out of retirement to keep her safe. But can the widowed single father protect her without losing his heart?

AN INCONVENIENT MARRIAGE
by Christina Miller

Widowed reverend Samuel Montgomery is excited to start over with his daughter in a new town—until he learns he'll lose his job if he doesn't marry. His only solution: a marriage in name only to local heiress Clarissa Adams, who needs a husband to win her inheritance.

LOOK FOR THESE AND OTHER LOVE INSPIRED BOOKS WHEREVER BOOKS ARE SOLD, INCLUDING MOST BOOKSTORES, SUPERMARKETS, DISCOUNT STORES AND DRUGSTORES.

Get 2 Free Books,
Plus 2 Free Gifts—
just for trying the Reader Service!

Love Inspired HISTORICAL

If you loved this story from
Love Inspired® Historical
be sure to discover more inspirational
stories to warm your heart from
Love Inspired® and
Love Inspired® Suspense!

Love Inspired stories show that
faith, forgiveness and hope have the power
to lift spirits and change lives—always.

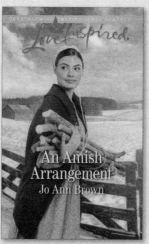 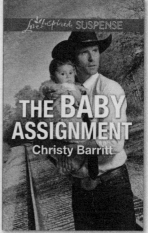

Look for six new romances every month
from **Love Inspired®** and
Love Inspired® Suspense!

SPECIAL EXCERPT FROM

Love Inspired HISTORICAL

Mail-order bride turned schoolteacher Emma Jones no longer wants a husband. But when the man she planned to marry returns to town after being called away for a family emergency, can she resist falling for Mason Chandler and the two little girls he's adopted?

Read on for a sneak preview of
SUDDENLY A FRONTIER FATHER
by **Lyn Cote**, *available February 2018*
from Love Inspired Historical!

Mason turned, startled when he heard his name being called. "Miss Jones. What can I do for you?"

"I'm glad to see you are walking without your crutch," she said, not replying to his question.

He didn't have to think about why this lady had come. Colton had repeatedly told him that Miss Jones wanted the girls in school. Evidently Emma was a woman to be reckoned with. His irritation over this vied with his unwelcome pleasure at seeing her here, so fine and determined. "I can guess why you've come. But I wasn't ready to send them to school yet."

"Your girls are ready. Do you think you are helping them, keeping them out?"

"I'm keeping them from being hurt. Children can be cruel," he said.

"And adults can be. Do you think keeping them out protects them from hurt? Don't you realize that keeping them home is hurting them, too?"

"I can teach them their letters and numbers."

"That's not what I mean. Isolating them is telling them that you don't think they can handle school. That they are lesser than the other children. Are you ashamed of Birdie and Charlotte?"

"No. They are wonderful little girls."

"Then bring them to school Monday." She turned as if to leave. "Have some trust in me, and trust in the children of this town."

She left him without a word to say.

The girls ran to him. "Did the lady teacher say we could come to school?" Birdie asked.

He looked down into Birdie's eager face. "Do you want to go to school?"

"Yes!" Birdie signed to Charlotte. "She says yes, too. We can see Lily and Colton. And meet other children."

He wondered if Birdie was capable of grasping the concept of prejudice.

"Some children will like us and some won't," Birdie said, answering his unspoken question. "But we want to go to school."

He hoped Miss Emma Jones knew what she was doing. He wanted everything good for his children. But he knew how cruel people could be.

At least no one knew the dark secret he must—above all else—keep hidden.

Don't miss
SUDDENLY A FRONTIER FATHER by Lyn Cote,
available February 2018 wherever
Love Inspired® Historical books and ebooks are sold.

www.LoveInspired.com

Looking for inspiration in tales
of hope, faith and heartfelt romance?

Check out **Love Inspired**® and
Love Inspired® **Suspense** books!

New books available every month!

LIGENRE2018

Love Inspired®

Inspirational Romance to Warm Your Heart and Soul

Join our social communities to connect with other readers who share your love!

Sign up for the Love Inspired newsletter at **www.LoveInspired.com** to be the first to find out about upcoming titles, special promotions and exclusive content.

CONNECT WITH US AT:

Harlequin.com/Community

 Facebook.com/LoveInspiredBooks

 Twitter.com/LoveInspiredBks

LISOCIAL2017